ONIBI
DIARY OF A YOKAI GHOST HUNTER

ATELIER SENTŌ

TUTTLE Publishing

Tokyo | Rutland, Vermont | Singapore

THIS STORY WAS INSPIRED BY ONE OF OUR TRIPS TO NIIGATA, DURING THE FALL OF 2014. WE DEDICATE IT TO THE PEOPLE WE'VE MET THERE. THEY WELCOMED US WITH OVERWHELMING GENEROSITY AND HELPED US DISCOVER THE REGION AND ITS SECRETS. SOME OF THESE PEOPLE APPEAR IN THIS BOOK. WE HOPE THEY WILL ENJOY IT.

WE ALSO THANK OUR FAMILIES AND FRIENDS WHO ENCOURAGED US DURING THE MAKING OF THIS BOOK.

CÉCILE & OLIVIER

Published as *Onibi: Carnets du Japon Invisible* by Issekinicho Éditions, Shiltigheim, France, 2016

www.tuttlepublishing.com

ISBN: 978-4-8053-1496-8

22 21 20 19   10 9 8 7 6 5 4 3 2   1812EP
Printed in Hong Kong

ABOUT TUTTLE
"Books to Span the East and West"

Our core mission at Tuttle Publishing is to create books which bring people together one page at a time. Tuttle was founded in 1832 in the small New England town of Rutland, Vermont (USA). Our fundamental values remain as strong today as they were then—to publish best-in-class books informing the English-speaking world about the countries and peoples of Asia. The world has become a smaller place today and Asia's economic, cultural and political influence has expanded, yet the need for meaningful dialogue and information about this diverse region has never been greater. Since 1948, Tuttle has been a leader in publishing books on the cultures, arts, cuisines, languages and literatures of Asia. Our authors and photographers have won numerous awards and Tuttle has published thousands of books on subjects ranging from martial arts to paper crafts. We welcome you to explore the wealth of information available on Asia at **www.tuttlepublishing.com**.

Distributed by

North America, Latin America & Europe
Tuttle Publishing
364 Innovation Drive
North Clarendon,
VT 05759-9436 U.S.A.
Tel: 1 (802) 773-8930
Fax: 1 (802) 773-6993
info@tuttlepublishing.com
www.tuttlepublishing.com

Japan
Tuttle Publishing
Yaekari Building, 3rd Floor
5-4-12 Osaki
Shinagawa-ku
Tokyo 141-0032
Tel: (81) 3 5437-0171
Fax: (81) 3 5437-0755
sales@tuttle.co.jp
www.tuttle.co.jp

Asia Pacific
Berkeley Books Pte. Ltd.
3 Kallang Sector #04-01
Singapore 349278
Tel: (65) 6741-2178
Fax: (65) 6741-2179
inquiries@periplus.com.sg
www.periplus.com

TUTTLE PUBLISHING® is a registered trademark of Tuttle Publishing, a division of Periplus Editions (HK) Ltd.

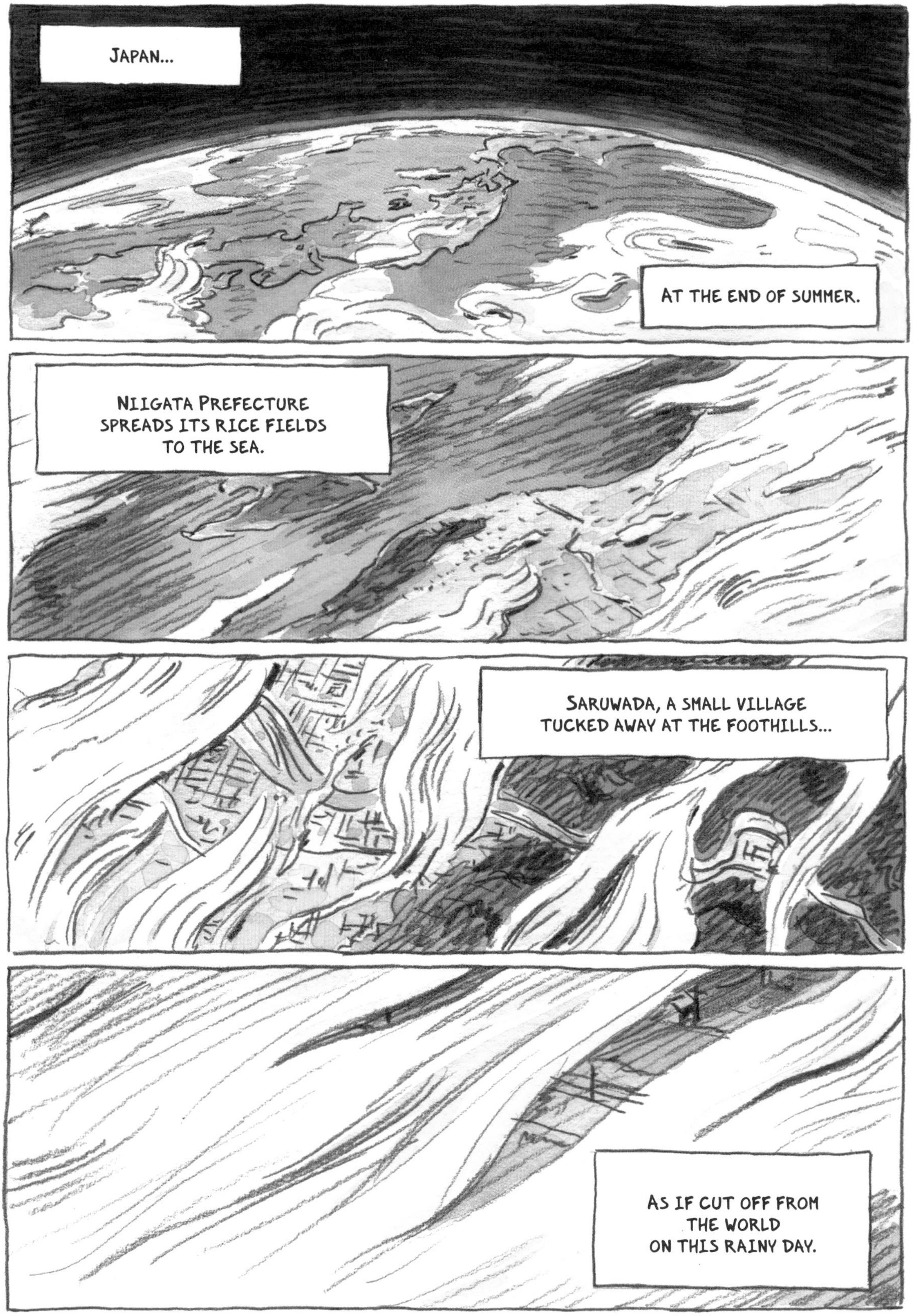
JAPAN...
AT THE END OF SUMMER.
NIIGATA PREFECTURE SPREADS ITS RICE FIELDS TO THE SEA.
SARUWADA, A SMALL VILLAGE TUCKED AWAY AT THE FOOTHILLS...
AS IF CUT OFF FROM THE WORLD ON THIS RAINY DAY.

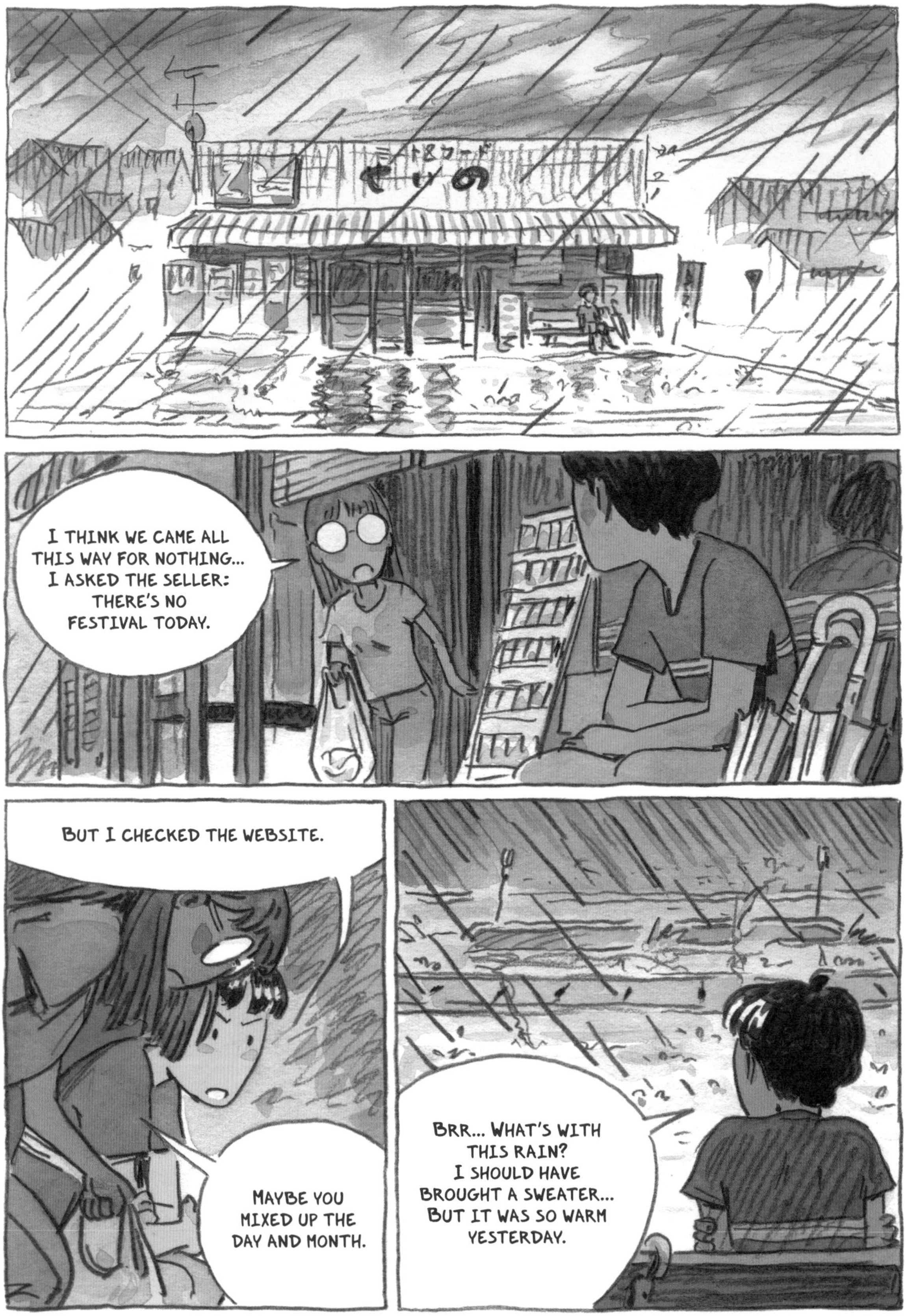
I THINK WE CAME ALL THIS WAY FOR NOTHING... I ASKED THE SELLER: THERE'S NO FESTIVAL TODAY.
BUT I CHECKED THE WEBSITE.
MAYBE YOU MIXED UP THE DAY AND MONTH.
BRR... WHAT'S WITH THIS RAIN? I SHOULD HAVE BROUGHT A SWEATER... BUT IT WAS SO WARM YESTERDAY.

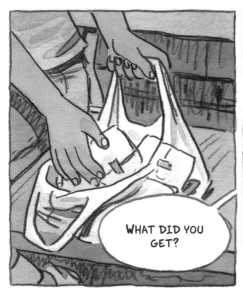

WHAT DID YOU GET?

SOME STEAMED BUNS AND A FEW PLAIN CROQUETTES.

MMM, IT'S SO GOOD. IT WARMS YOU UP.

IT LOOKS LIKE IT'S DYING DOWN.

BOM

BOM

BOM

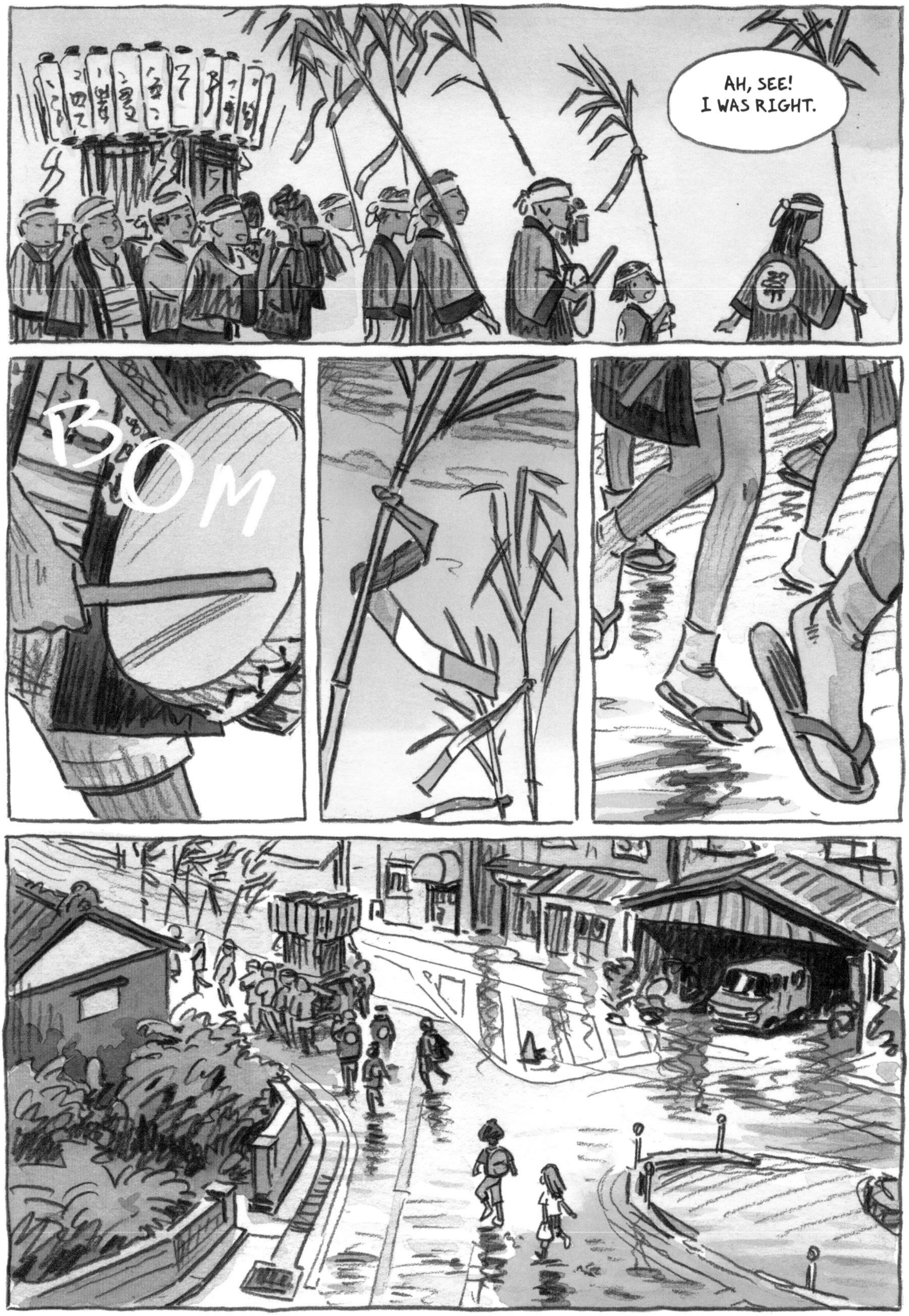
AH, SEE!
I WAS RIGHT.
BOM

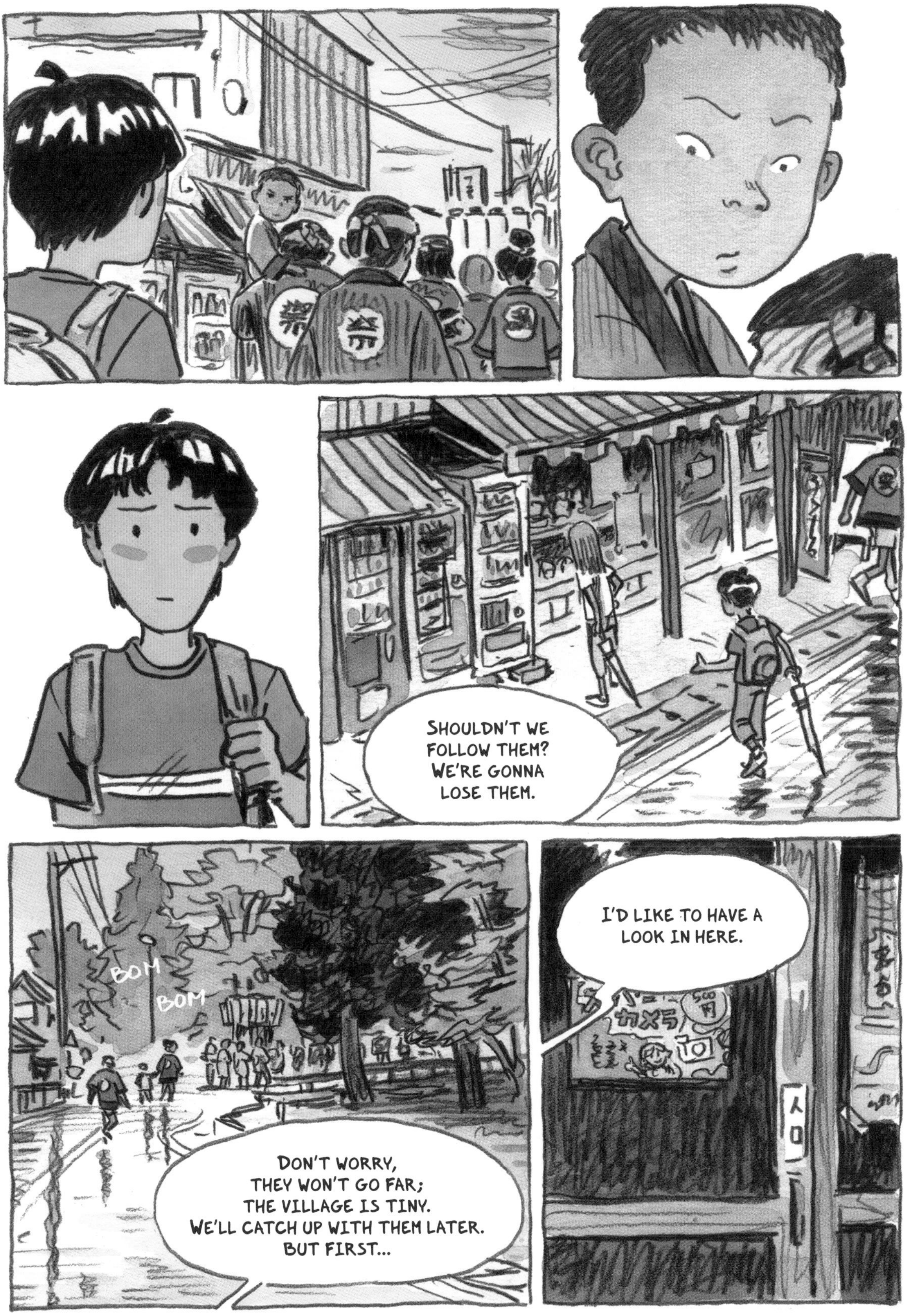
SHOULDN'T WE FOLLOW THEM? WE'RE GONNA LOSE THEM.
BOM
BOM
DON'T WORRY, THEY WON'T GO FAR; THE VILLAGE IS TINY. WE'LL CATCH UP WITH THEM LATER. BUT FIRST...
I'D LIKE TO HAVE A LOOK IN HERE.

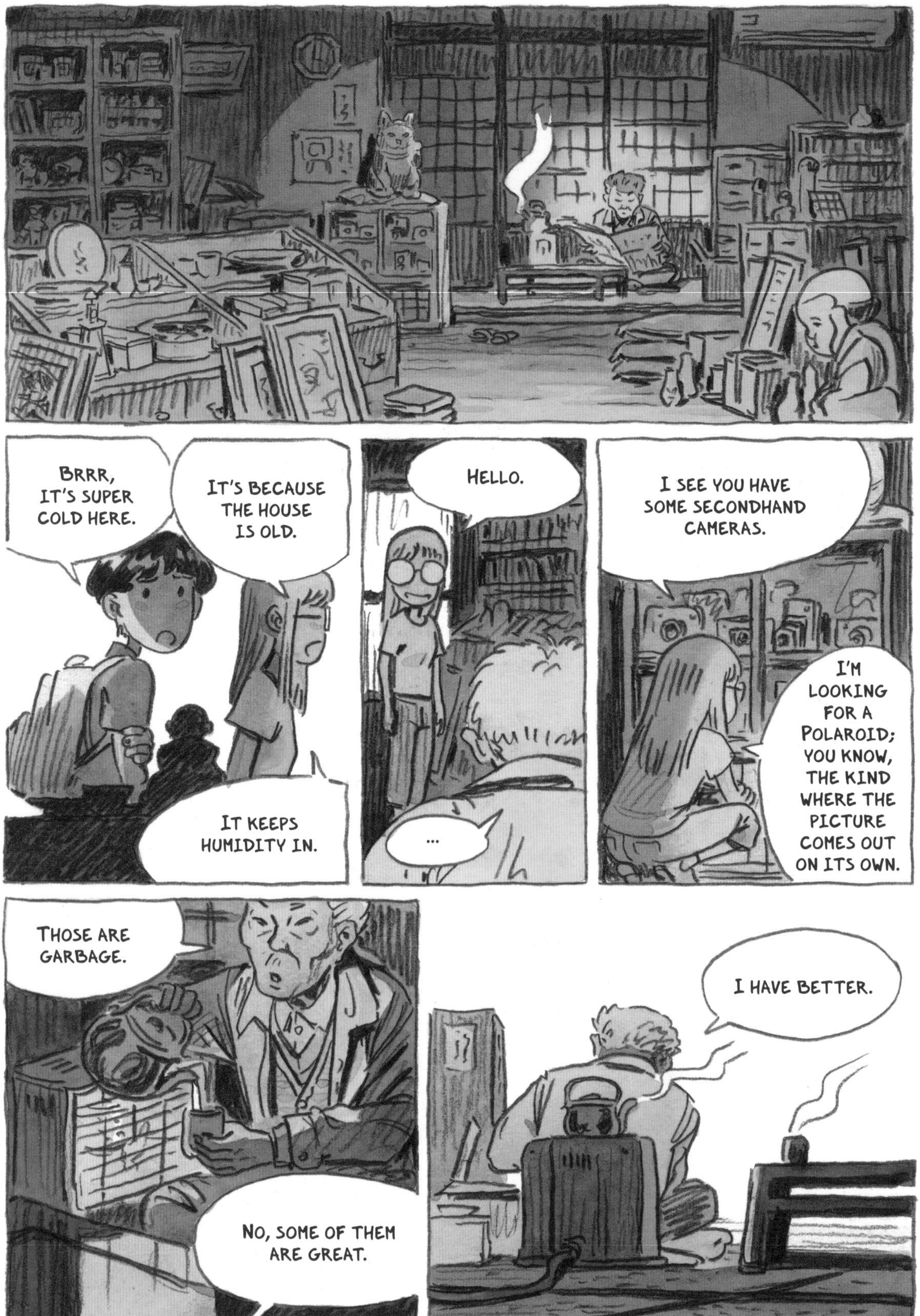
Brrr, it's super cold here.
It's because the house is old.
It keeps humidity in.
Hello.
...
I see you have some secondhand cameras.
I'm looking for a Polaroid; you know, the kind where the picture comes out on its own.
Those are garbage.
No, some of them are great.
I have better.

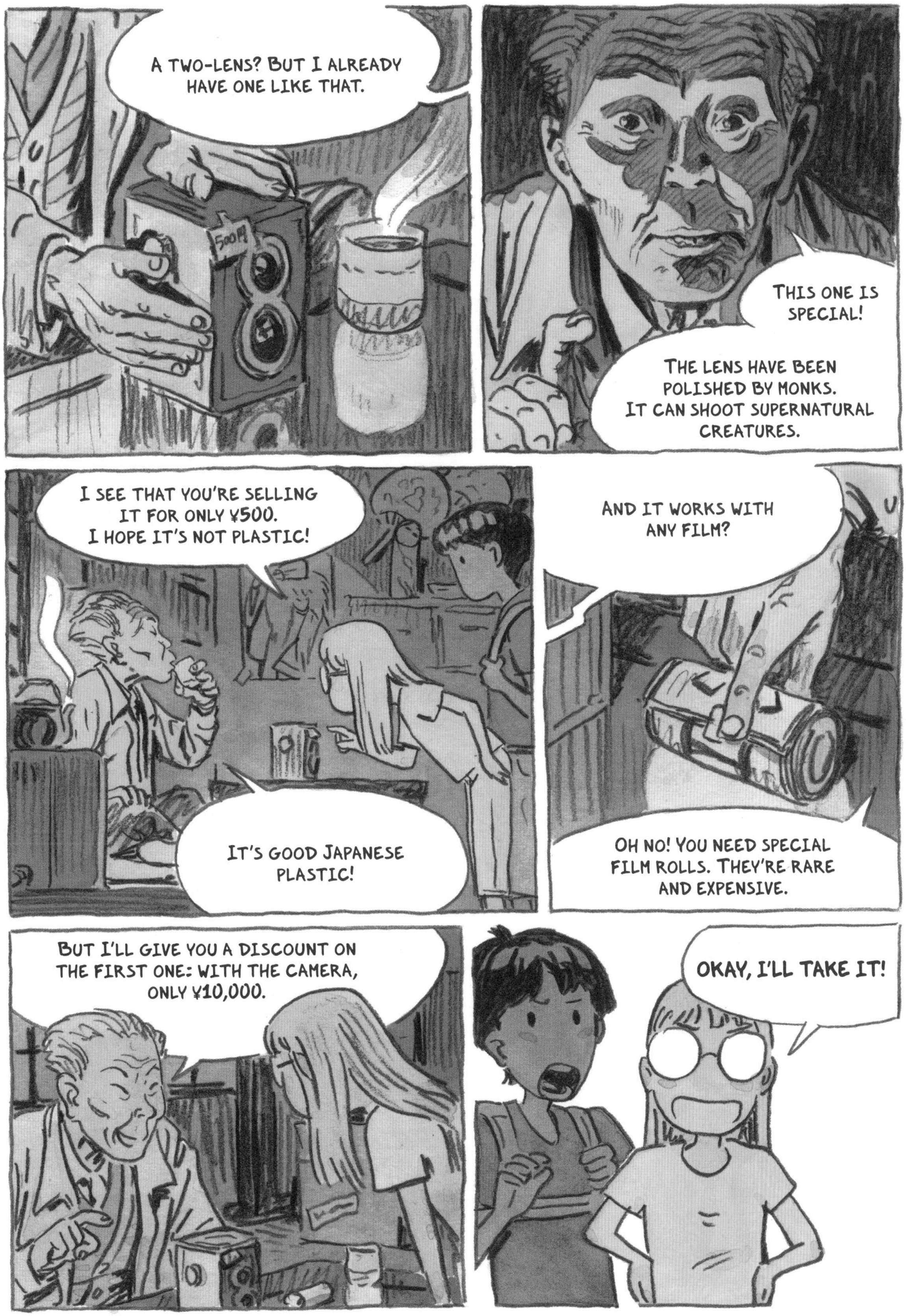
A TWO-LENS? BUT I ALREADY HAVE ONE LIKE THAT.
THIS ONE IS SPECIAL!
THE LENS HAVE BEEN POLISHED BY MONKS. IT CAN SHOOT SUPERNATURAL CREATURES.
I SEE THAT YOU'RE SELLING IT FOR ONLY ¥500. I HOPE IT'S NOT PLASTIC!
IT'S GOOD JAPANESE PLASTIC!
AND IT WORKS WITH ANY FILM?
OH NO! YOU NEED SPECIAL FILM ROLLS. THEY'RE RARE AND EXPENSIVE.
BUT I'LL GIVE YOU A DISCOUNT ON THE FIRST ONE: WITH THE CAMERA, ONLY ¥10,000.
OKAY, I'LL TAKE IT!

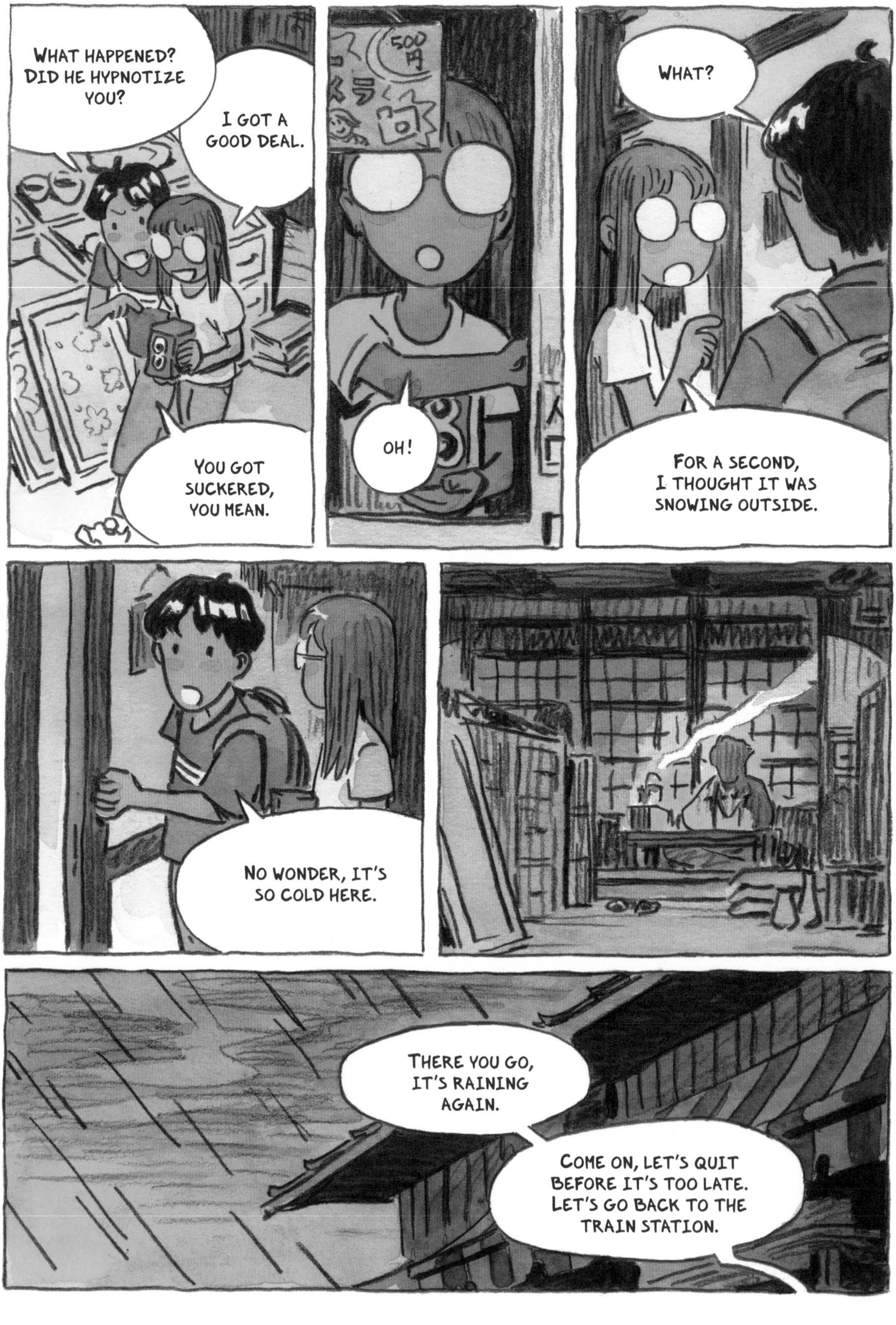
WHAT HAPPENED? DID HE HYPNOTIZE YOU?
I GOT A GOOD DEAL.
YOU GOT SUCKERED, YOU MEAN.
500 円
OH!
WHAT?
FOR A SECOND, I THOUGHT IT WAS SNOWING OUTSIDE.
NO WONDER, IT'S SO COLD HERE.
THERE YOU GO, IT'S RAINING AGAIN.
COME ON, LET'S QUIT BEFORE IT'S TOO LATE. LET'S GO BACK TO THE TRAIN STATION.

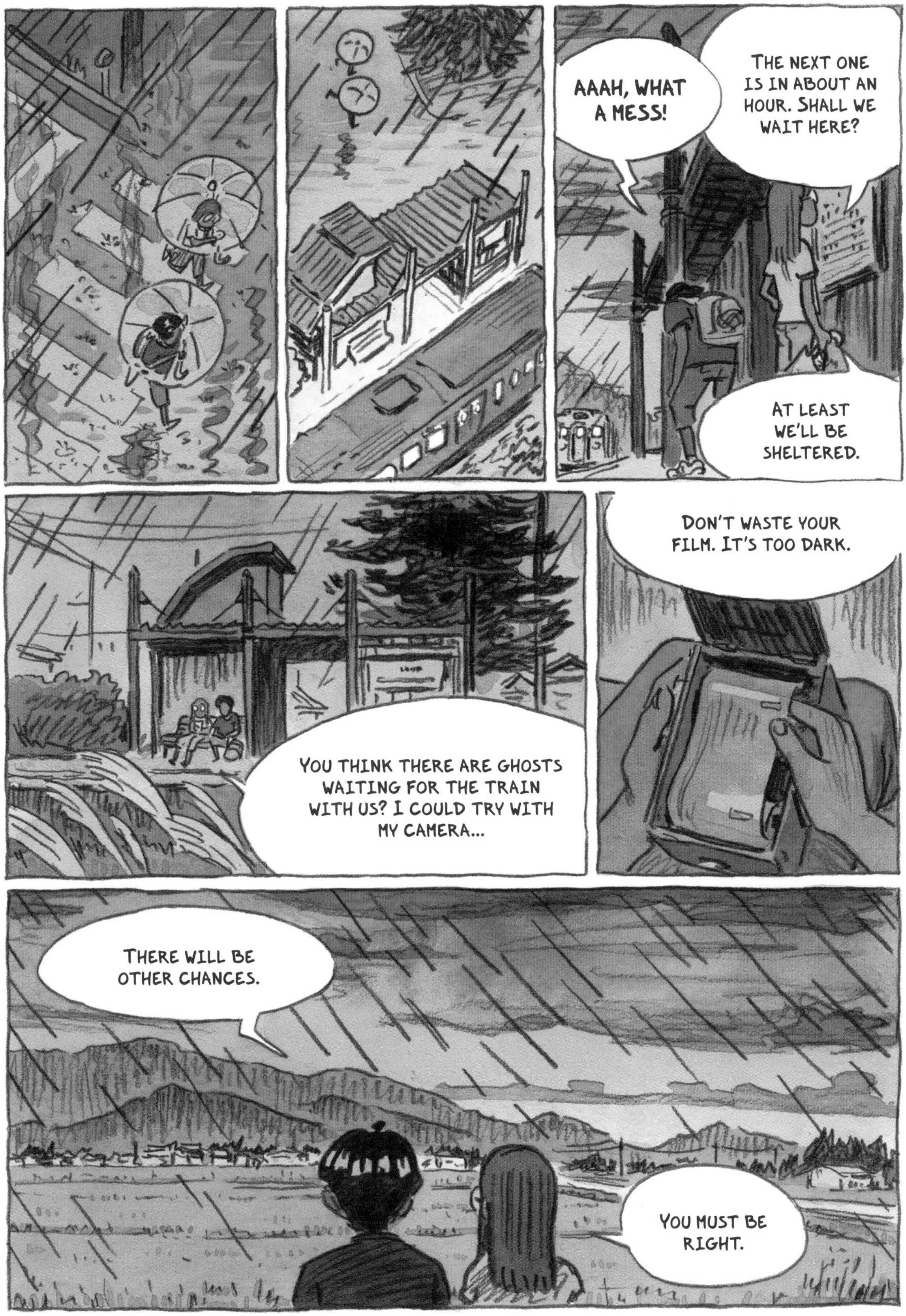
AAAH, WHAT A MESS!
THE NEXT ONE IS IN ABOUT AN HOUR. SHALL WE WAIT HERE?
AT LEAST WE'LL BE SHELTERED.
YOU THINK THERE ARE GHOSTS WAITING FOR THE TRAIN WITH US? I COULD TRY WITH MY CAMERA...
DON'T WASTE YOUR FILM. IT'S TOO DARK.
THERE WILL BE OTHER CHANCES.
YOU MUST BE RIGHT.

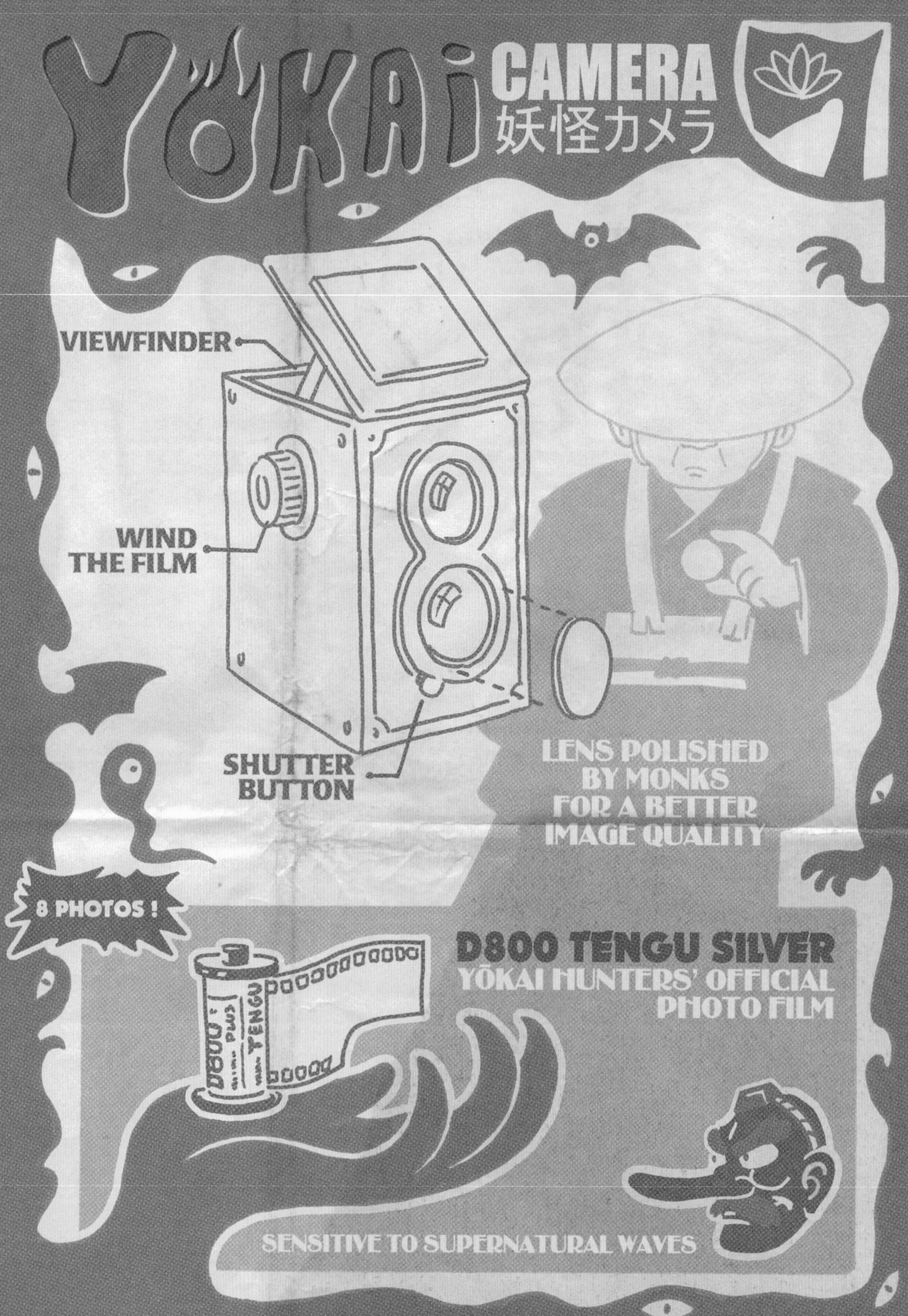

YŌKAI CAMERA
妖怪カメラ
VIEWFINDER
WIND THE FILM
SHUTTER BUTTON
LENS POLISHED BY MONKS FOR A BETTER IMAGE QUALITY
8 PHOTOS !
D800 TENGU SILVER
YŌKAI HUNTERS' OFFICIAL PHOTO FILM
SENSITIVE TO SUPERNATURAL WAVES

INSTRUCTIONS

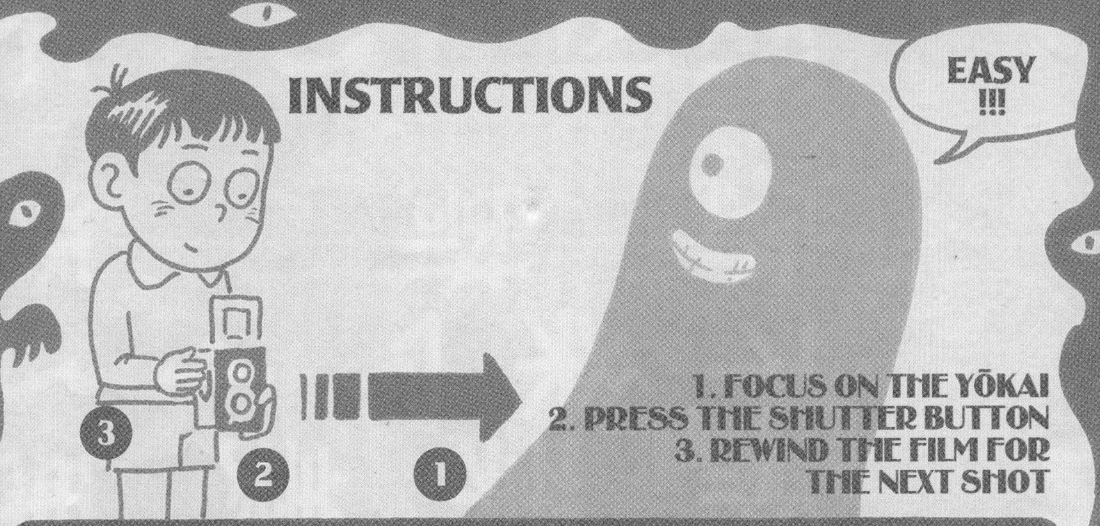
EASY !!!
3
2
1

1. FOCUS ON THE YŌKAI
2. PRESS THE SHUTTER BUTTON
3. REWIND THE FILM FOR THE NEXT SHOT

AN ADVANCED TECHNOLOGY FOR STEALTH

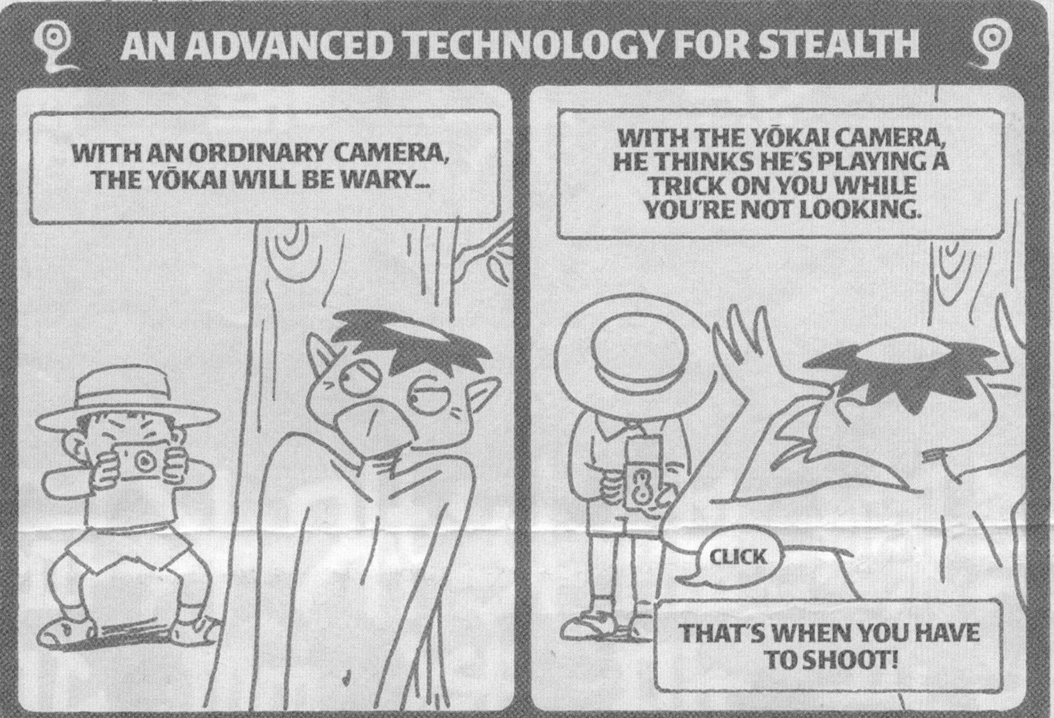
WITH AN ORDINARY CAMERA, THE YŌKAI WILL BE WARY...
WITH THE YŌKAI CAMERA, HE THINKS HE'S PLAYING A TRICK ON YOU WHILE YOU'RE NOT LOOKING.
CLICK
THAT'S WHEN YOU HAVE TO SHOOT!

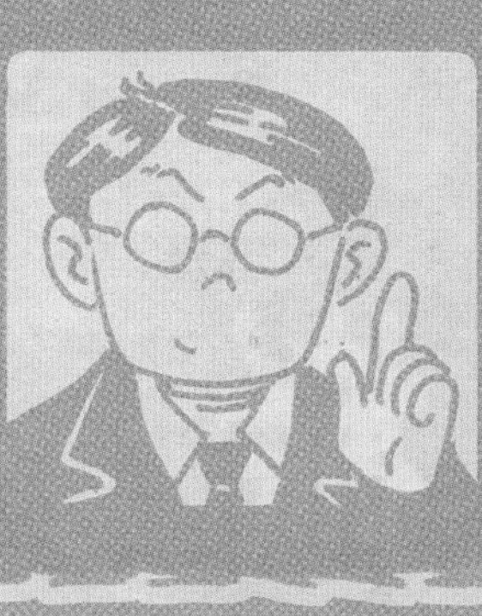

HINTS FROM A PRO

PROFESSOR TAKADA FROM TOKYO UNIVERSITY

1.KNOW YOUR OPPONENT. MY YŌKAI ENCYCLOPEDIA (¥3200 PLUS TAXES) IS THE PERFECT TOOL.
2.FIND THE PROPER LURE TO ATTRACT YOUR PREY. YŌKAI ARE FOOD-GREEDY, SO WATCH OUT!
3.STAY STEALTHY AND NEVER LOOK YOUR TARGET IN THE EYES. FLASH IS NOT RECOMMENDED.
4.NEVER PET A YŌKAI, EVEN IF IT'S CUTE.

1

Uchino Foxes

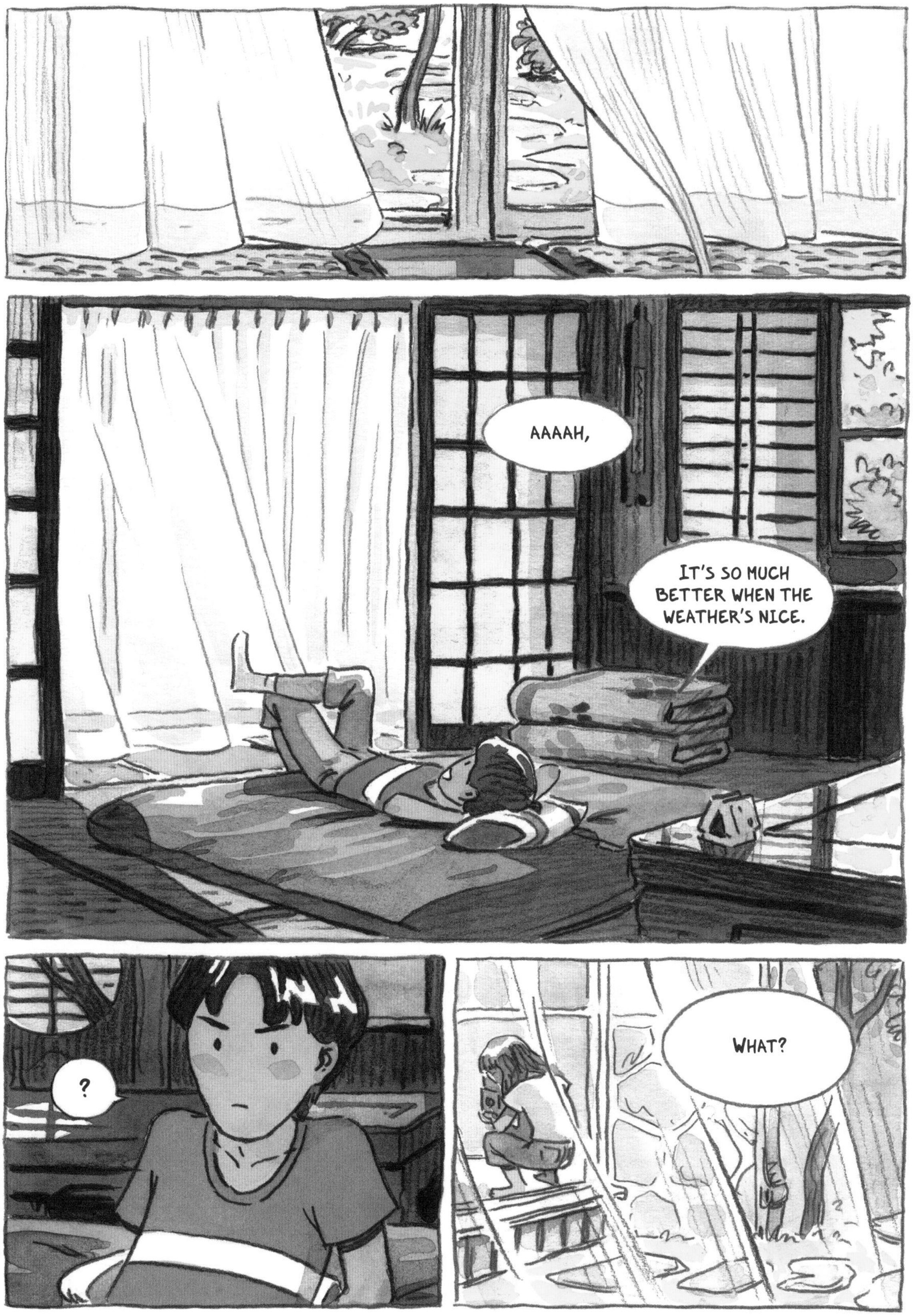
AAAAH,
IT'S SO MUCH BETTER WHEN THE WEATHER'S NICE.
?
WHAT?

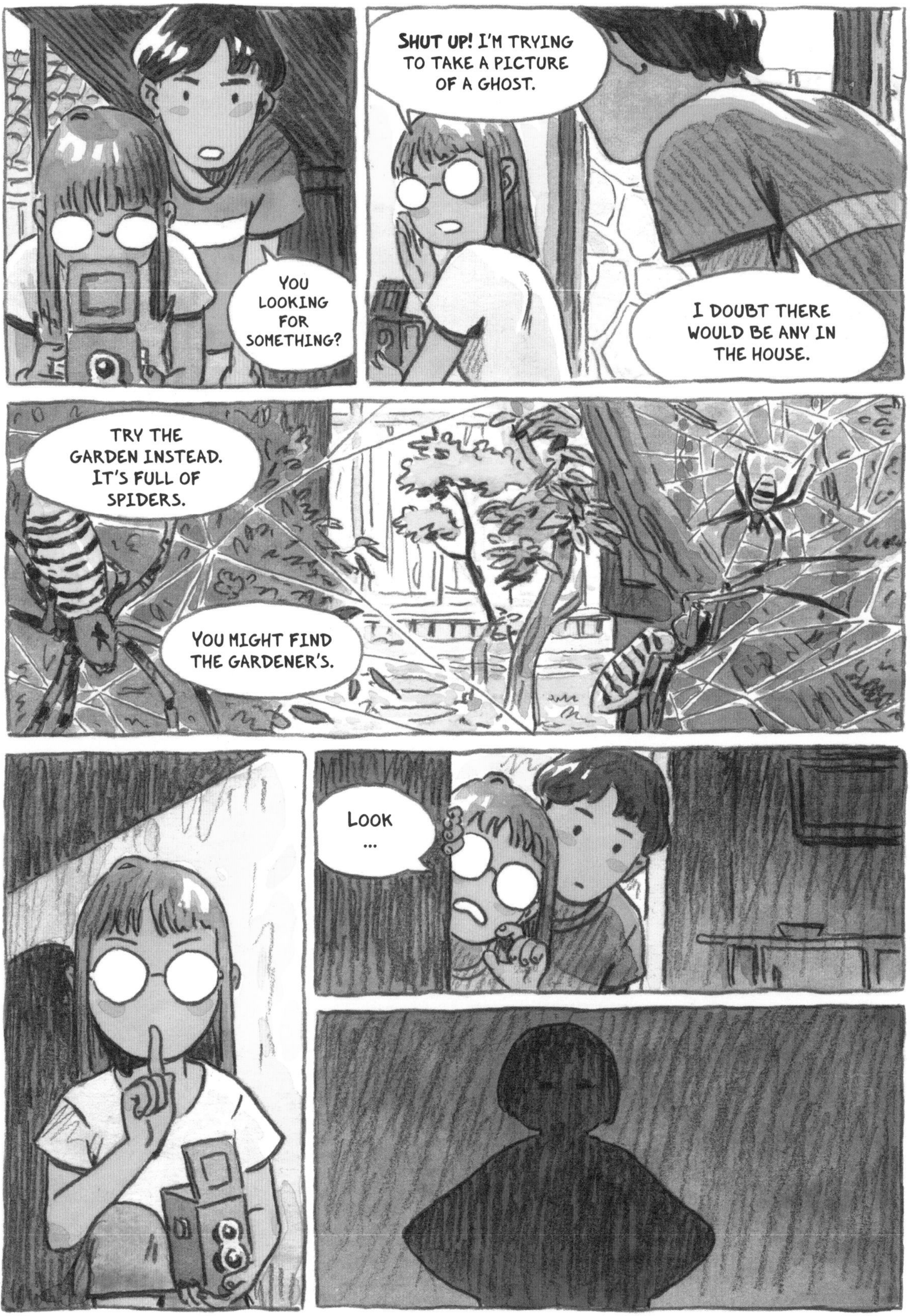
YOU LOOKING FOR SOMETHING?
SHUT UP! I'M TRYING TO TAKE A PICTURE OF A GHOST.
I DOUBT THERE WOULD BE ANY IN THE HOUSE.
TRY THE GARDEN INSTEAD. IT'S FULL OF SPIDERS.
YOU MIGHT FIND THE GARDENER'S.
LOOK ...

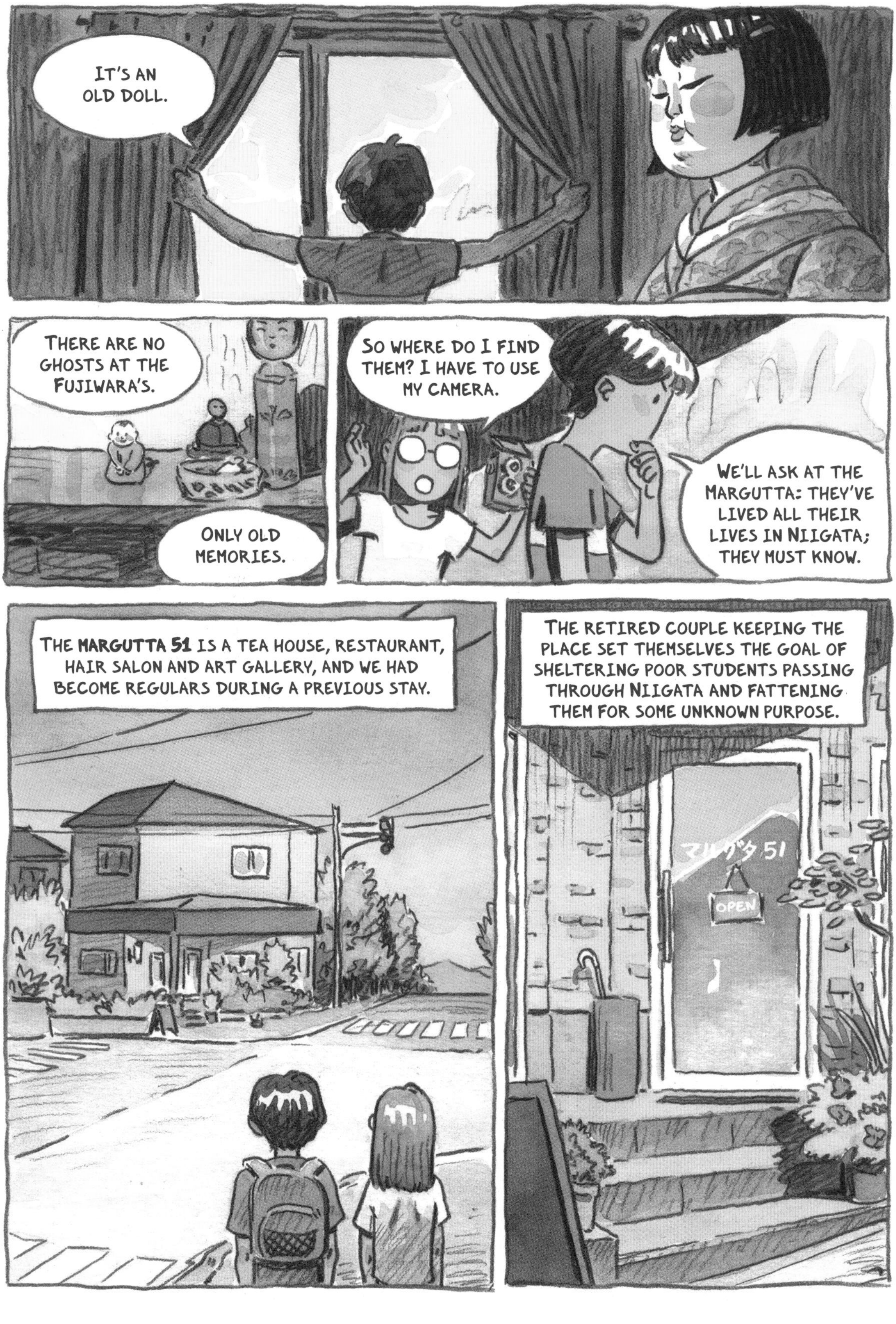
IT'S AN OLD DOLL.
THERE ARE NO GHOSTS AT THE FUJIWARA'S.
ONLY OLD MEMORIES.
SO WHERE DO I FIND THEM? I HAVE TO USE MY CAMERA.
WE'LL ASK AT THE MARGUTTA: THEY'VE LIVED ALL THEIR LIVES IN NIIGATA; THEY MUST KNOW.
THE **MARGUTTA 51** IS A TEA HOUSE, RESTAURANT, HAIR SALON AND ART GALLERY, AND WE HAD BECOME REGULARS DURING A PREVIOUS STAY.
THE RETIRED COUPLE KEEPING THE PLACE SET THEMSELVES THE GOAL OF SHELTERING POOR STUDENTS PASSING THROUGH NIIGATA AND FATTENING THEM FOR SOME UNKNOWN PURPOSE.
マルグタ 51
OPEN

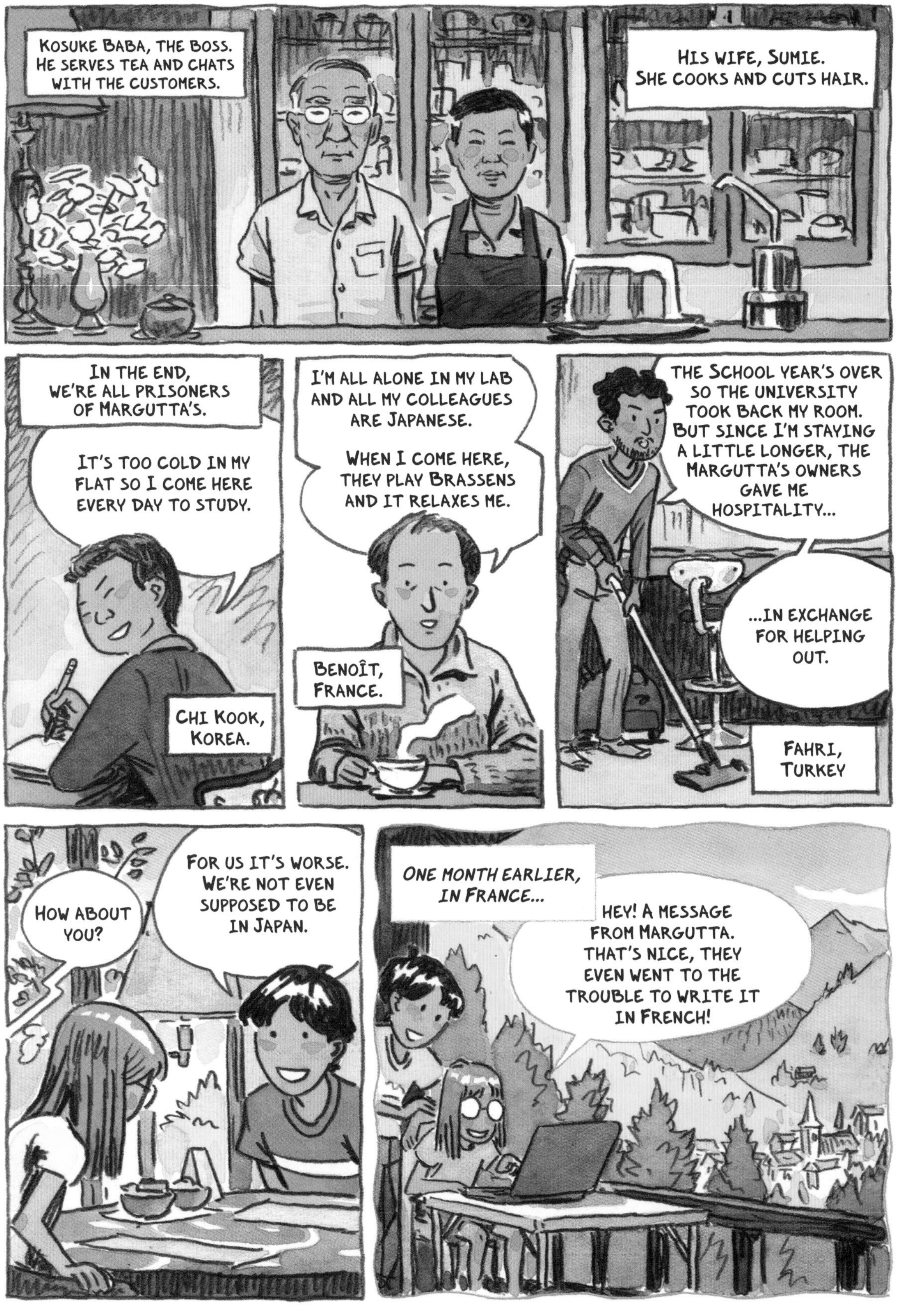
KOSUKE BABA, THE BOSS. HE SERVES TEA AND CHATS WITH THE CUSTOMERS.
HIS WIFE, SUMIE. SHE COOKS AND CUTS HAIR.
IN THE END, WE'RE ALL PRISONERS OF MARGUTTA'S.
IT'S TOO COLD IN MY FLAT SO I COME HERE EVERY DAY TO STUDY.
CHI KOOK, KOREA.
I'M ALL ALONE IN MY LAB AND ALL MY COLLEAGUES ARE JAPANESE.
WHEN I COME HERE, THEY PLAY BRASSENS AND IT RELAXES ME.
BENOÎT, FRANCE.
THE SCHOOL YEAR'S OVER SO THE UNIVERSITY TOOK BACK MY ROOM. BUT SINCE I'M STAYING A LITTLE LONGER, THE MARGUTTA'S OWNERS GAVE ME HOSPITALITY...
...IN EXCHANGE FOR HELPING OUT.
FAHRI, TURKEY
HOW ABOUT YOU?
FOR US IT'S WORSE. WE'RE NOT EVEN SUPPOSED TO BE IN JAPAN.
ONE MONTH EARLIER, IN FRANCE...
HEY! A MESSAGE FROM MARGUTTA. THAT'S NICE, THEY EVEN WENT TO THE TROUBLE TO WRITE IT IN FRENCH!

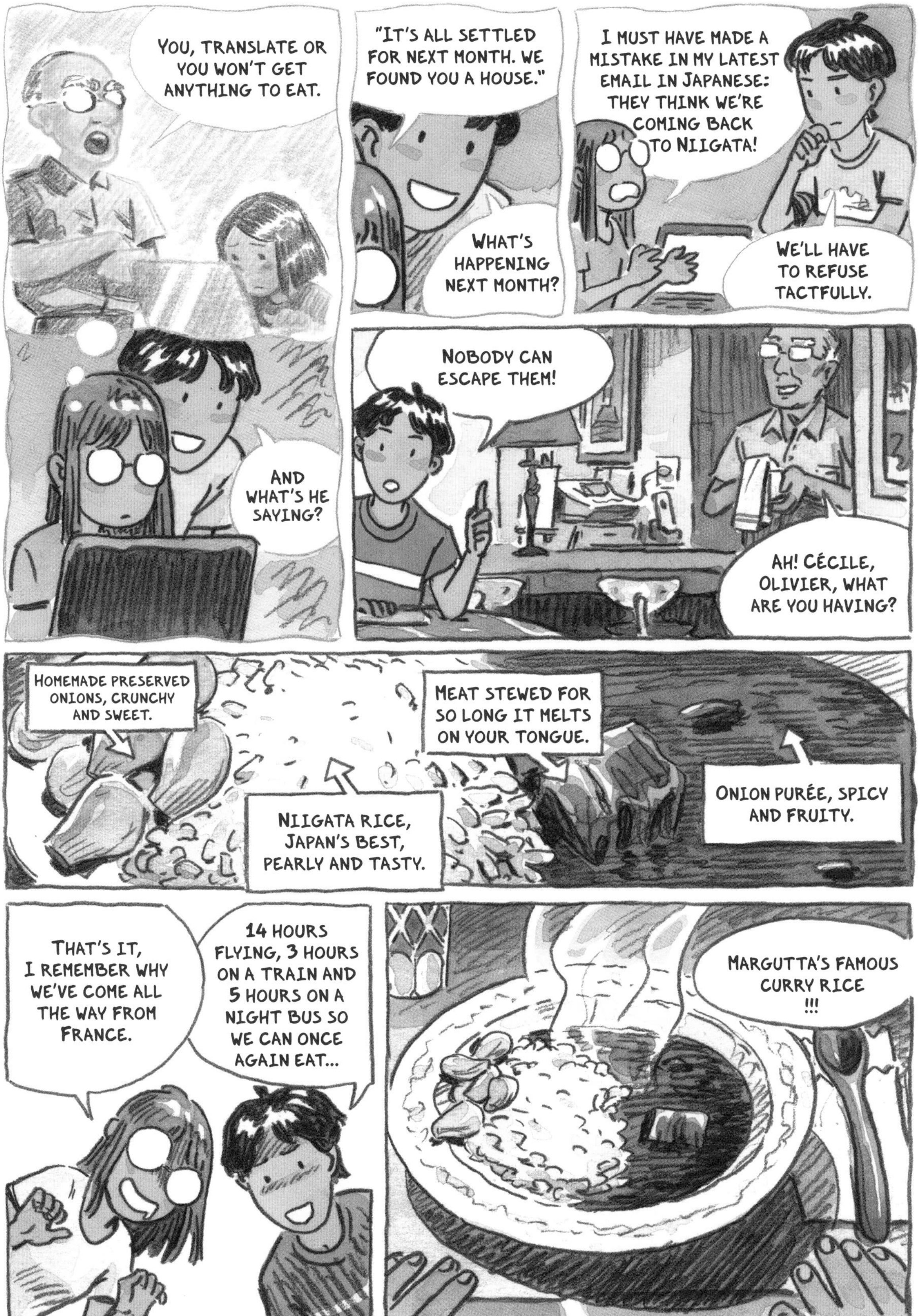

YOU, TRANSLATE OR YOU WON'T GET ANYTHING TO EAT.
"IT'S ALL SETTLED FOR NEXT MONTH. WE FOUND YOU A HOUSE."
WHAT'S HAPPENING NEXT MONTH?
I MUST HAVE MADE A MISTAKE IN MY LATEST EMAIL IN JAPANESE: THEY THINK WE'RE COMING BACK TO NIIGATA!
WE'LL HAVE TO REFUSE TACTFULLY.
AND WHAT'S HE SAYING?
NOBODY CAN ESCAPE THEM!
AH! CÉCILE, OLIVIER, WHAT ARE YOU HAVING?
HOMEMADE PRESERVED ONIONS, CRUNCHY AND SWEET.
NIIGATA RICE, JAPAN'S BEST, PEARLY AND TASTY.
MEAT STEWED FOR SO LONG IT MELTS ON YOUR TONGUE.
ONION PURÉE, SPICY AND FRUITY.
THAT'S IT, I REMEMBER WHY WE'VE COME ALL THE WAY FROM FRANCE.
14 HOURS FLYING, 3 HOURS ON A TRAIN AND 5 HOURS ON A NIGHT BUS SO WE CAN ONCE AGAIN EAT...
MARGUTTA'S FAMOUS CURRY RICE !!!

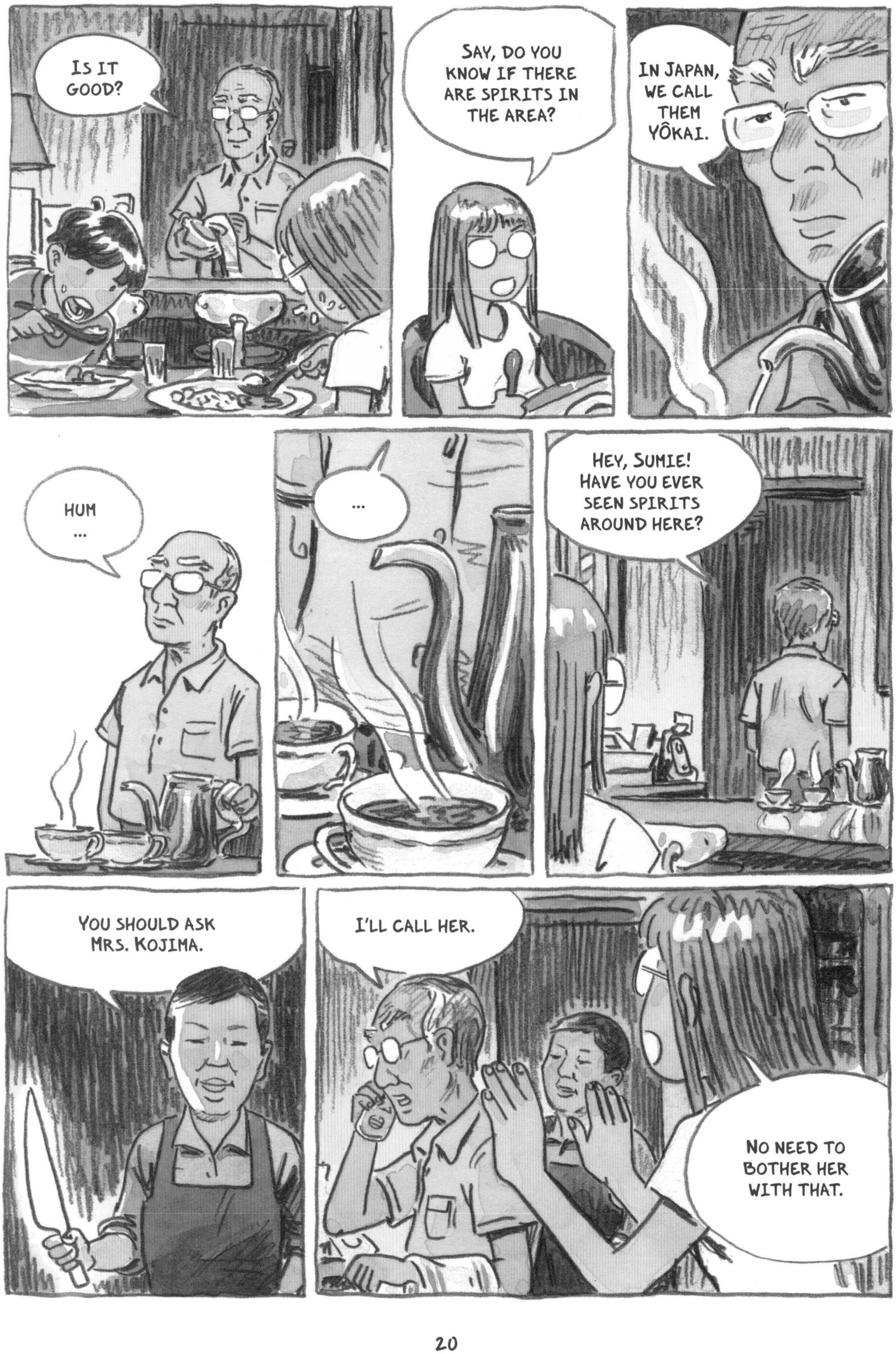
Is it good?
Say, do you know if there are spirits in the area?
In Japan, we call them yôkai.
Hum ...
...
Hey, Sumie! Have you ever seen spirits around here?
You should ask Mrs. Kojima.
I'll call her.
No need to bother her with that.

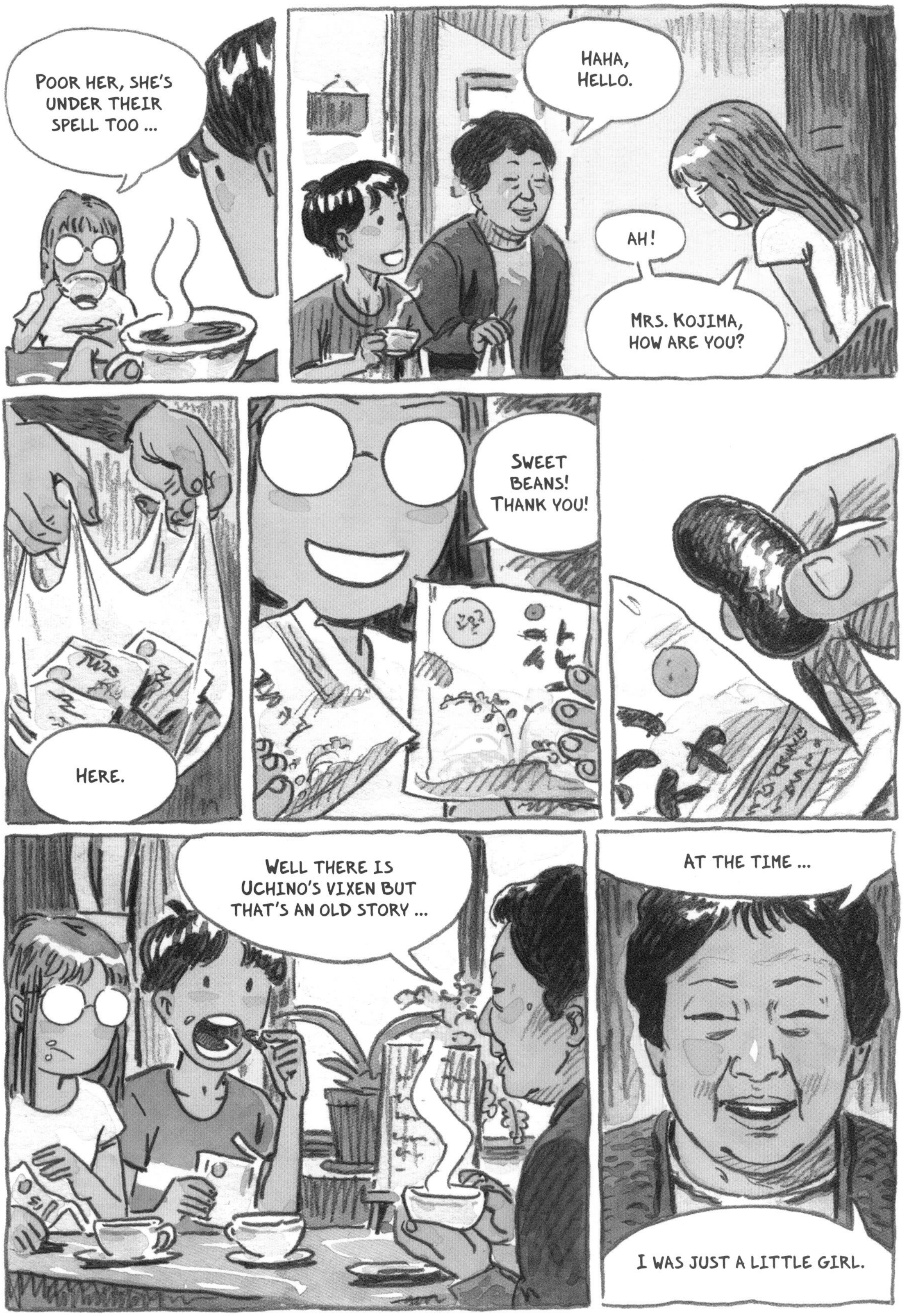
POOR HER, SHE'S UNDER THEIR SPELL TOO ...
HAHA, HELLO.
AH!
MRS. KOJIMA, HOW ARE YOU?
HERE.
SWEET BEANS! THANK YOU!
WELL THERE IS UCHINO'S VIXEN BUT THAT'S AN OLD STORY ...
AT THE TIME ...
I WAS JUST A LITTLE GIRL.

MRS. KOJIMA'S TALE

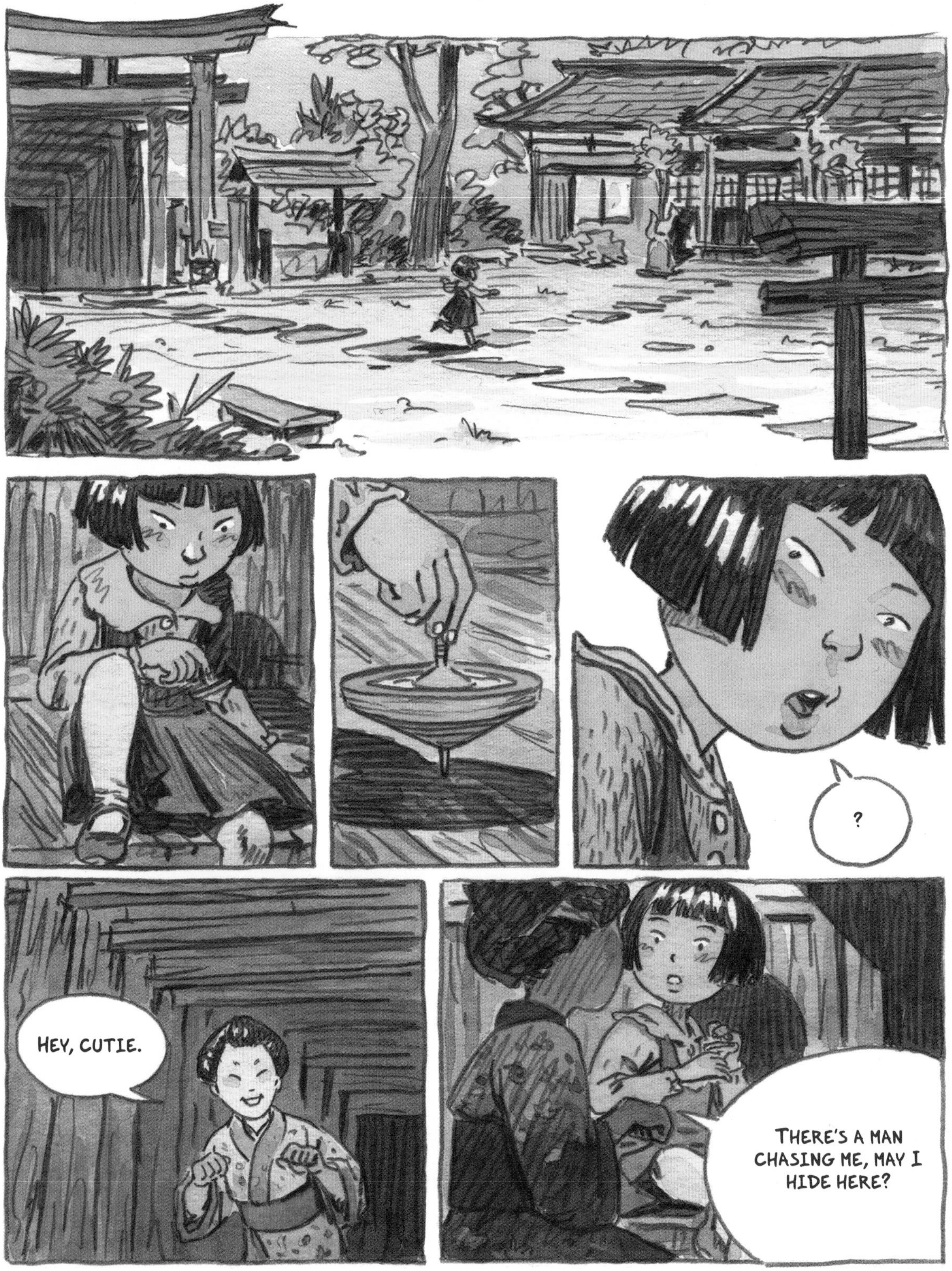
?
HEY, CUTIE.
THERE'S A MAN CHASING ME, MAY I HIDE HERE?

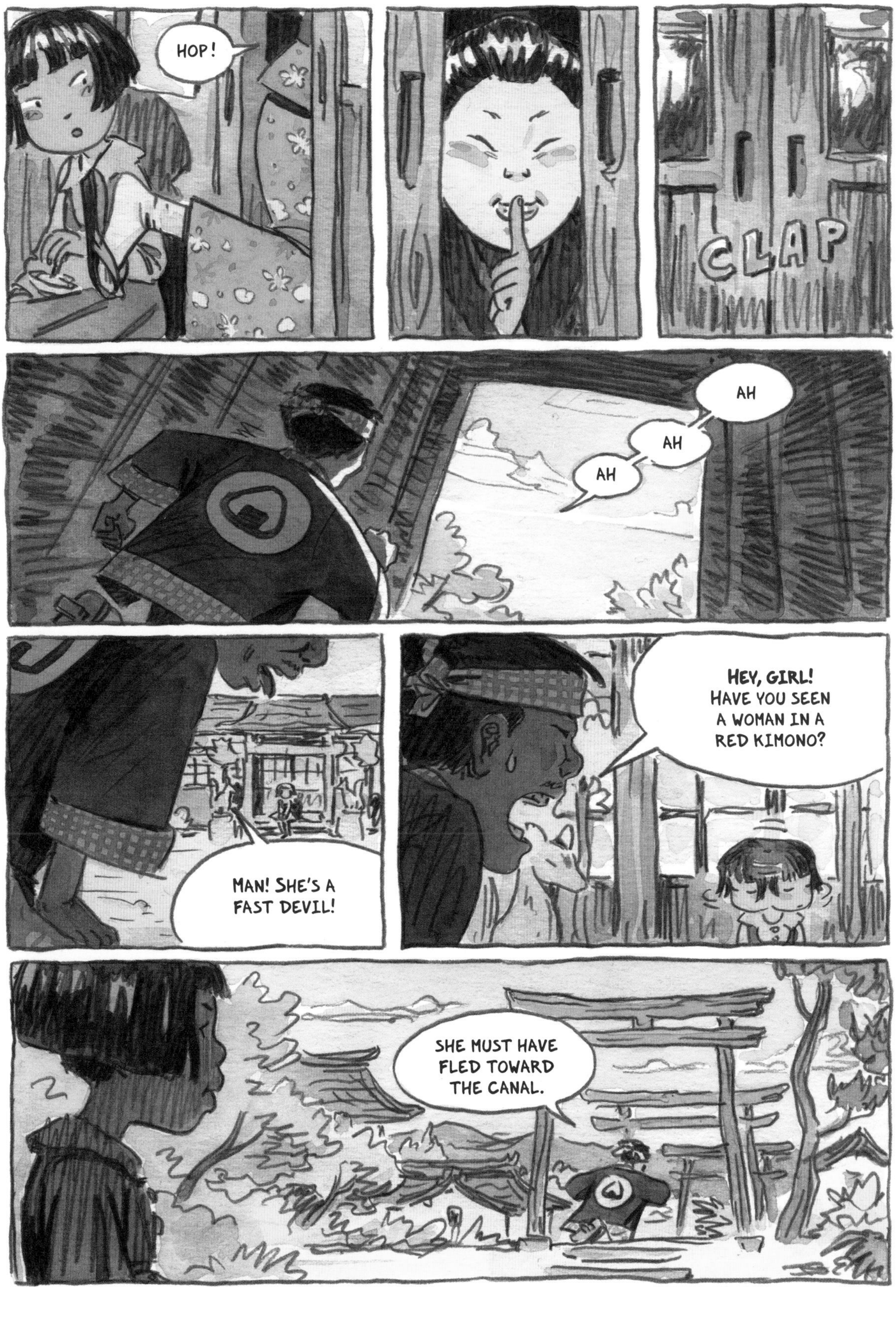
HOP!
CLAP
AH
AH
AH
MAN! SHE'S A FAST DEVIL!
HEY, GIRL! HAVE YOU SEEN A WOMAN IN A RED KIMONO?
SHE MUST HAVE FLED TOWARD THE CANAL.

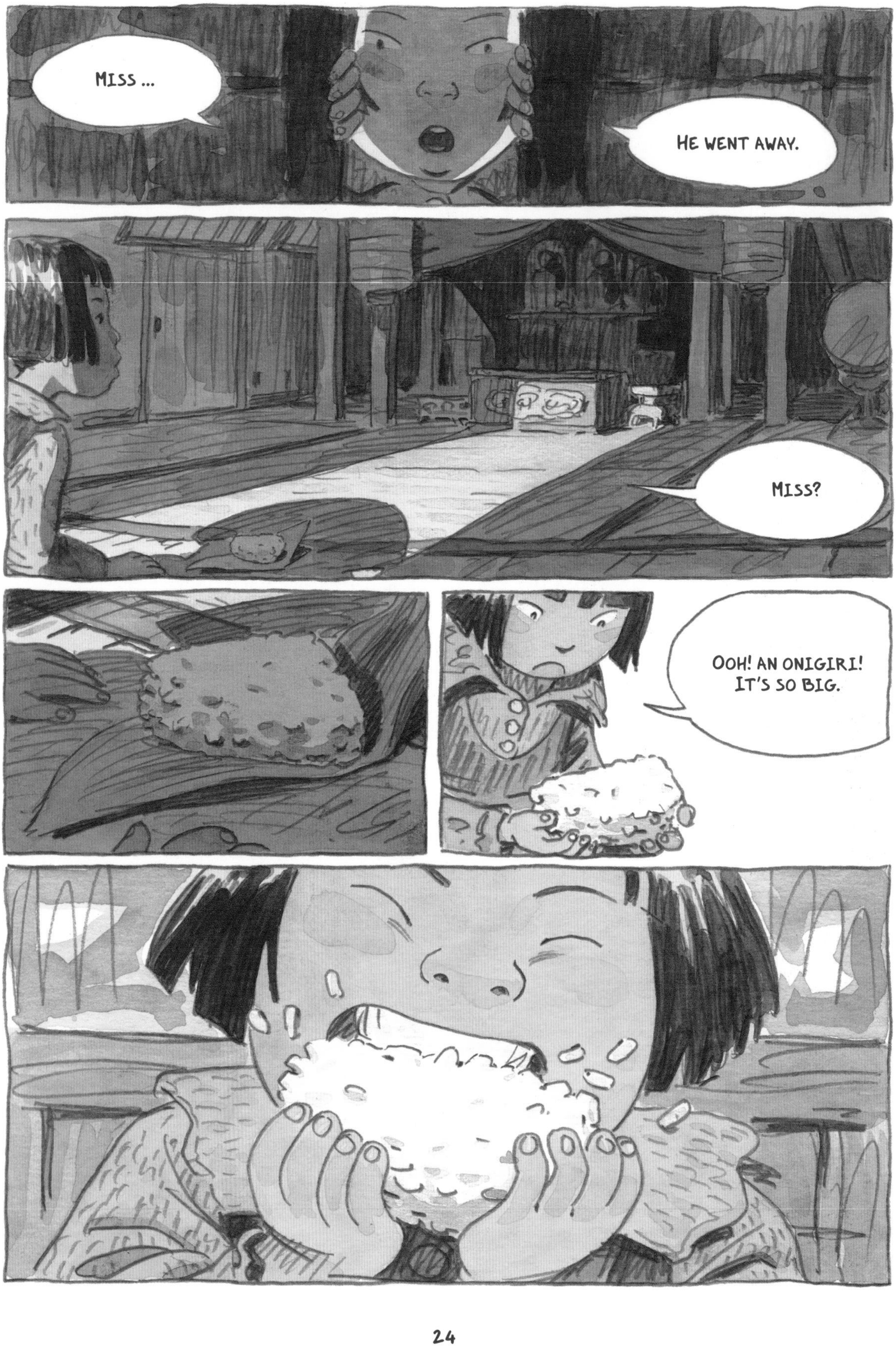
MISS ...
HE WENT AWAY.
MISS?
OOH! AN ONIGIRI! IT'S SO BIG.

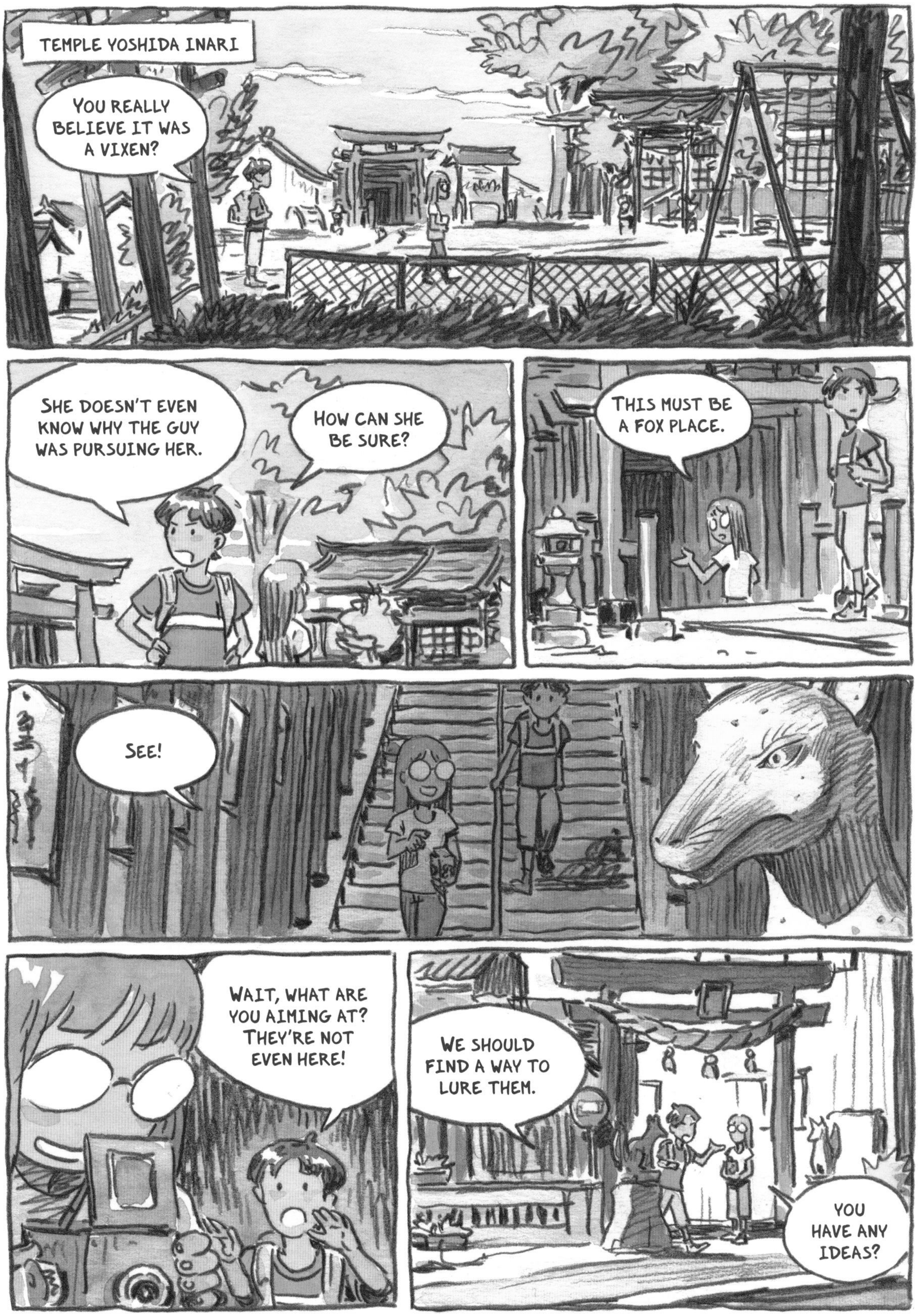
TEMPLE YOSHIDA INARI
YOU REALLY BELIEVE IT WAS A VIXEN?
SHE DOESN'T EVEN KNOW WHY THE GUY WAS PURSUING HER.
HOW CAN SHE BE SURE?
THIS MUST BE A FOX PLACE.
SEE!
WAIT, WHAT ARE YOU AIMING AT? THEY'RE NOT EVEN HERE!
WE SHOULD FIND A WAY TO LURE THEM.
YOU HAVE ANY IDEAS?

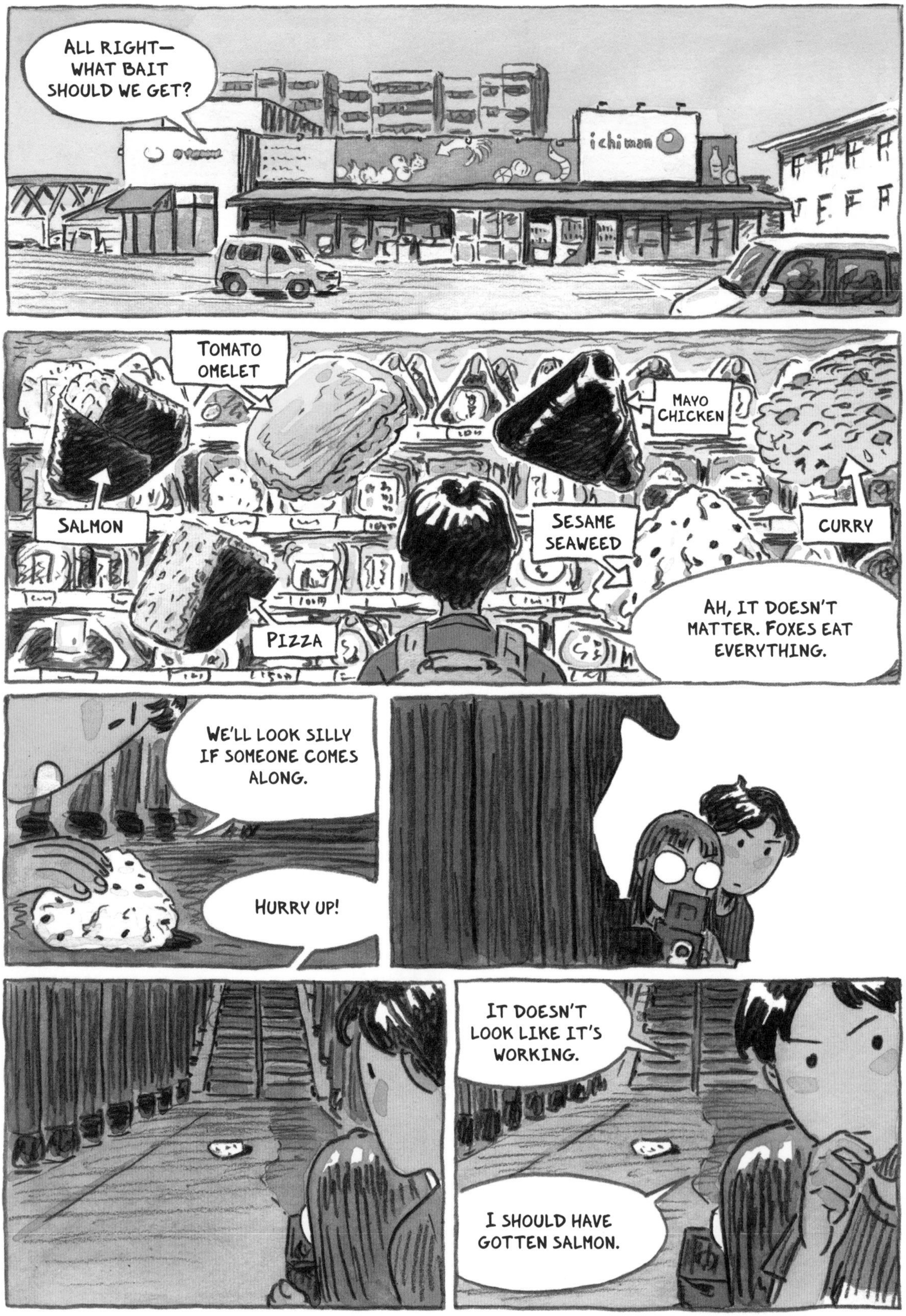
ALL RIGHT—
WHAT BAIT
SHOULD WE GET?
ichiman
TOMATO OMELET
MAYO CHICKEN
SALMON
SESAME SEAWEED
CURRY
PIZZA
AH, IT DOESN'T MATTER. FOXES EAT EVERYTHING.
WE'LL LOOK SILLY IF SOMEONE COMES ALONG.
HURRY UP!
IT DOESN'T LOOK LIKE IT'S WORKING.
I SHOULD HAVE GOTTEN SALMON.

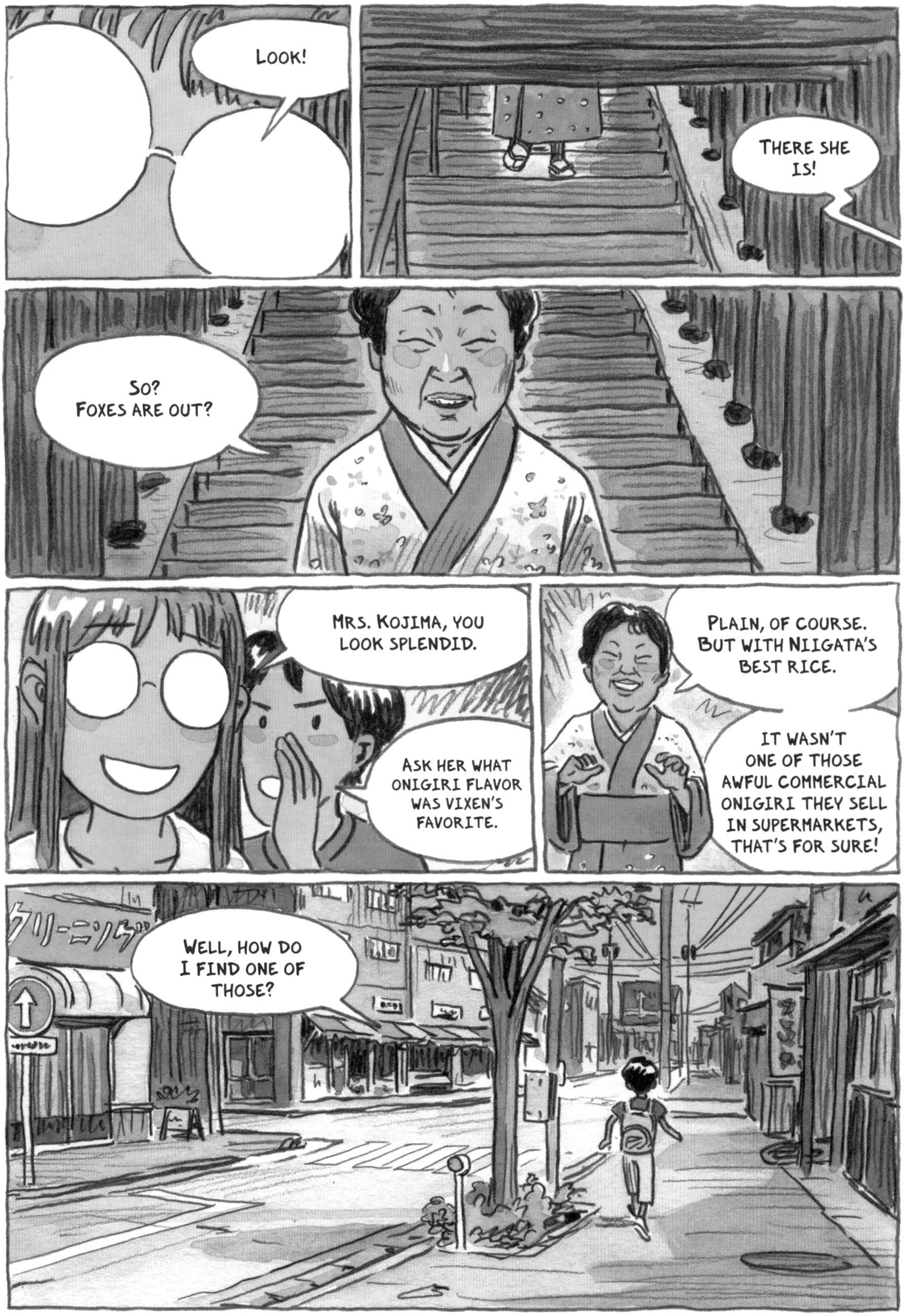
LOOK!
THERE SHE IS!
SO? FOXES ARE OUT?
MRS. KOJIMA, YOU LOOK SPLENDID.
ASK HER WHAT ONIGIRI FLAVOR WAS VIXEN'S FAVORITE.
PLAIN, OF COURSE. BUT WITH NIIGATA'S BEST RICE.
IT WASN'T ONE OF THOSE AWFUL COMMERCIAL ONIGIRI THEY SELL IN SUPERMARKETS, THAT'S FOR SURE!
クリーニング
WELL, HOW DO I FIND ONE OF THOSE?

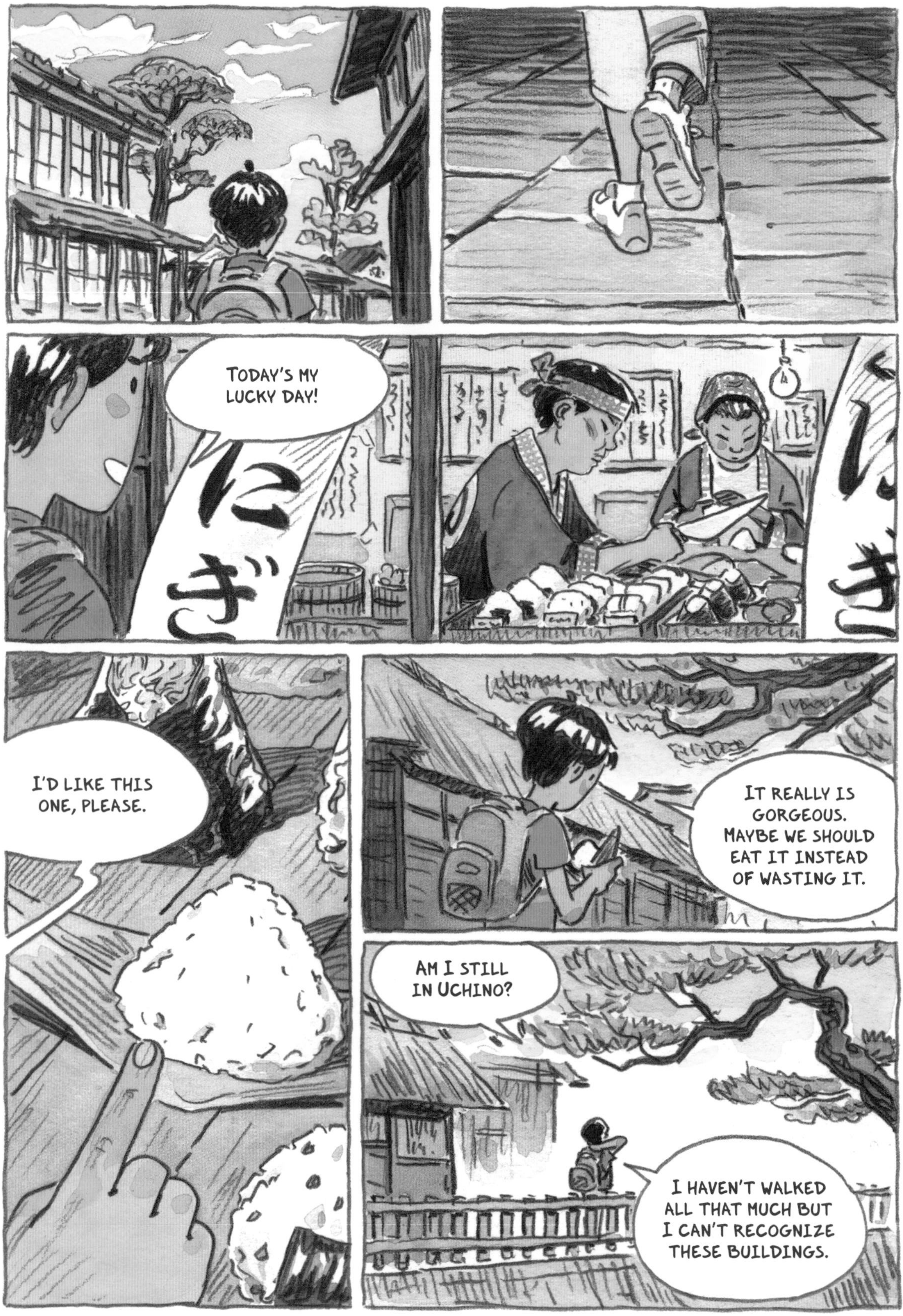
TODAY'S MY LUCKY DAY!
にぎ
にぎ
I'D LIKE THIS ONE, PLEASE.
IT REALLY IS GORGEOUS. MAYBE WE SHOULD EAT IT INSTEAD OF WASTING IT.
AM I STILL IN UCHINO?
I HAVEN'T WALKED ALL THAT MUCH BUT I CAN'T RECOGNIZE THESE BUILDINGS.

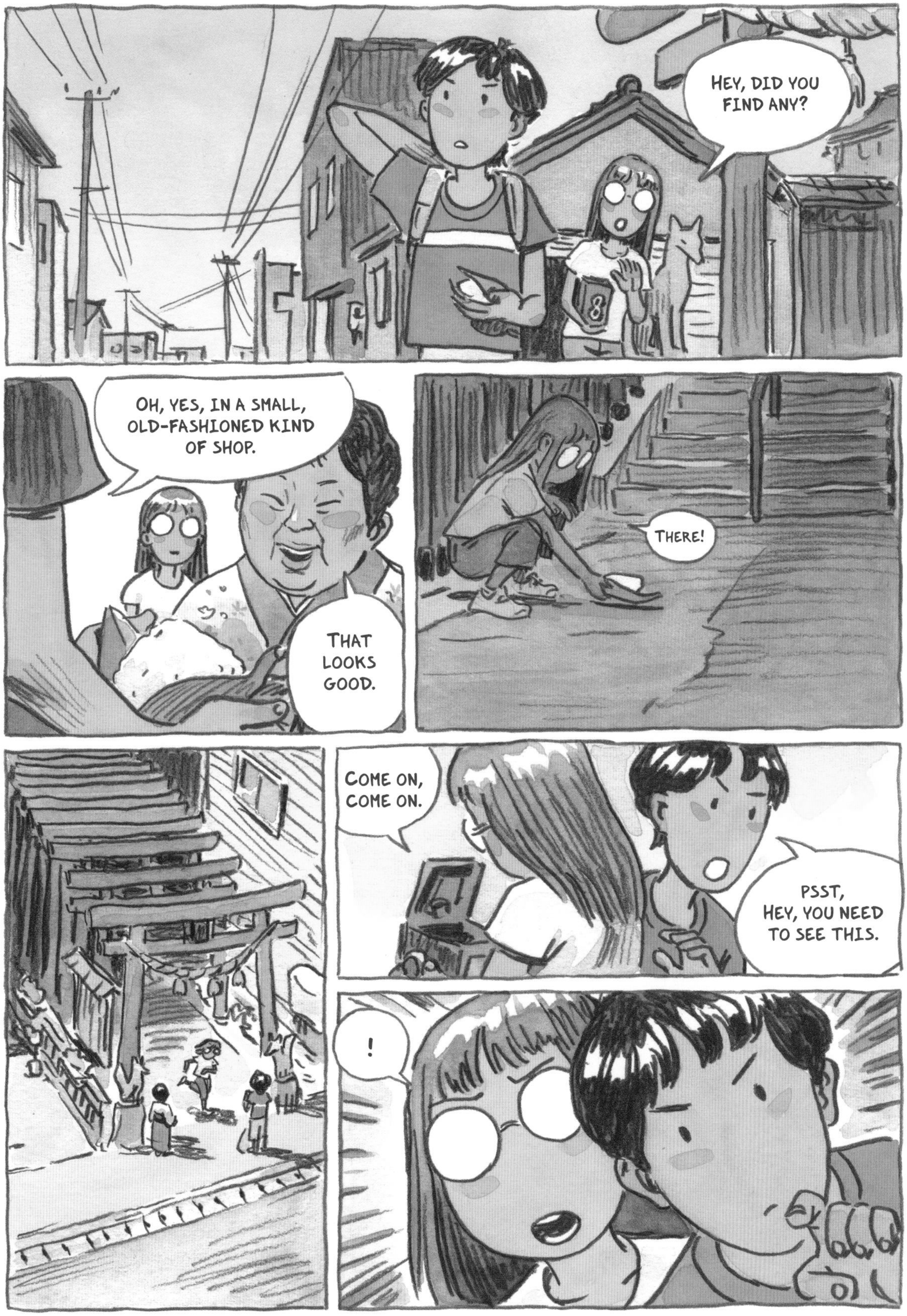
HEY, DID YOU FIND ANY?
OH, YES, IN A SMALL, OLD-FASHIONED KIND OF SHOP.
THAT LOOKS GOOD.
THERE!
COME ON, COME ON.
PSST, HEY, YOU NEED TO SEE THIS.
!

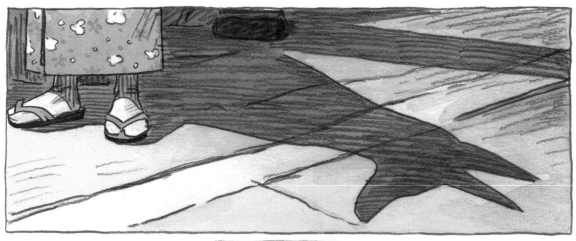

AH.

IT DISAPPEARED.

OH, NO. WE'VE MISSED IT!

WHAT DO I DO? DO I STILL TAKE THE PICTURE?

WHY NOT? GO AHEAD. YOU NEVER KNOW: THERE MIGHT BE ONE NAPPING.

WELL, WHERE'S MRS. KOJIMA?

CLICK

DON'T KNOW. SHE MUST HAVE HAD AN ERRAND.

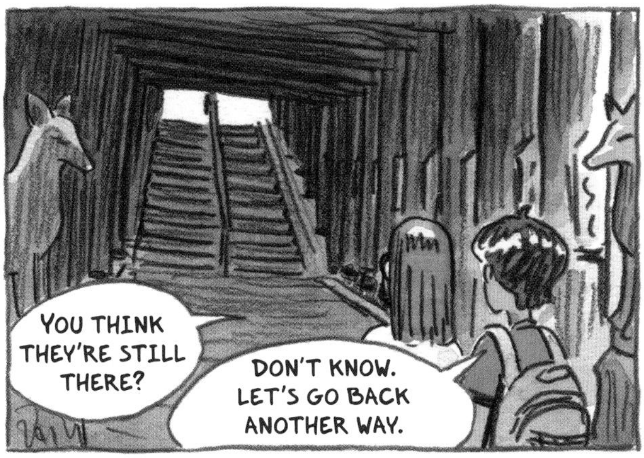
YOU THINK THEY'RE STILL THERE?
DON'T KNOW. LET'S GO BACK ANOTHER WAY.

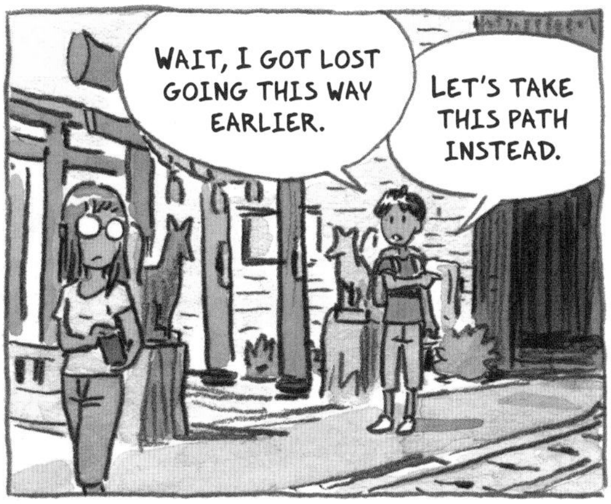
WAIT, I GOT LOST GOING THIS WAY EARLIER.
LET'S TAKE THIS PATH INSTEAD.

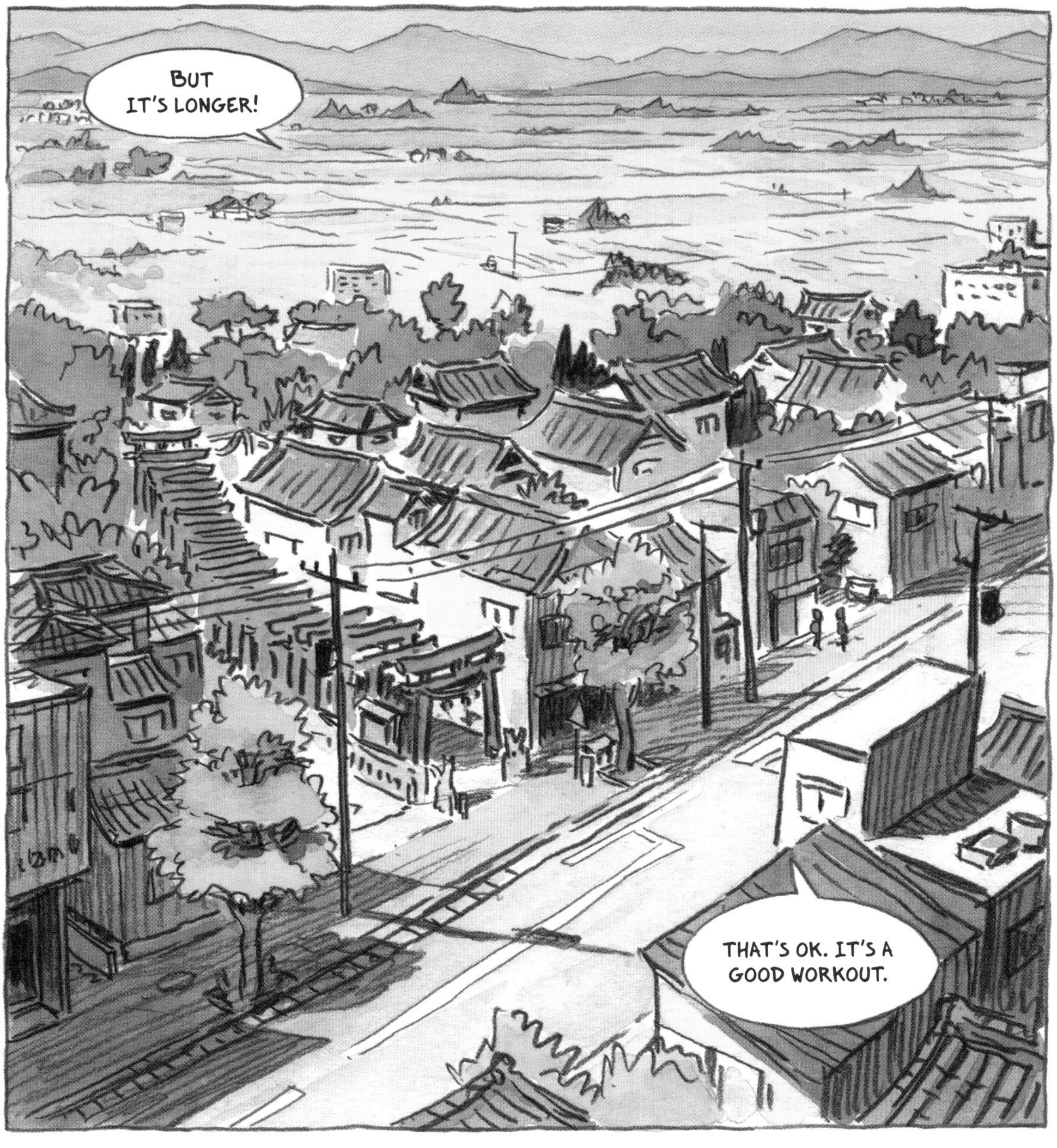
BUT IT'S LONGER!
THAT'S OK. IT'S A GOOD WORKOUT.

Photo 1/8

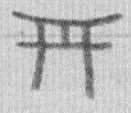

The torii path
(foxes)

Uchino
9/18/2014
Lightly cloudy sky

Settings:

Light 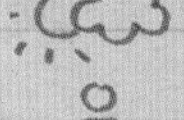

Distance 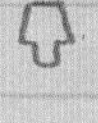

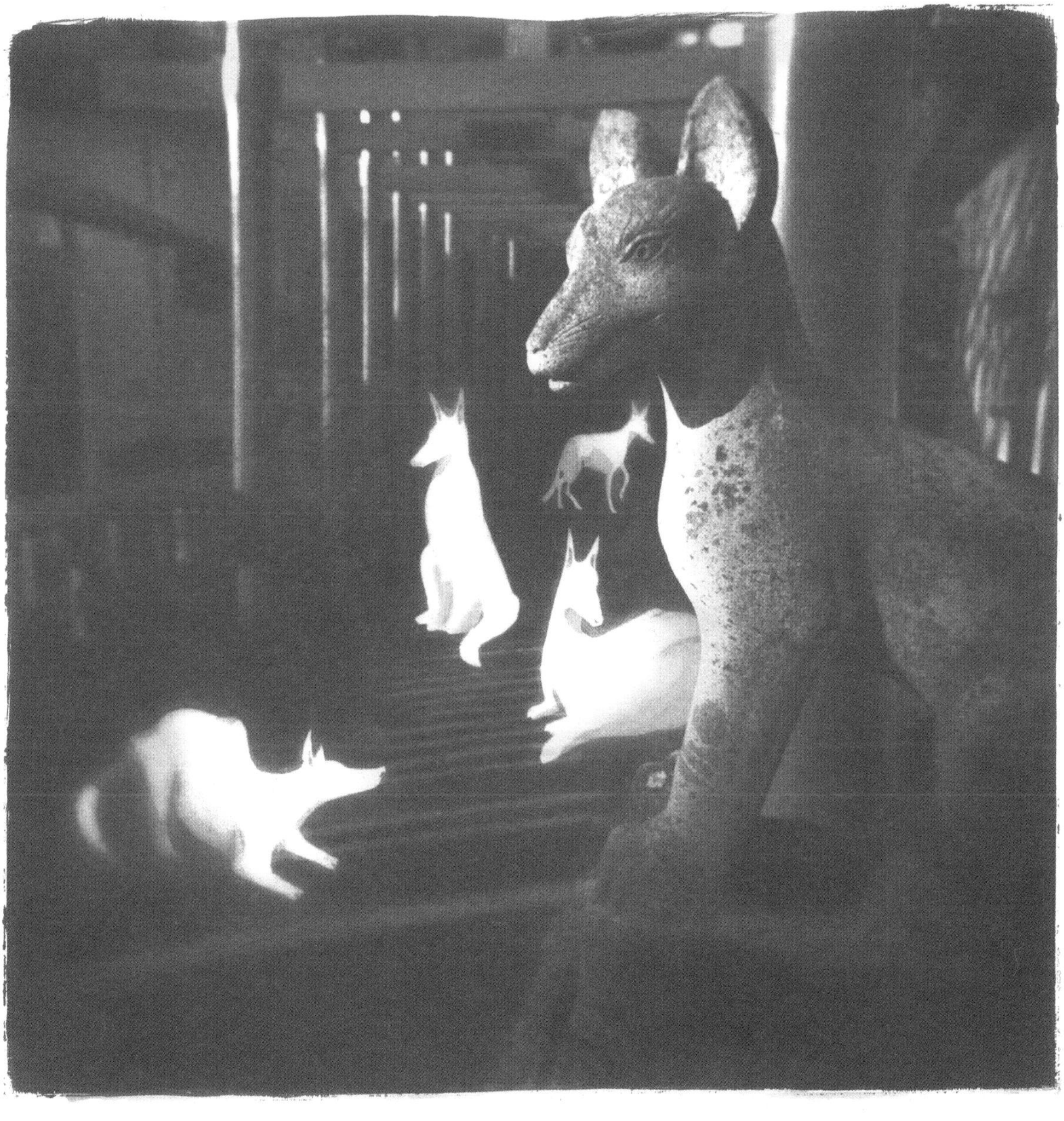

2

The magical forest

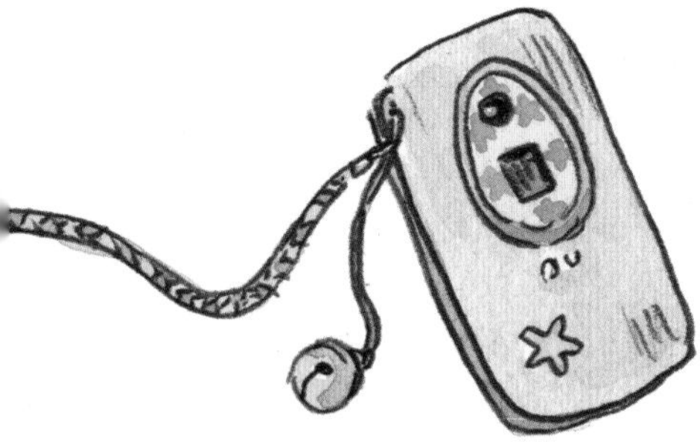
au

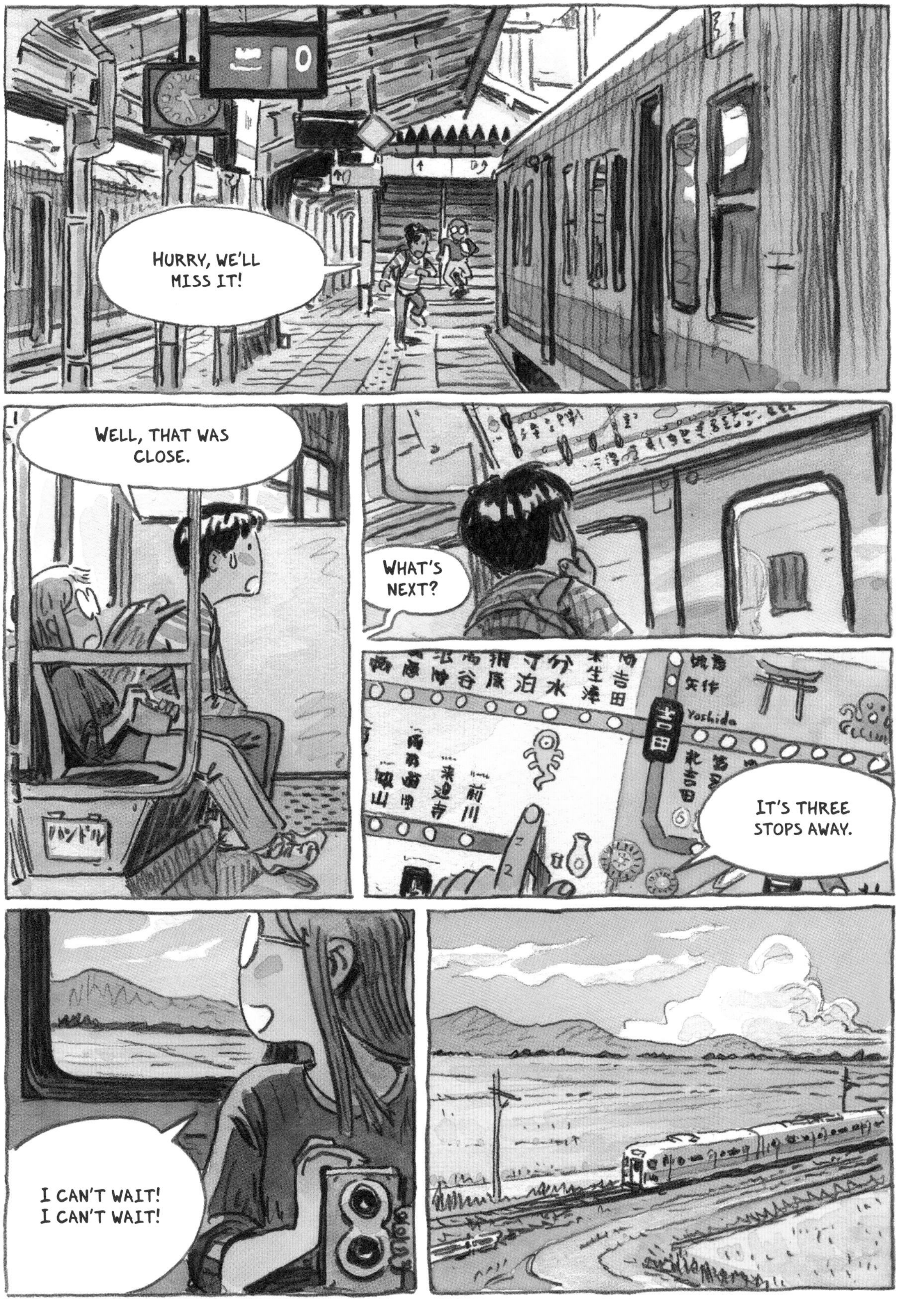
HURRY, WE'LL MISS IT!
WELL, THAT WAS CLOSE.
ハンドル
WHAT'S NEXT?
吉田
Yoshida
IT'S THREE STOPS AWAY.
I CAN'T WAIT! I CAN'T WAIT!

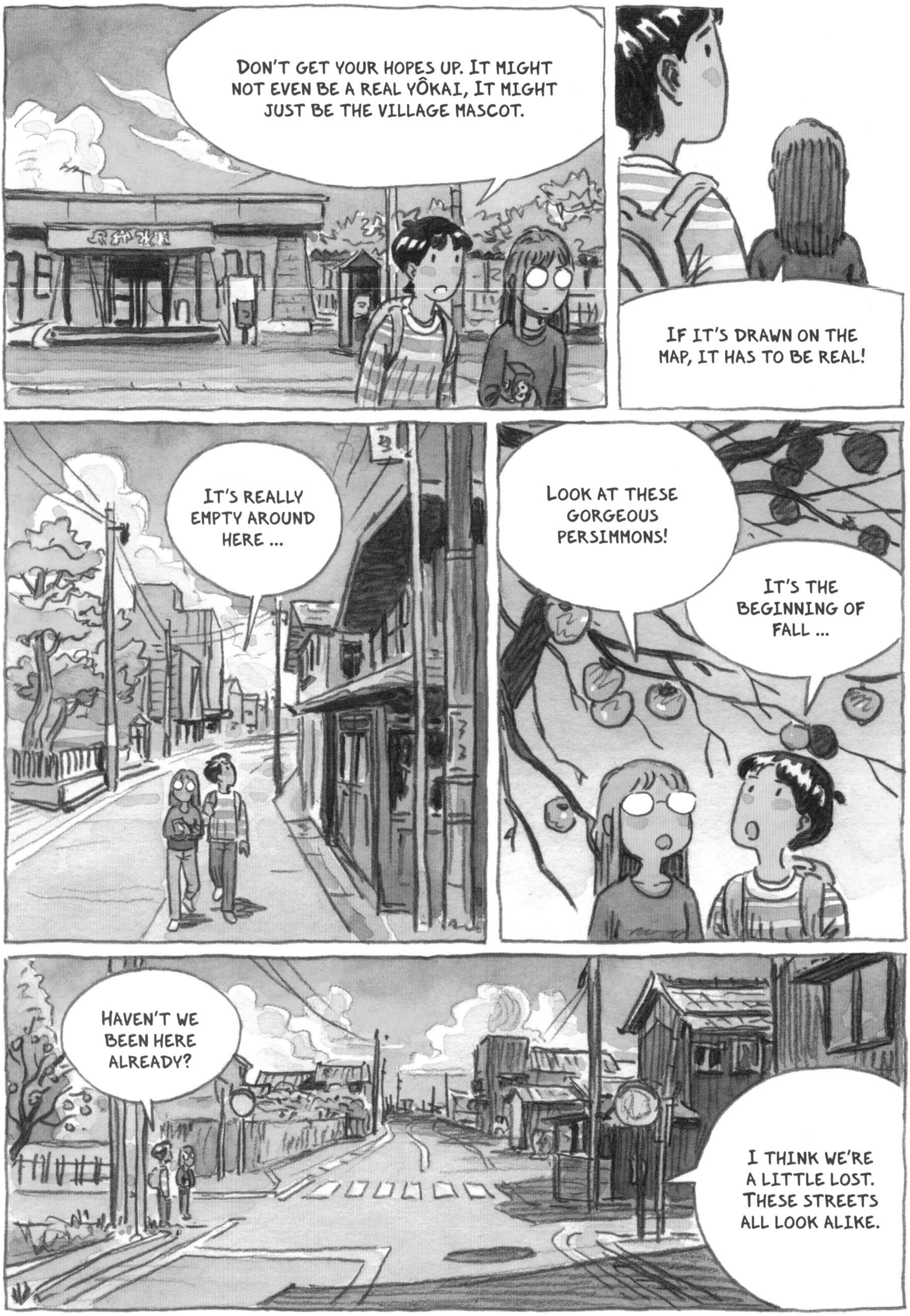
DON'T GET YOUR HOPES UP. IT MIGHT NOT EVEN BE A REAL YÔKAI, IT MIGHT JUST BE THE VILLAGE MASCOT.
IF IT'S DRAWN ON THE MAP, IT HAS TO BE REAL!
IT'S REALLY EMPTY AROUND HERE ...
LOOK AT THESE GORGEOUS PERSIMMONS!
IT'S THE BEGINNING OF FALL ...
HAVEN'T WE BEEN HERE ALREADY?
I THINK WE'RE A LITTLE LOST. THESE STREETS ALL LOOK ALIKE.

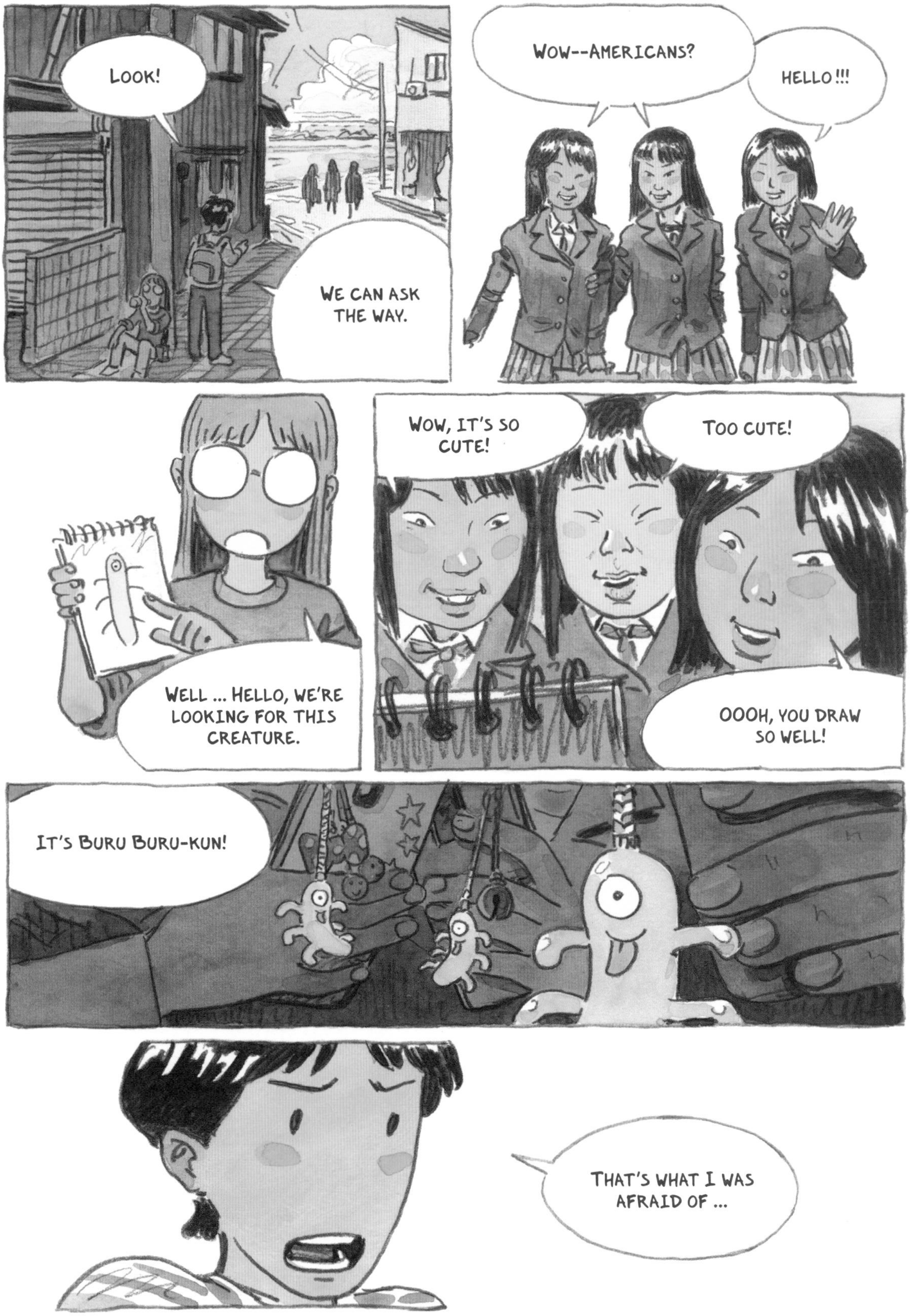

LOOK!
WE CAN ASK THE WAY.
WOW--AMERICANS?
HELLO!!!
WELL ... HELLO, WE'RE LOOKING FOR THIS CREATURE.
WOW, IT'S SO CUTE!
TOO CUTE!
OOOH, YOU DRAW SO WELL!
IT'S BURU BURU-KUN!
THAT'S WHAT I WAS AFRAID OF ...

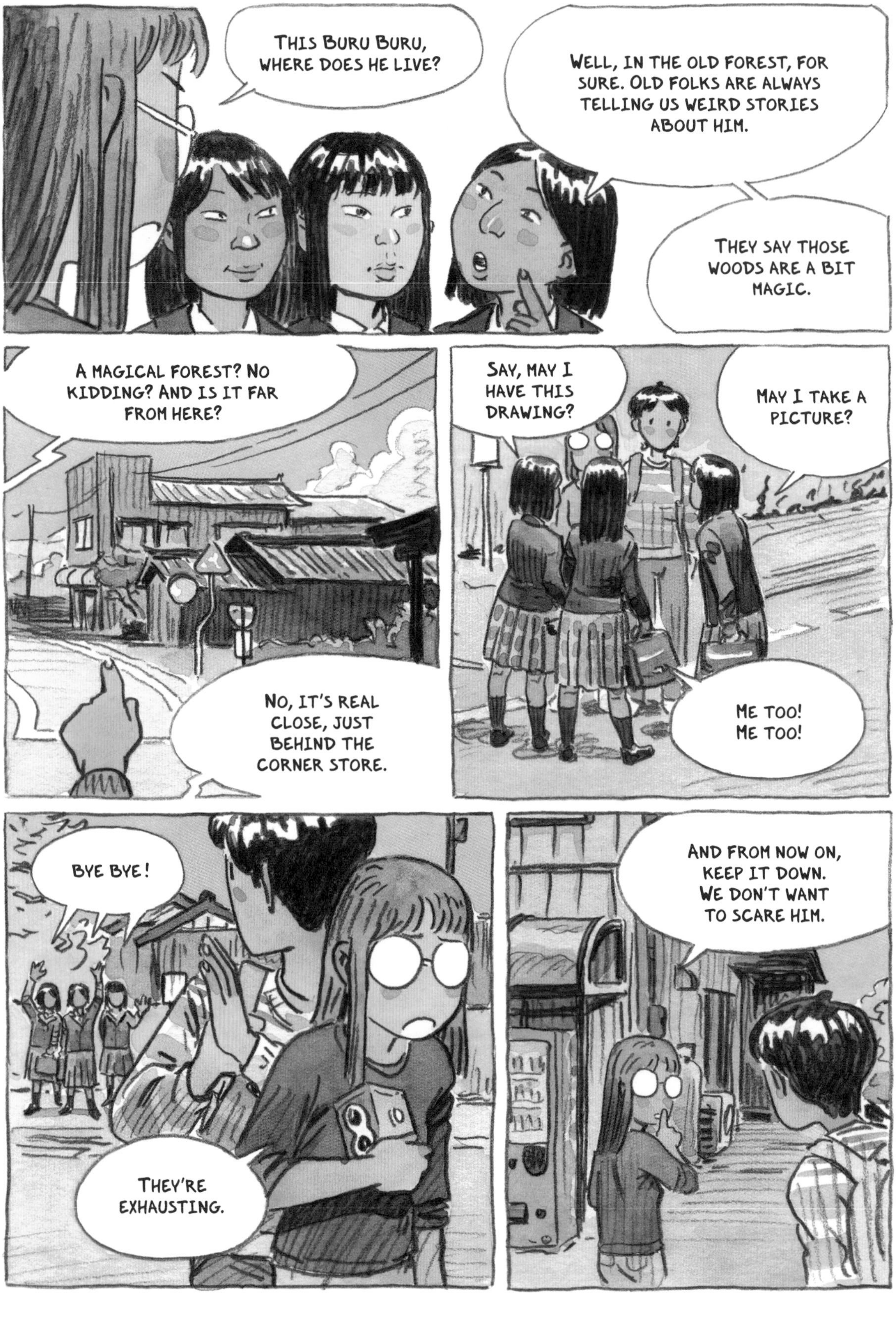
THIS BURU BURU, WHERE DOES HE LIVE?
WELL, IN THE OLD FOREST, FOR SURE. OLD FOLKS ARE ALWAYS TELLING US WEIRD STORIES ABOUT HIM.
THEY SAY THOSE WOODS ARE A BIT MAGIC.
A MAGICAL FOREST? NO KIDDING? AND IS IT FAR FROM HERE?
NO, IT'S REAL CLOSE, JUST BEHIND THE CORNER STORE.
SAY, MAY I HAVE THIS DRAWING?
MAY I TAKE A PICTURE?
ME TOO! ME TOO!
BYE BYE!
THEY'RE EXHAUSTING.
AND FROM NOW ON, KEEP IT DOWN. WE DON'T WANT TO SCARE HIM.

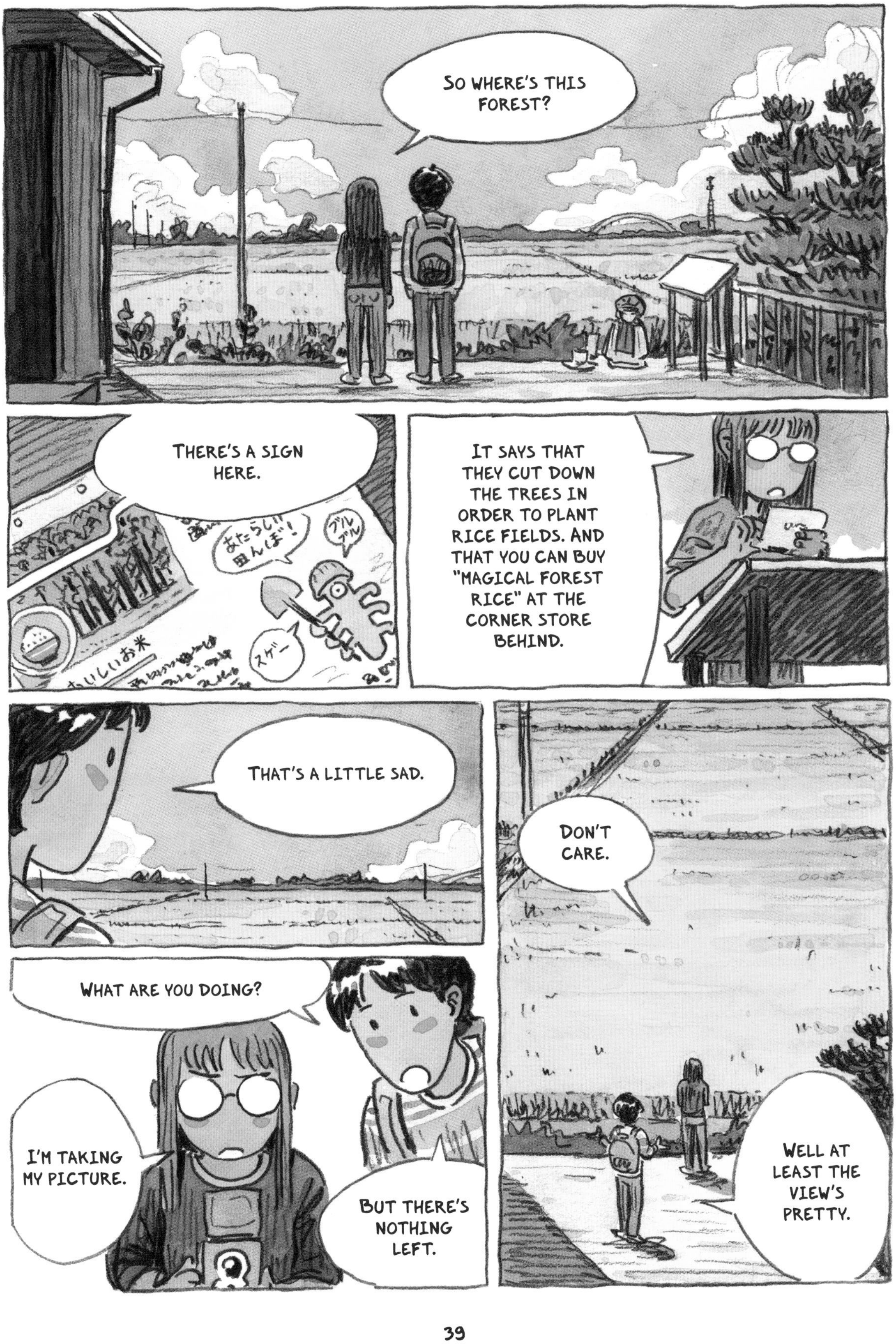

SO WHERE'S THIS FOREST?
THERE'S A SIGN HERE.
あたらしい田んぼ！
ブルブル
スゲー
おいしいお米
IT SAYS THAT THEY CUT DOWN THE TREES IN ORDER TO PLANT RICE FIELDS. AND THAT YOU CAN BUY "MAGICAL FOREST RICE" AT THE CORNER STORE BEHIND.
THAT'S A LITTLE SAD.
DON'T CARE.
WHAT ARE YOU DOING?
I'M TAKING MY PICTURE.
BUT THERE'S NOTHING LEFT.
WELL AT LEAST THE VIEW'S PRETTY.

Photo 2/8

Magical Forest
(Buru Buru)

Bunsui
10/2/2014
Clear weather

Settings:

Light 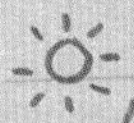
Distance 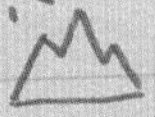

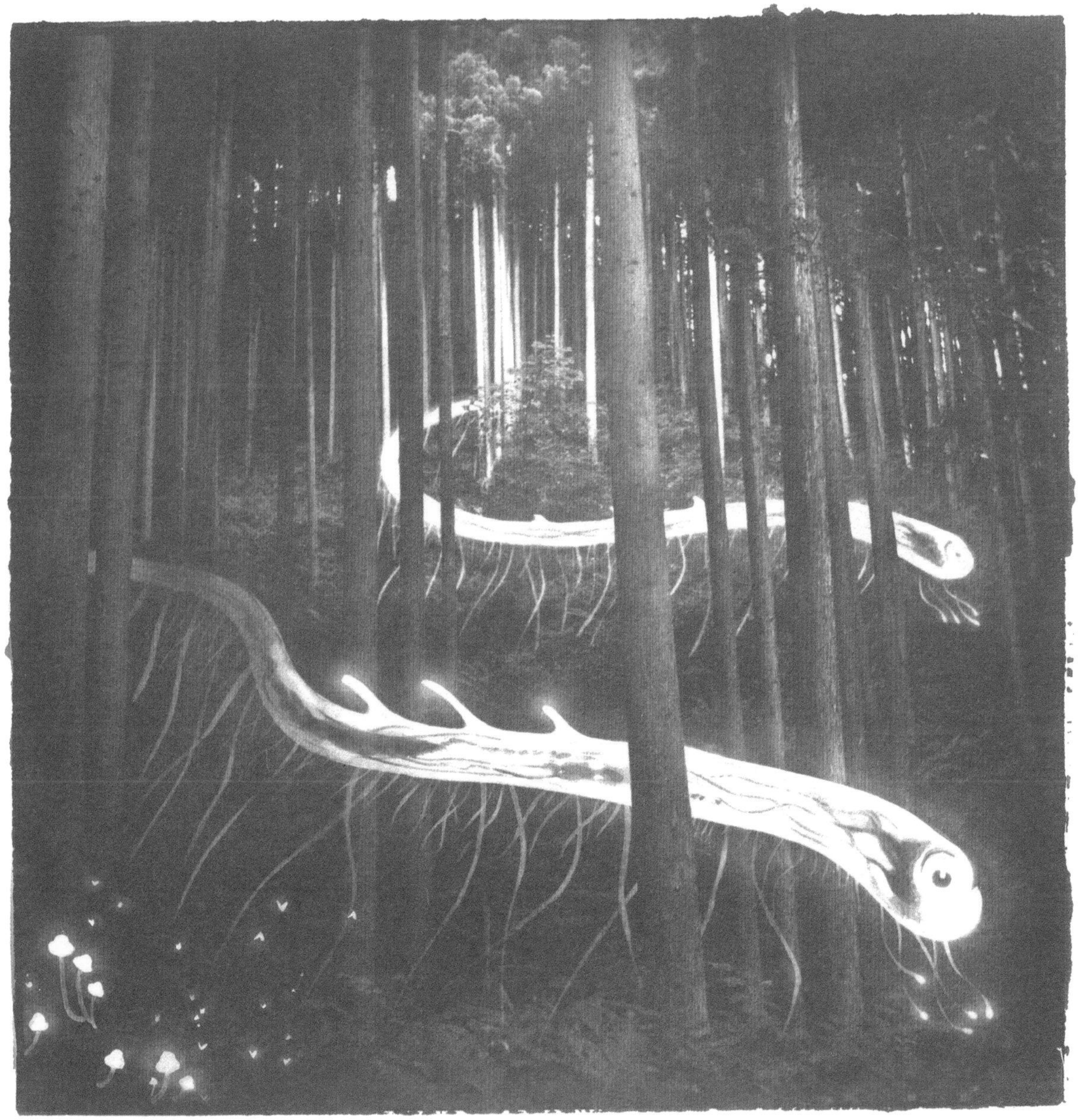

The Floating World

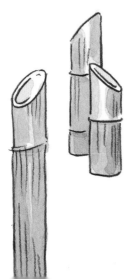

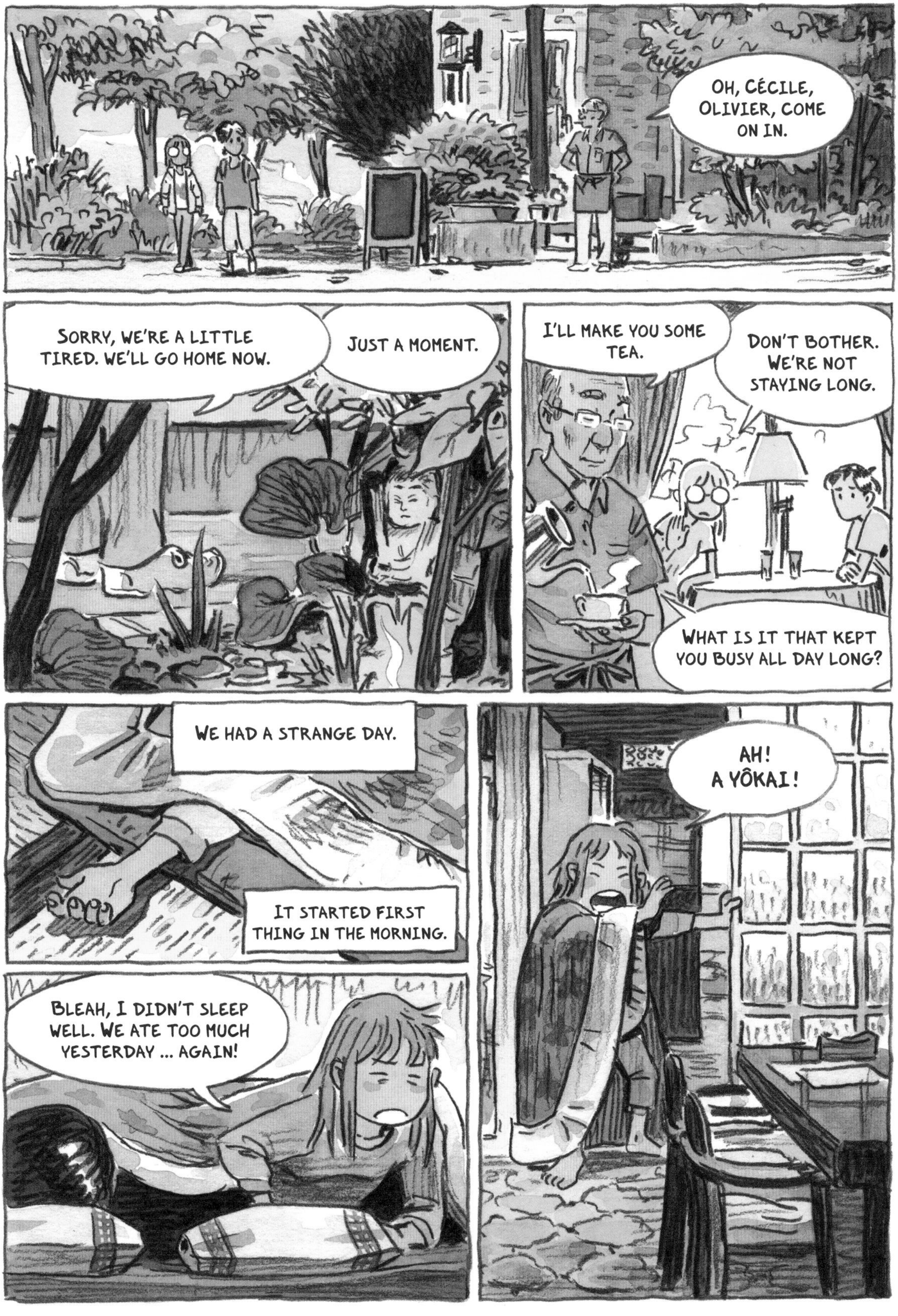
OH, CÉCILE, OLIVIER, COME ON IN.
SORRY, WE'RE A LITTLE TIRED. WE'LL GO HOME NOW.
JUST A MOMENT.
I'LL MAKE YOU SOME TEA.
DON'T BOTHER. WE'RE NOT STAYING LONG.
WHAT IS IT THAT KEPT YOU BUSY ALL DAY LONG?
WE HAD A STRANGE DAY.
IT STARTED FIRST THING IN THE MORNING.
BLEAH, I DIDN'T SLEEP WELL. WE ATE TOO MUCH YESTERDAY ... AGAIN!
AH! A YÔKAI!

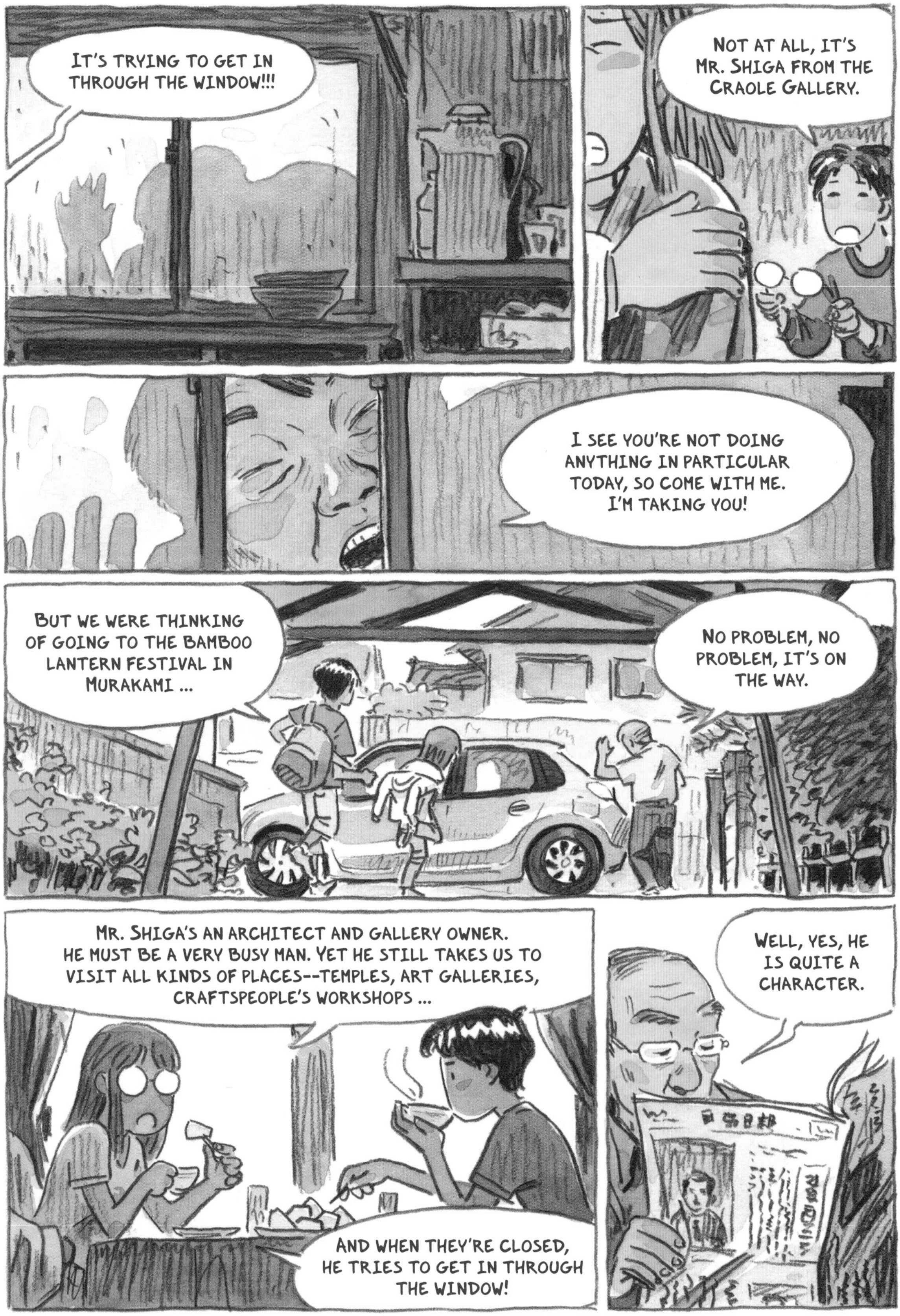
IT'S TRYING TO GET IN THROUGH THE WINDOW!!!
NOT AT ALL, IT'S MR. SHIGA FROM THE CRAOLE GALLERY.
I SEE YOU'RE NOT DOING ANYTHING IN PARTICULAR TODAY, SO COME WITH ME. I'M TAKING YOU!
BUT WE WERE THINKING OF GOING TO THE BAMBOO LANTERN FESTIVAL IN MURAKAMI ...
NO PROBLEM, NO PROBLEM, IT'S ON THE WAY.
MR. SHIGA'S AN ARCHITECT AND GALLERY OWNER. HE MUST BE A VERY BUSY MAN. YET HE STILL TAKES US TO VISIT ALL KINDS OF PLACES--TEMPLES, ART GALLERIES, CRAFTSPEOPLE'S WORKSHOPS ...
AND WHEN THEY'RE CLOSED, HE TRIES TO GET IN THROUGH THE WINDOW!
WELL, YES, HE IS QUITE A CHARACTER.

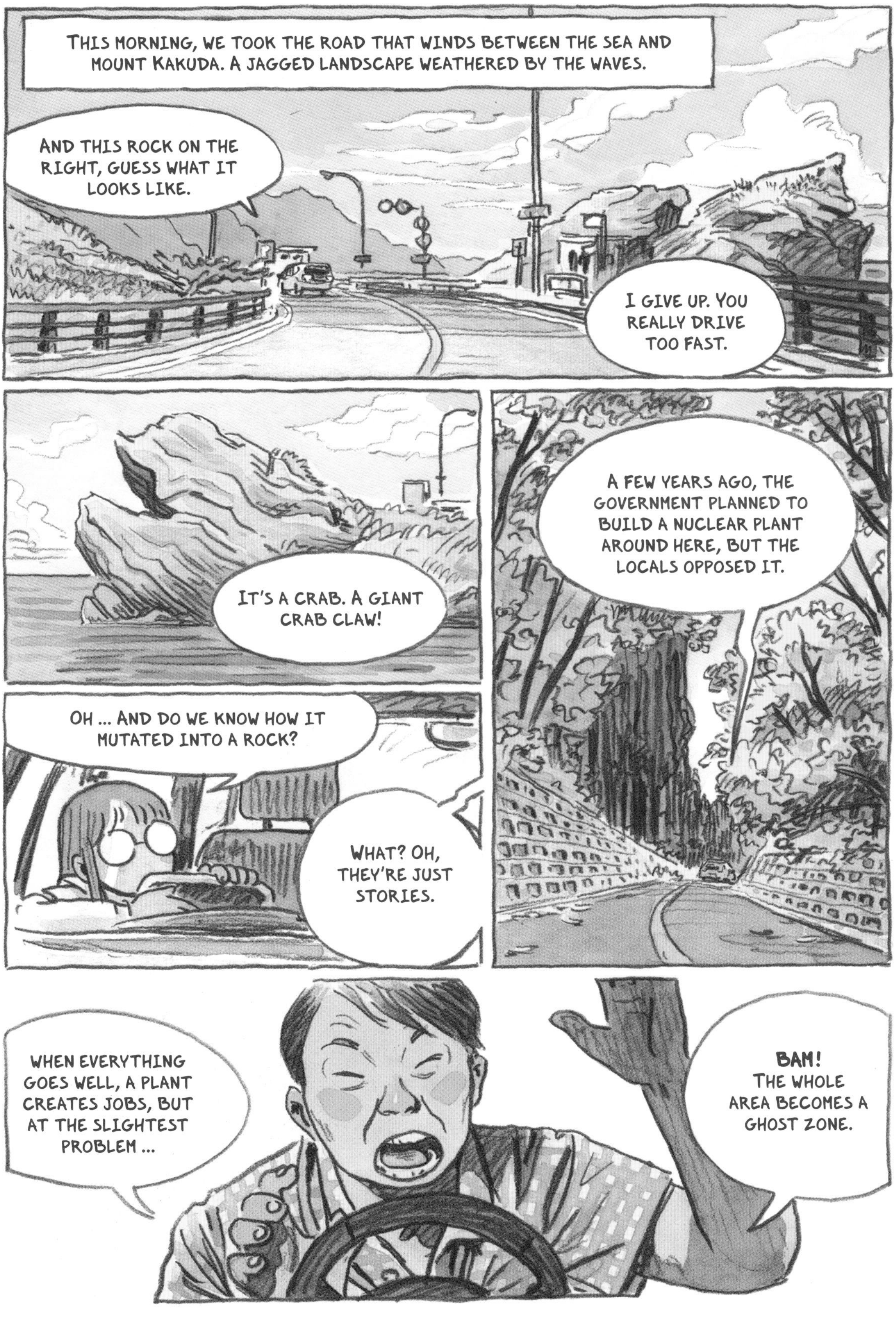
THIS MORNING, WE TOOK THE ROAD THAT WINDS BETWEEN THE SEA AND MOUNT KAKUDA. A JAGGED LANDSCAPE WEATHERED BY THE WAVES.
AND THIS ROCK ON THE RIGHT, GUESS WHAT IT LOOKS LIKE.
I GIVE UP. YOU REALLY DRIVE TOO FAST.
IT'S A CRAB. A GIANT CRAB CLAW!
OH ... AND DO WE KNOW HOW IT MUTATED INTO A ROCK?
WHAT? OH, THEY'RE JUST STORIES.
A FEW YEARS AGO, THE GOVERNMENT PLANNED TO BUILD A NUCLEAR PLANT AROUND HERE, BUT THE LOCALS OPPOSED IT.
WHEN EVERYTHING GOES WELL, A PLANT CREATES JOBS, BUT AT THE SLIGHTEST PROBLEM ...
BAM! THE WHOLE AREA BECOMES A GHOST ZONE.

THEY SAY NUCLEAR PLANTS GIVE OFF A BLUE GLOW. LIKE THE ONIBI, THESE WILL-O'-THE WISP THAT COME BEFORE THE APPARITION OF SPECTRES ... IT'S A MORBID LIGHT. IT CAN SUCK IN THE SPIRIT OF ANYONE WHO CROSSES ITS PATH.

WE CREATED MODERN MONSTERS TO REPLACE THE TRADITIONAL ONES.

THIS MOUNTAIN, WE HAVE TO PROTECT IT. IT HAS A WHOLE STORY.

BACK IN THE DAY, THERE WAS A FAMOUS MONK WHO LIVED HERE. RYOKAN WAS HIS NAME.

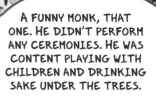

A FUNNY MONK, THAT ONE. HE DIDN'T PERFORM ANY CEREMONIES. HE WAS CONTENT PLAYING WITH CHILDREN AND DRINKING SAKE UNDER THE TREES.

HE LIVED HERE, IN THIS HUT.

SITTING LIKE THIS IN THE SUN IN THE ANCIENT MONUMENT, MR. SHIGA SEEMED AT PEACE, BUT SOMETHING CAUGHT OUR EYE ...

A SPOT OF LIGHT IN THE SHADE.

IT WAS A SMALL STONE DEMON OBSERVING US INTENTLY.

FROM THIS MOMENT ON, EVERYTHING BECAME WEIRDER.
WE GOT ON THE ROAD FOR MURAKAMI ...

THE LANTERN FESTIVAL WAS
AWASH IN A TROUBLING
ATMOSPHERE.

WATCHING THIS PARADE OF WASHED-OUT SILHOUETTES,
WE ALMOST EXPECTED A YŌKAI TO APPEAR FROM THE SHADOWS.

ONE OF THE SILHOUETTES
LEFT ITS GROUP AND
CAME TOWARDS US.

WITH A CLEAR
VOICE, IT
TOLD US ...

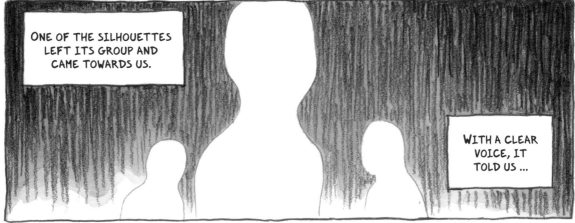

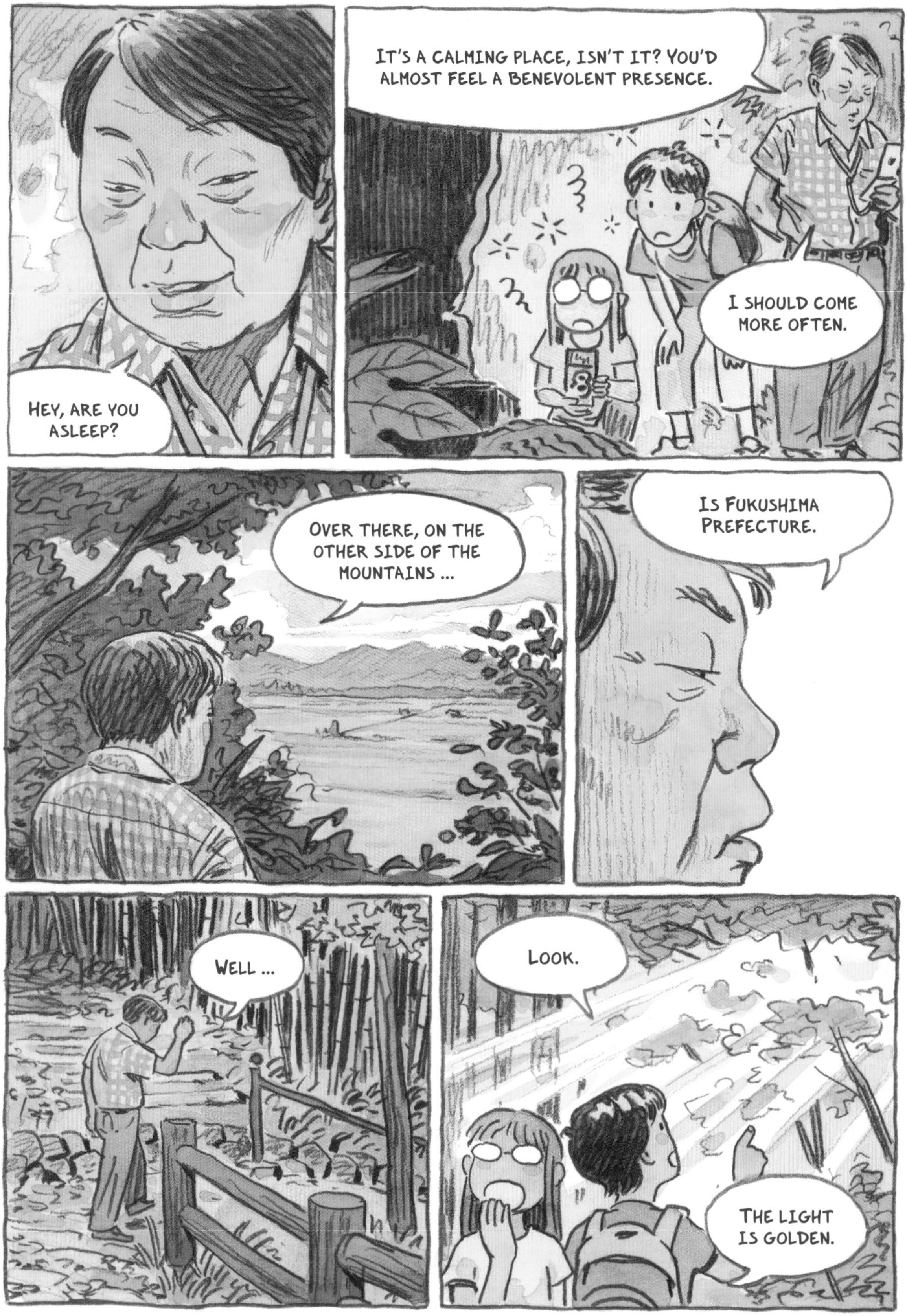
Hey, are you asleep?
It's a calming place, isn't it? You'd almost feel a benevolent presence.
I should come more often.
Over there, on the other side of the mountains ...
Is Fukushima Prefecture.
Well ...
Look.
The light is golden.

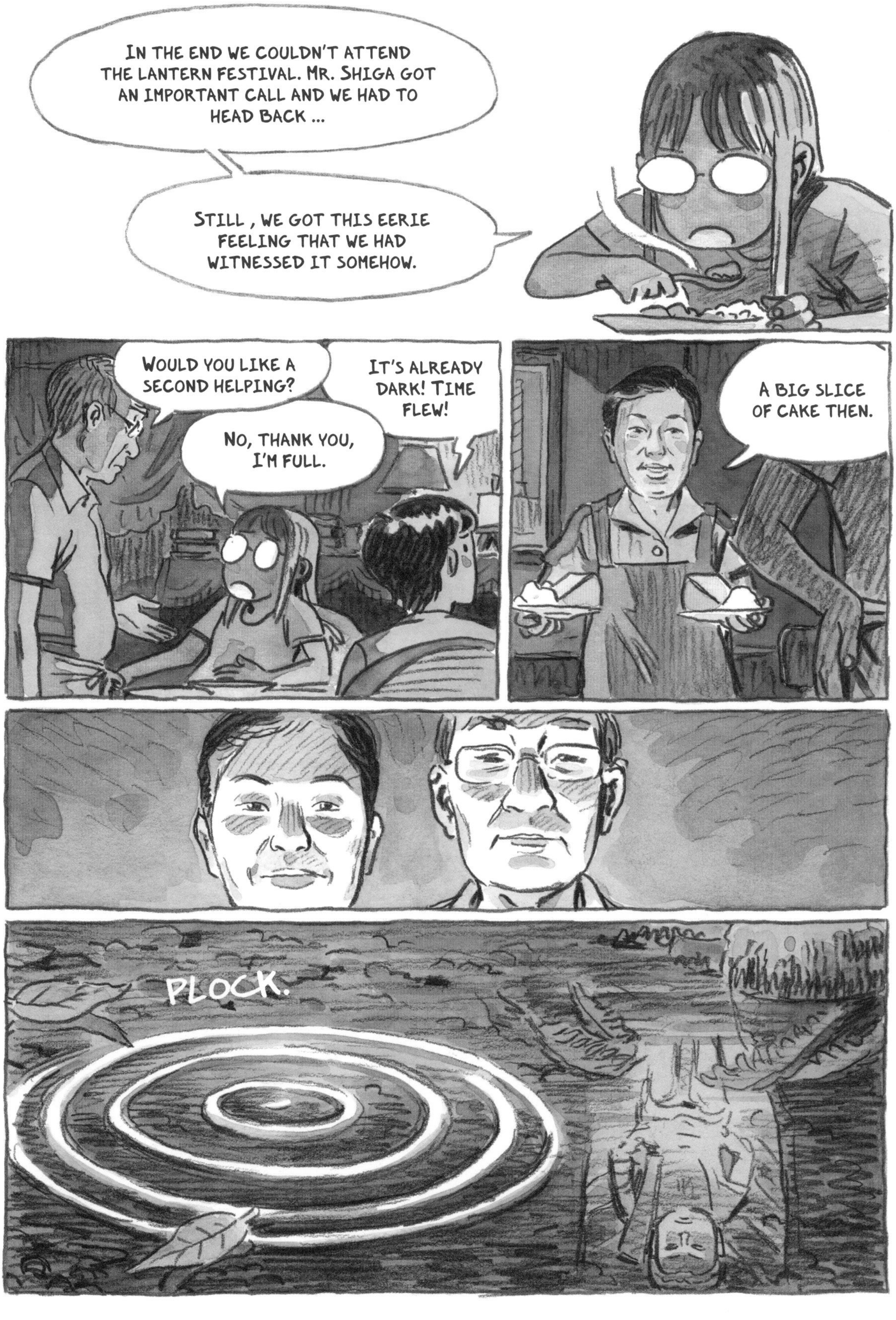
In the end we couldn't attend the lantern festival. Mr. Shiga got an important call and we had to head back ...
Still , we got this eerie feeling that we had witnessed it somehow.
Would you like a second helping?
No, thank you, I'm full.
It's already dark! Time flew!
A big slice of cake then.
PLOCK.

Stone Demon
(Onibi)

Ryokan's hut
(between Yahiko and Bunsui)
October 13, 2014
Clear sky but shot
in a dark corner.

Settings:
Light
Distance

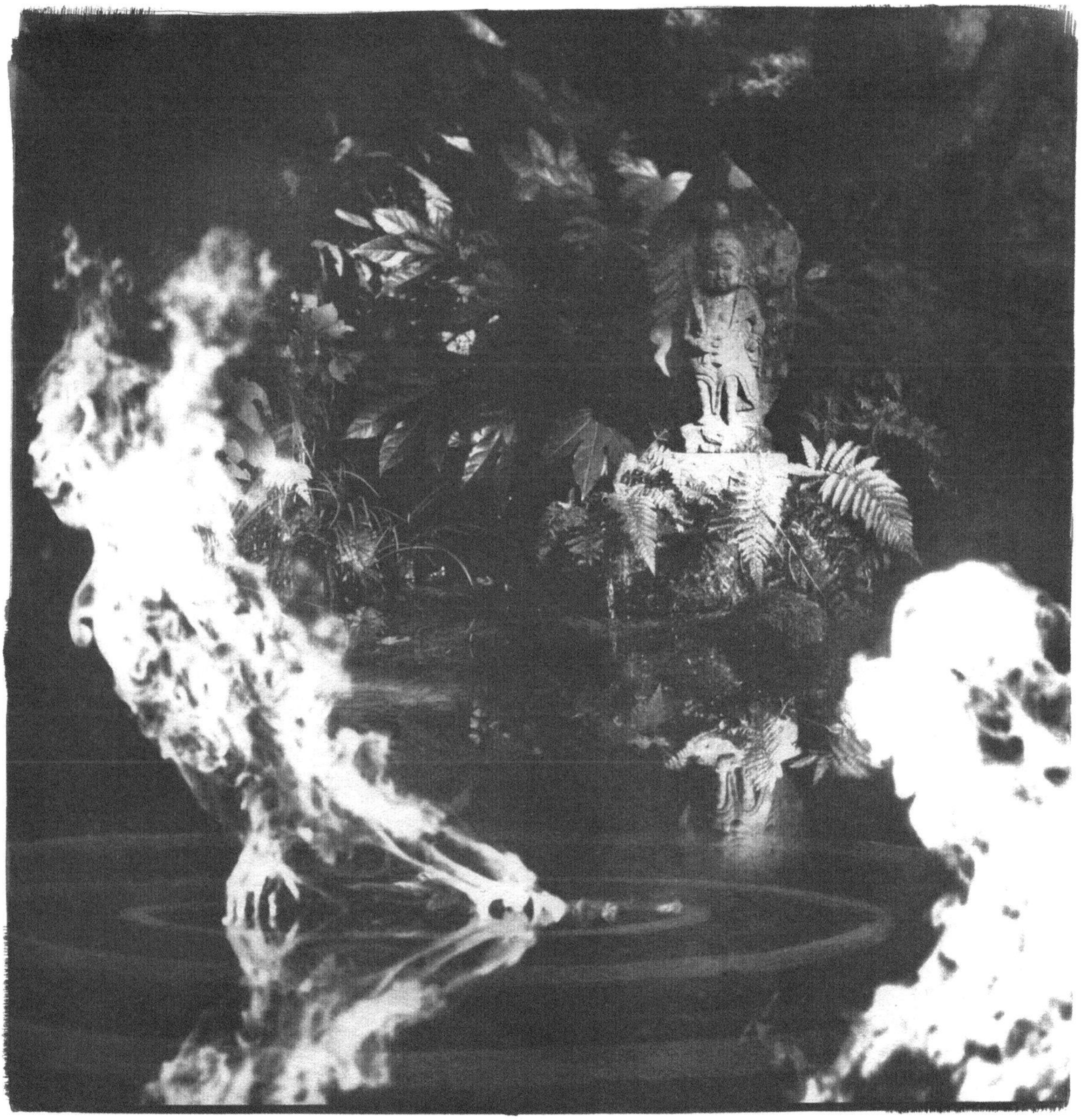

Mountain's shadow

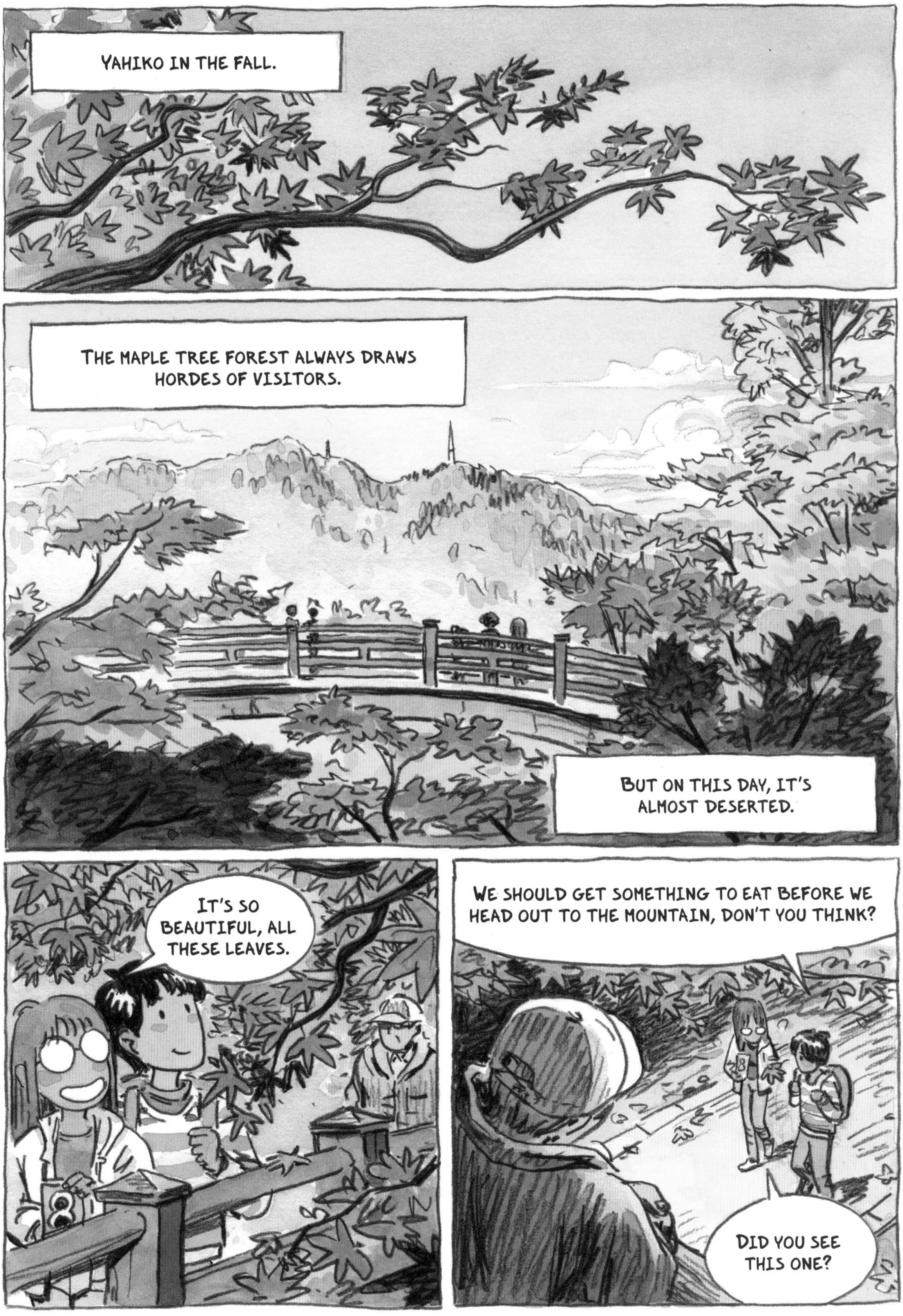

YAHIKO IN THE FALL.
THE MAPLE TREE FOREST ALWAYS DRAWS HORDES OF VISITORS.
BUT ON THIS DAY, IT'S ALMOST DESERTED.
IT'S SO BEAUTIFUL, ALL THESE LEAVES.
WE SHOULD GET SOMETHING TO EAT BEFORE WE HEAD OUT TO THE MOUNTAIN, DON'T YOU THINK?
DID YOU SEE THIS ONE?

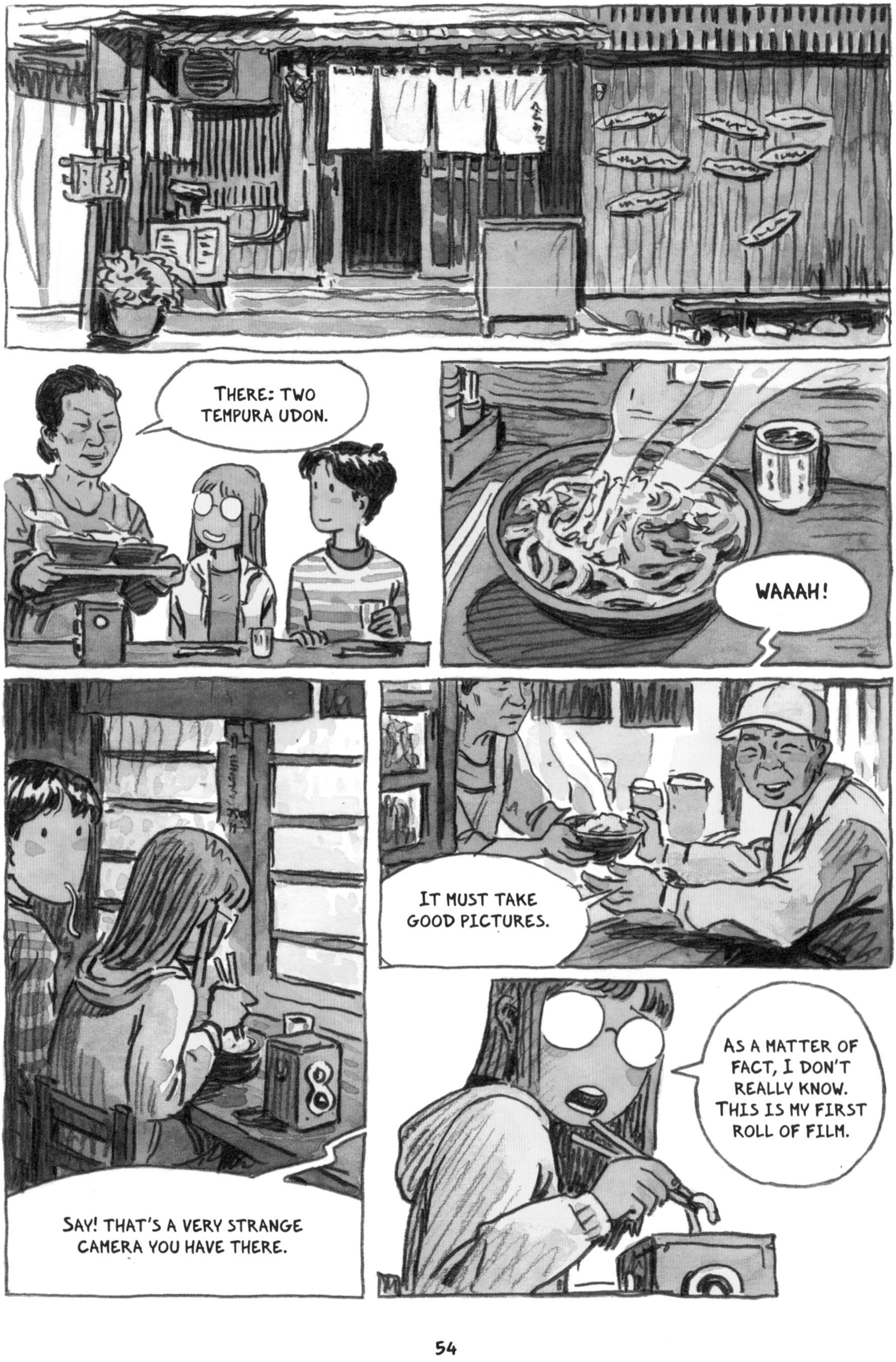
THERE: TWO TEMPURA UDON.
WAAAH!
IT MUST TAKE GOOD PICTURES.
SAY! THAT'S A VERY STRANGE CAMERA YOU HAVE THERE.
AS A MATTER OF FACT, I DON'T REALLY KNOW. THIS IS MY FIRST ROLL OF FILM.

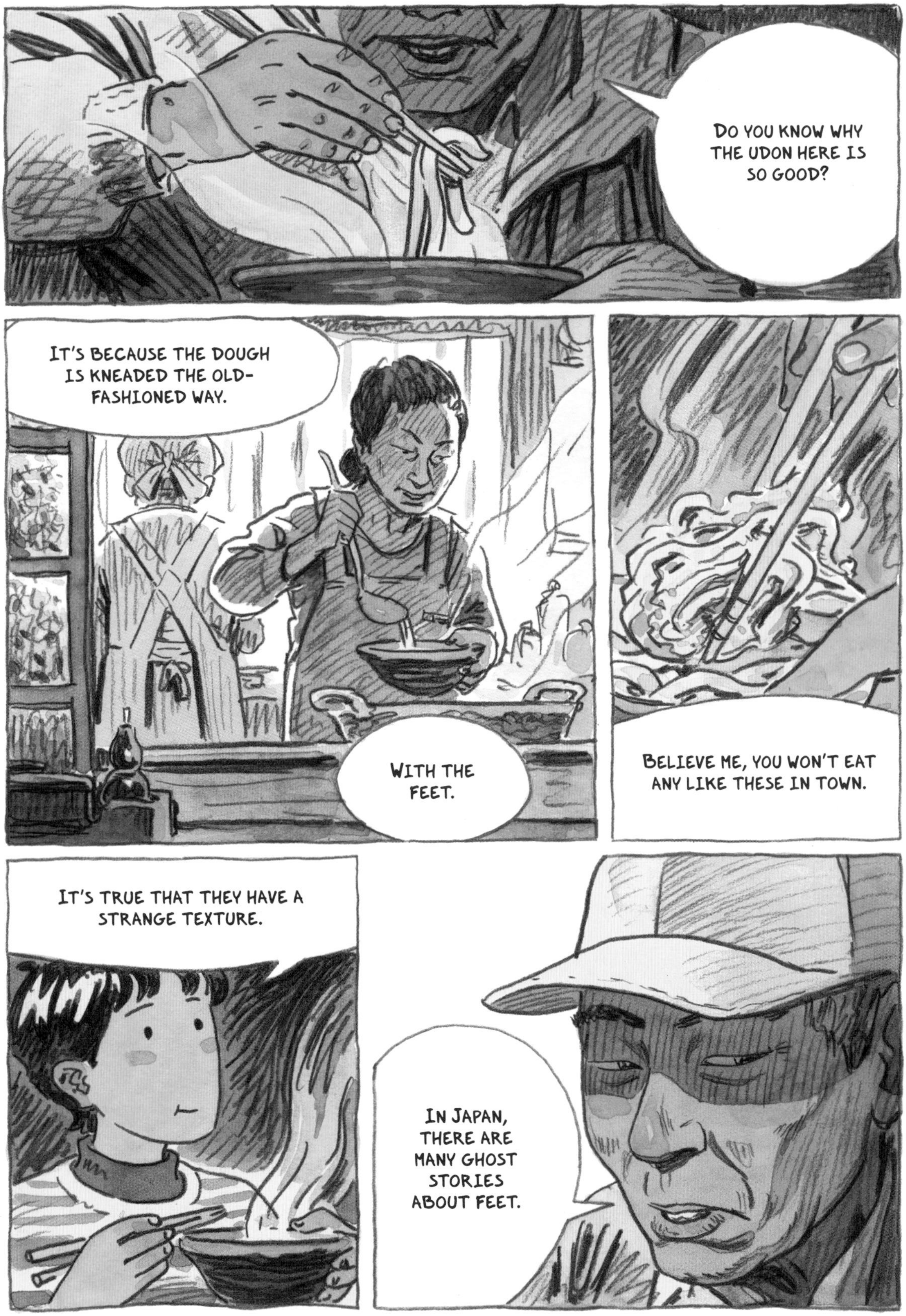
Do you know why the udon here is so good?
It's because the dough is kneaded the old-fashioned way.
With the feet.
Believe me, you won't eat any like these in town.
It's true that they have a strange texture.
In Japan, there are many ghost stories about feet.

ARE YOU MESSING WITH US?

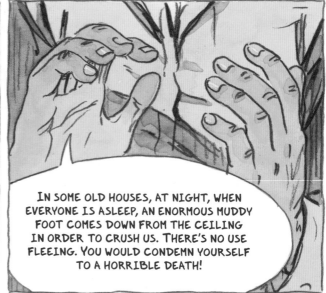

IN SOME OLD HOUSES, AT NIGHT, WHEN EVERYONE IS ASLEEP, AN ENORMOUS MUDDY FOOT COMES DOWN FROM THE CEILING IN ORDER TO CRUSH US. THERE'S NO USE FLEEING. YOU WOULD CONDEMN YOURSELF TO A HORRIBLE DEATH!

BUT IF YOU STAY QUIET AND WASH THE FOOT, IT LEAVES ON ITS OWN.

I MEAN, WHO WOULD MISS OUT ON A GOOD BATH?

THERE ARE FAMOUS ONSEN IN THE AREA. YOU SHOULD MAKE THE ROUNDS IF YOU LIKE HOT SPRINGS.

AND WHAT ABOUT YÔKAI?

DO YOU KNOW WHERE TO FIND THEM?

56

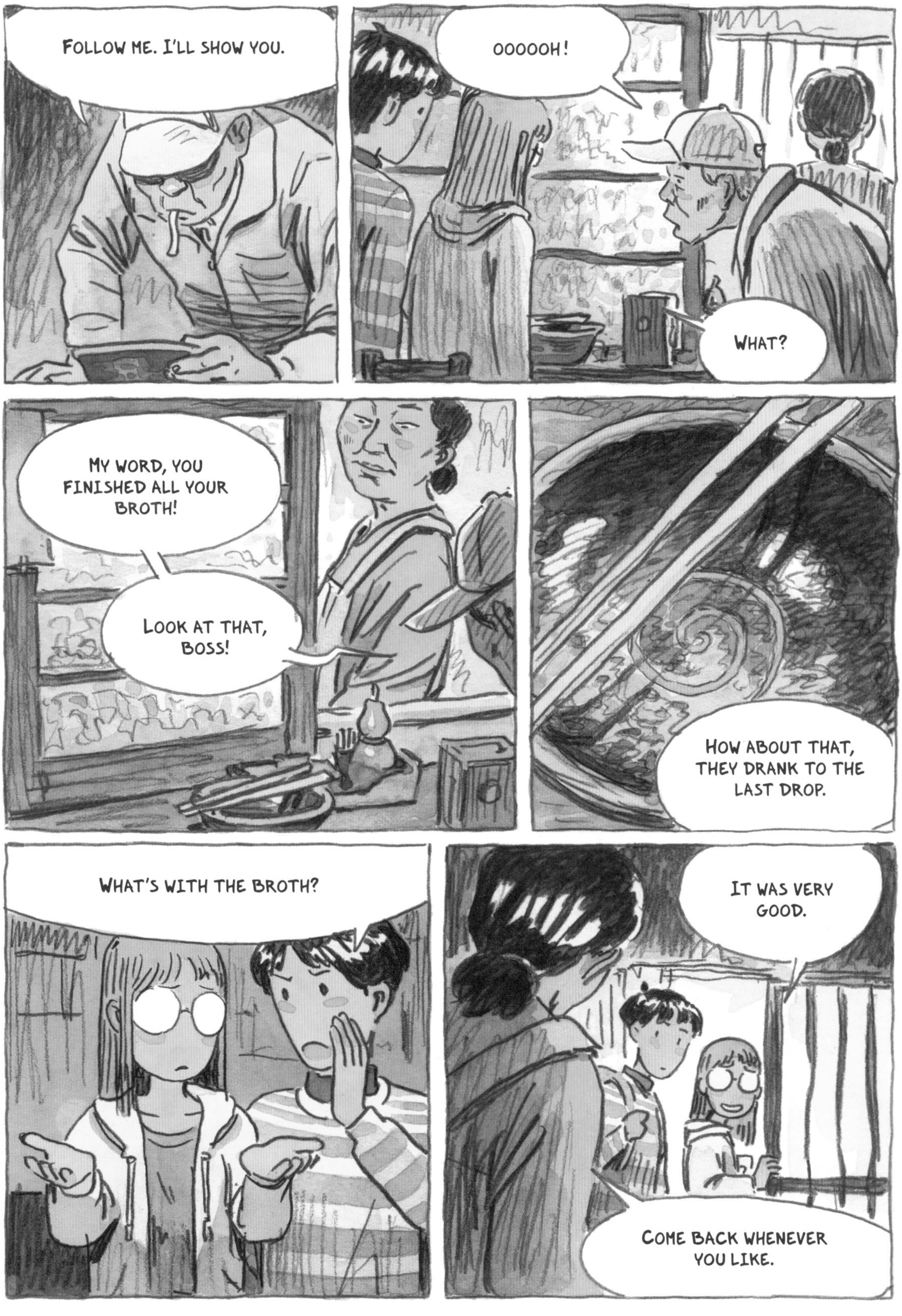
Follow me. I'll show you.
OOOOOH!
What?
My word, you finished all your broth!
Look at that, boss!
How about that, they drank to the last drop.
What's with the broth?
It was very good.
Come back whenever you like.

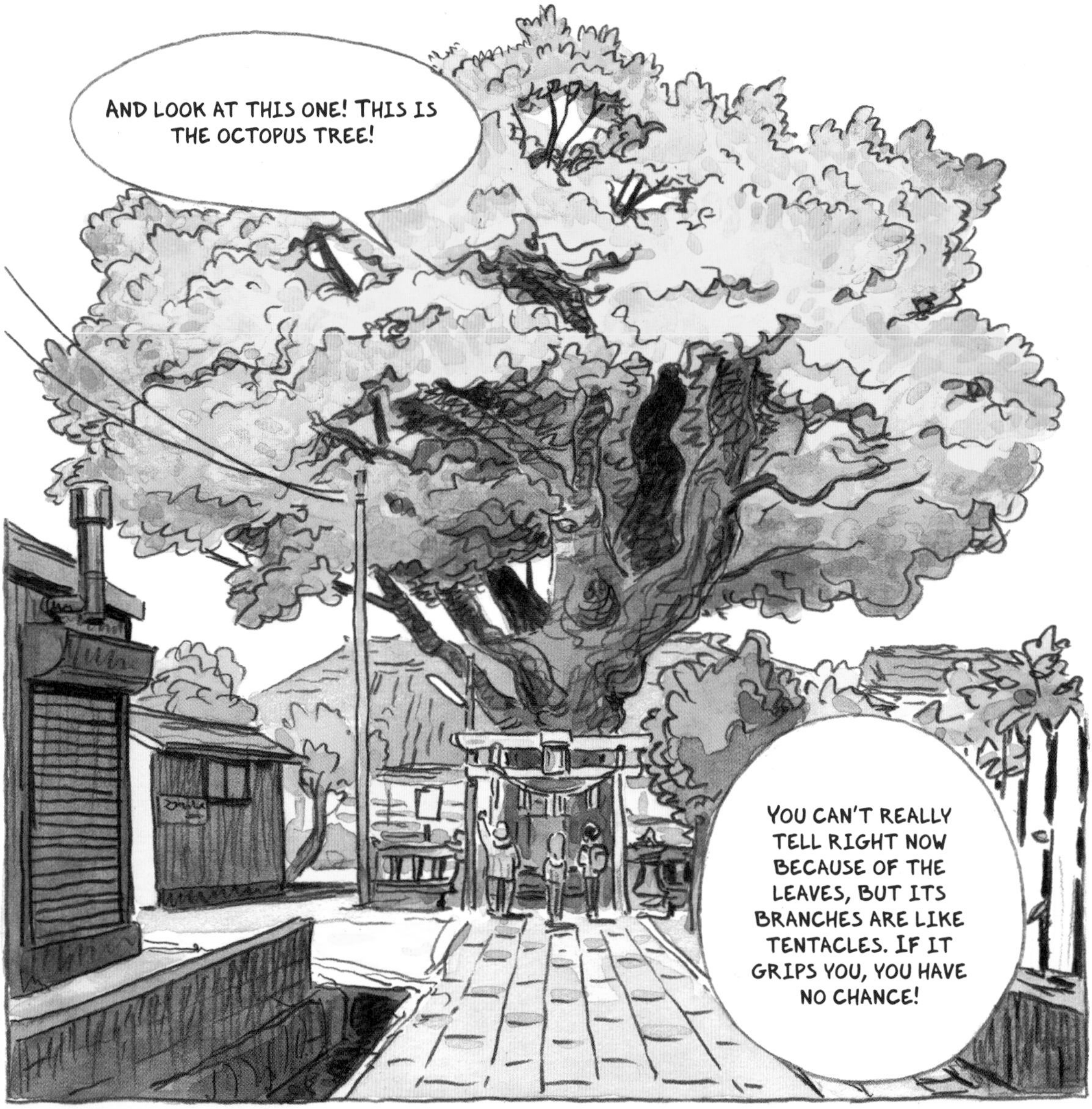
AND LOOK AT THIS ONE! THIS IS THE OCTOPUS TREE!
YOU CAN'T REALLY TELL RIGHT NOW BECAUSE OF THE LEAVES, BUT ITS BRANCHES ARE LIKE TENTACLES. IF IT GRIPS YOU, YOU HAVE NO CHANCE!

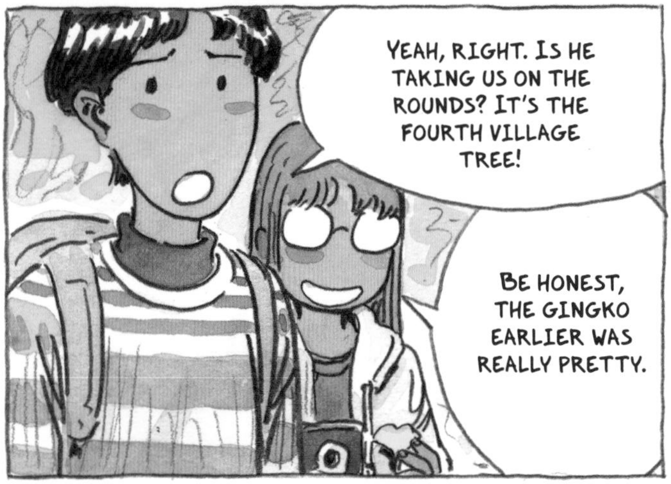
YEAH, RIGHT. IS HE TAKING US ON THE ROUNDS? IT'S THE FOURTH VILLAGE TREE!
BE HONEST, THE GINGKO EARLIER WAS REALLY PRETTY.

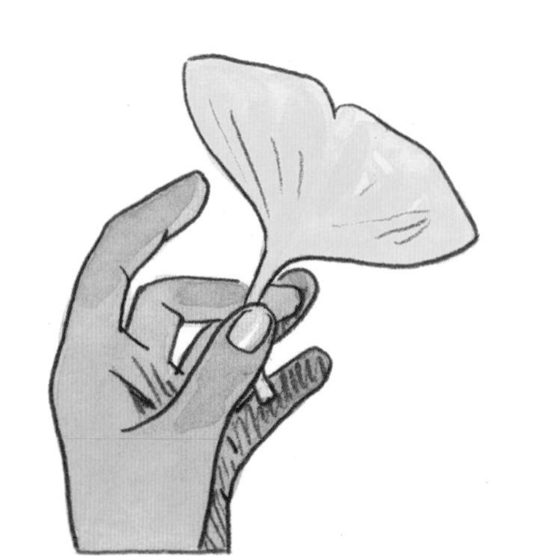

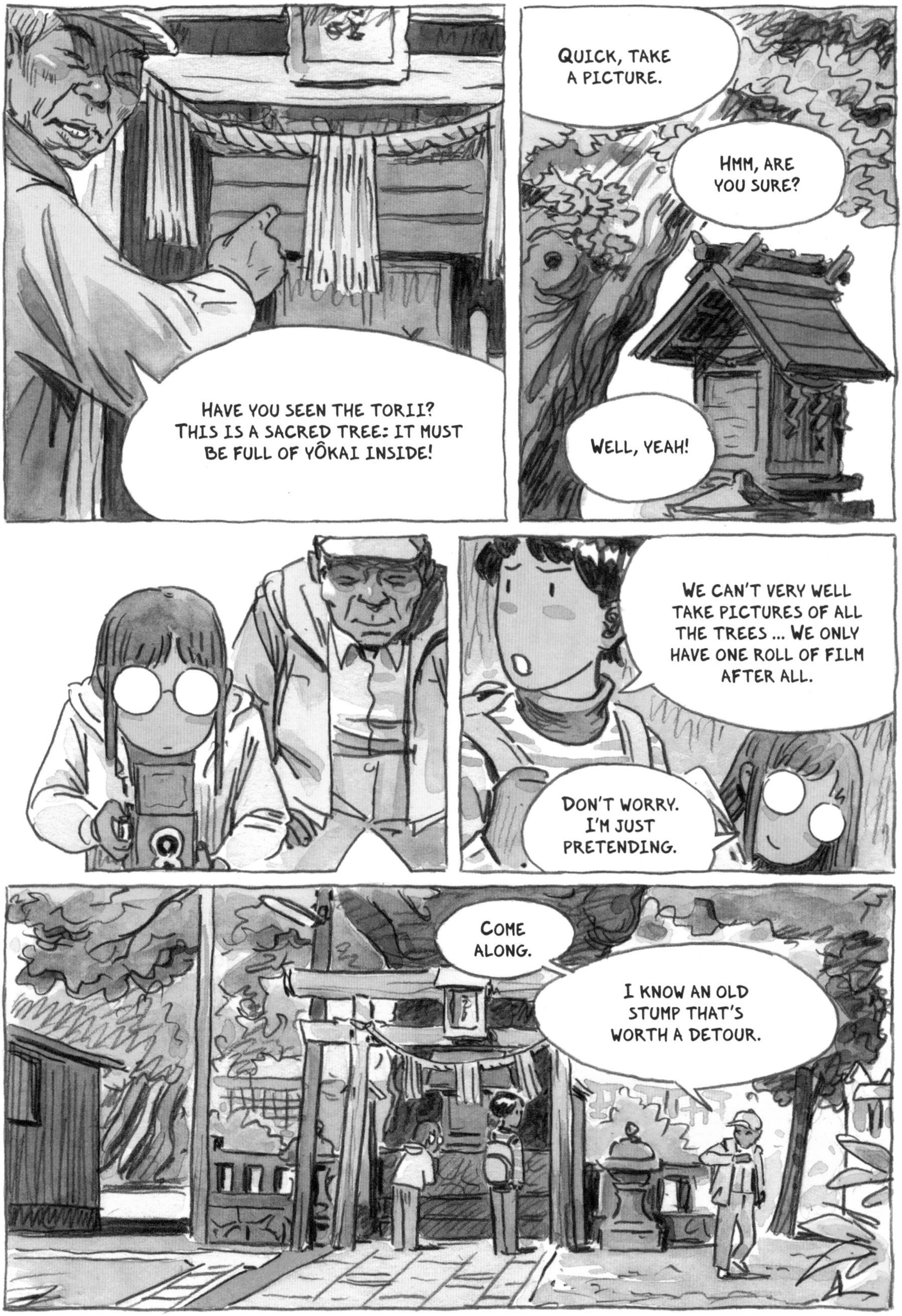
HAVE YOU SEEN THE TORII? THIS IS A SACRED TREE: IT MUST BE FULL OF YÔKAI INSIDE!
QUICK, TAKE A PICTURE.
HMM, ARE YOU SURE?
WELL, YEAH!
WE CAN'T VERY WELL TAKE PICTURES OF ALL THE TREES ... WE ONLY HAVE ONE ROLL OF FILM AFTER ALL.
DON'T WORRY. I'M JUST PRETENDING.
COME ALONG.
I KNOW AN OLD STUMP THAT'S WORTH A DETOUR.

IT LOOKS LIKE A DIFFERENT PLANET, DOESN'T IT?

HAVE A GOOD LOOK AT THIS HOLE, HERE. DO YOU KNOW WHERE IT LEADS?

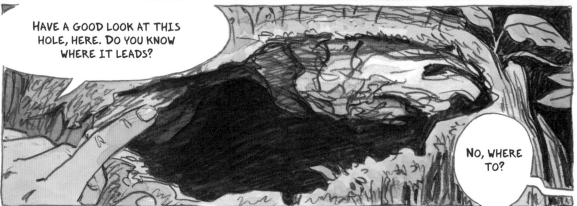

NO, WHERE TO?

NOBODY KNOWS.

HEY, I HAVE AN IDEA! TAKE MY PICTURE IN FRONT OF THE TEMPLE.

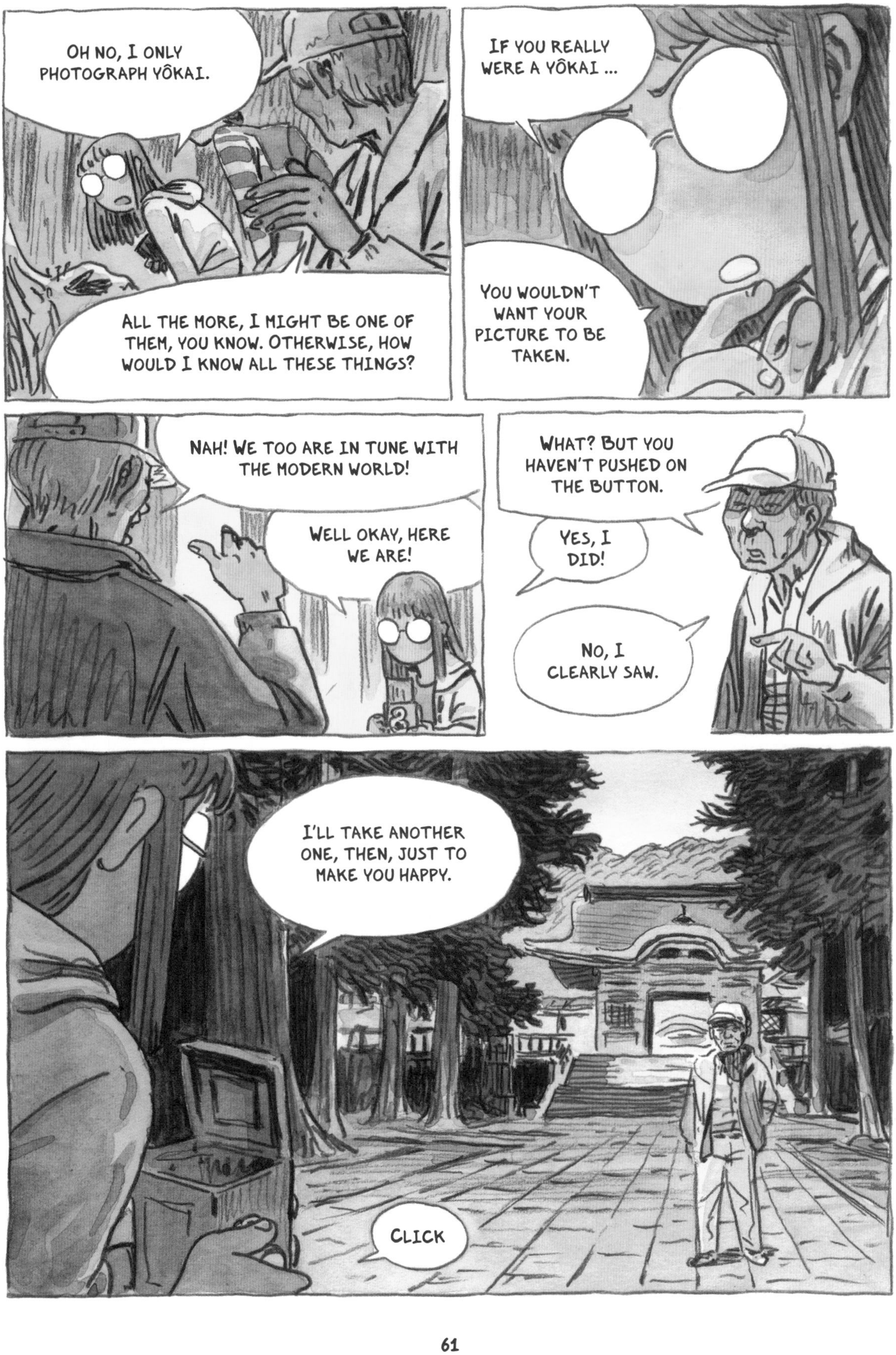
OH NO, I ONLY PHOTOGRAPH YÔKAI.
ALL THE MORE, I MIGHT BE ONE OF THEM, YOU KNOW. OTHERWISE, HOW WOULD I KNOW ALL THESE THINGS?
IF YOU REALLY WERE A YÔKAI ...
YOU WOULDN'T WANT YOUR PICTURE TO BE TAKEN.
NAH! WE TOO ARE IN TUNE WITH THE MODERN WORLD!
WELL OKAY, HERE WE ARE!
WHAT? BUT YOU HAVEN'T PUSHED ON THE BUTTON.
YES, I DID!
NO, I CLEARLY SAW.
I'LL TAKE ANOTHER ONE, THEN, JUST TO MAKE YOU HAPPY.
CLICK

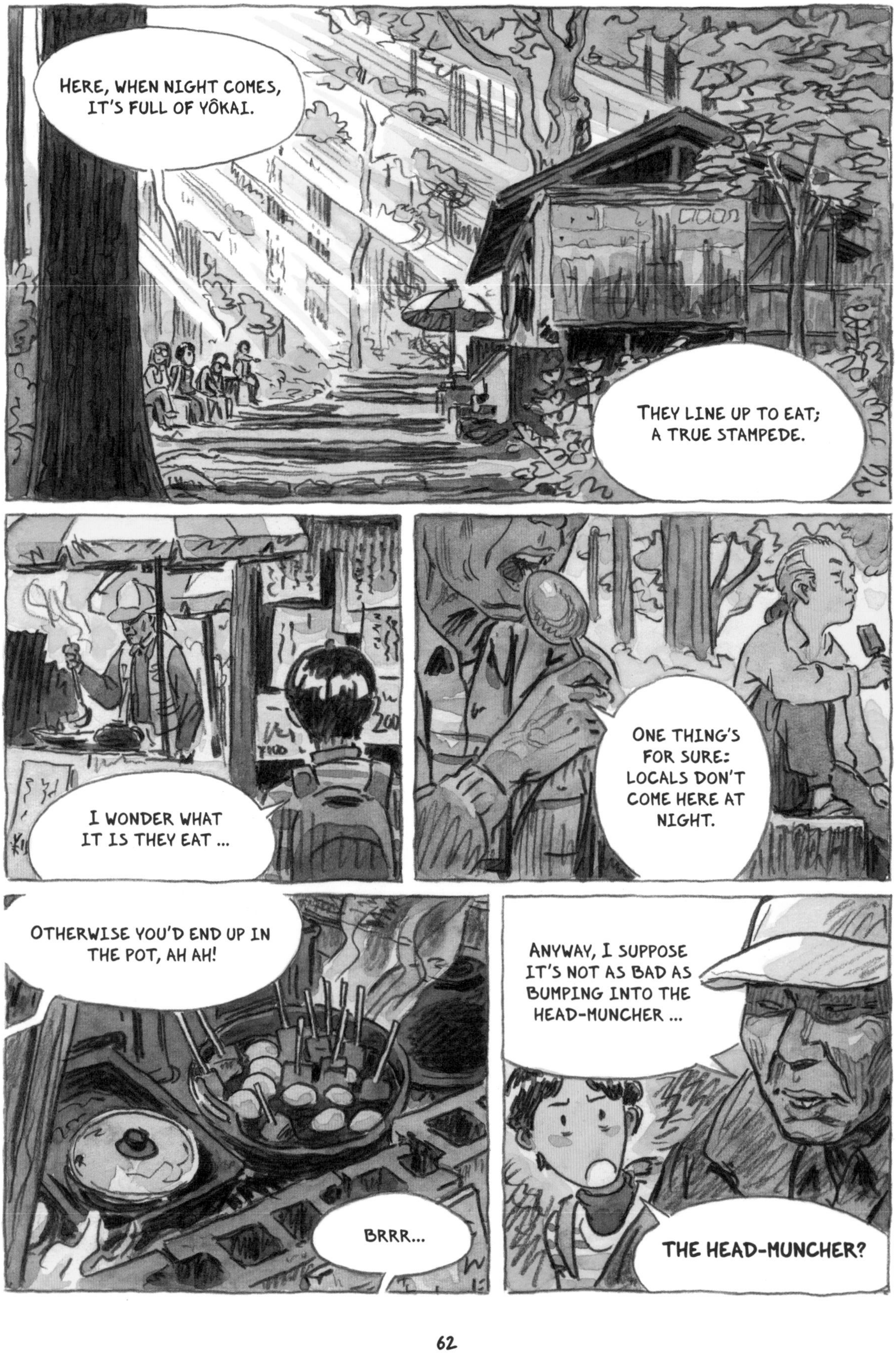
HERE, WHEN NIGHT COMES, IT'S FULL OF YÔKAI.
THEY LINE UP TO EAT; A TRUE STAMPEDE.
I WONDER WHAT IT IS THEY EAT ...
ONE THING'S FOR SURE: LOCALS DON'T COME HERE AT NIGHT.
OTHERWISE YOU'D END UP IN THE POT, AH AH!
BRRR...
ANYWAY, I SUPPOSE IT'S NOT AS BAD AS BUMPING INTO THE HEAD-MUNCHER ...
THE HEAD-MUNCHER?

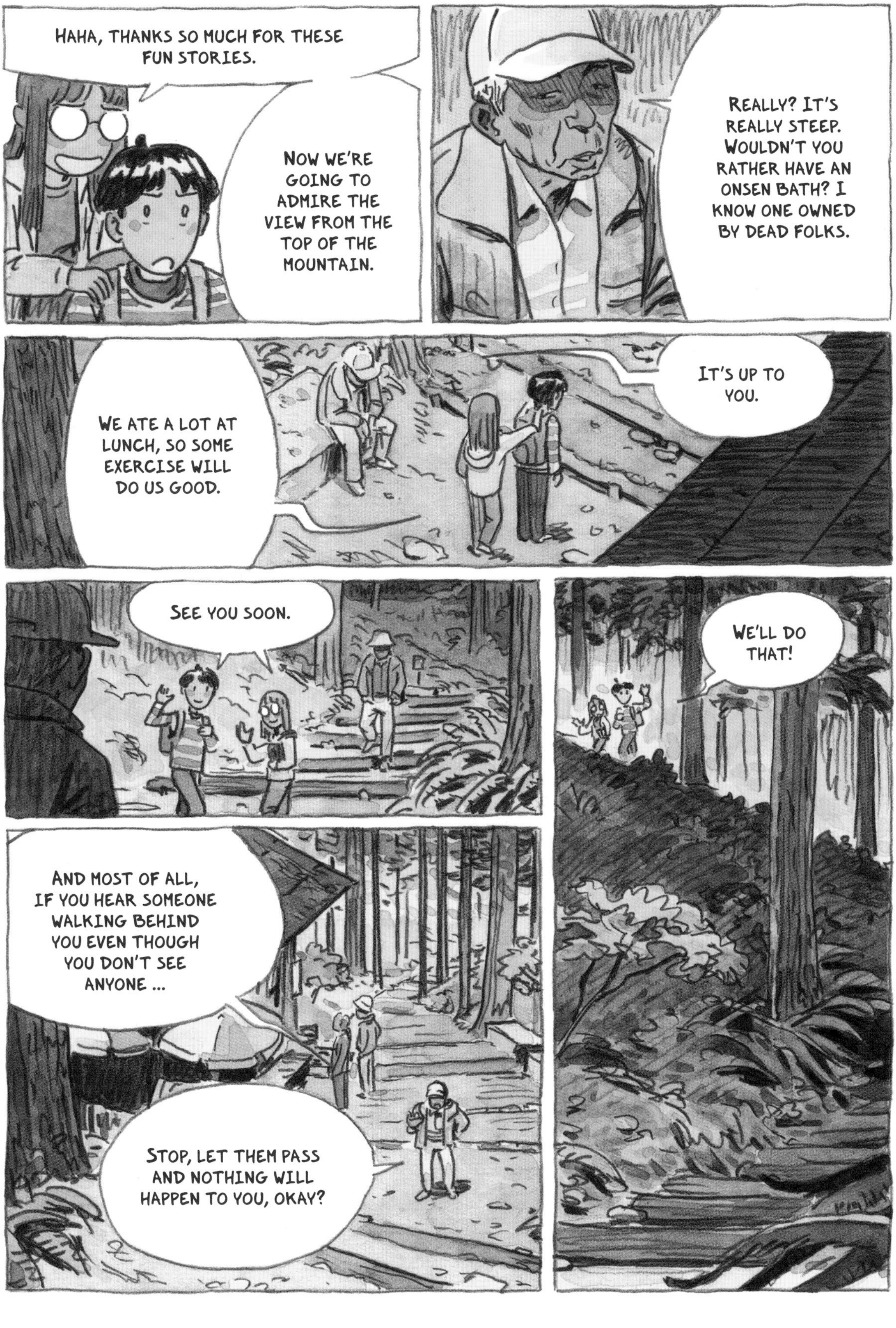
HAHA, THANKS SO MUCH FOR THESE FUN STORIES.
NOW WE'RE GOING TO ADMIRE THE VIEW FROM THE TOP OF THE MOUNTAIN.
REALLY? IT'S REALLY STEEP. WOULDN'T YOU RATHER HAVE AN ONSEN BATH? I KNOW ONE OWNED BY DEAD FOLKS.
WE ATE A LOT AT LUNCH, SO SOME EXERCISE WILL DO US GOOD.
IT'S UP TO YOU.
SEE YOU SOON.
WE'LL DO THAT!
AND MOST OF ALL, IF YOU HEAR SOMEONE WALKING BEHIND YOU EVEN THOUGH YOU DON'T SEE ANYONE ...
STOP, LET THEM PASS AND NOTHING WILL HAPPEN TO YOU, OKAY?

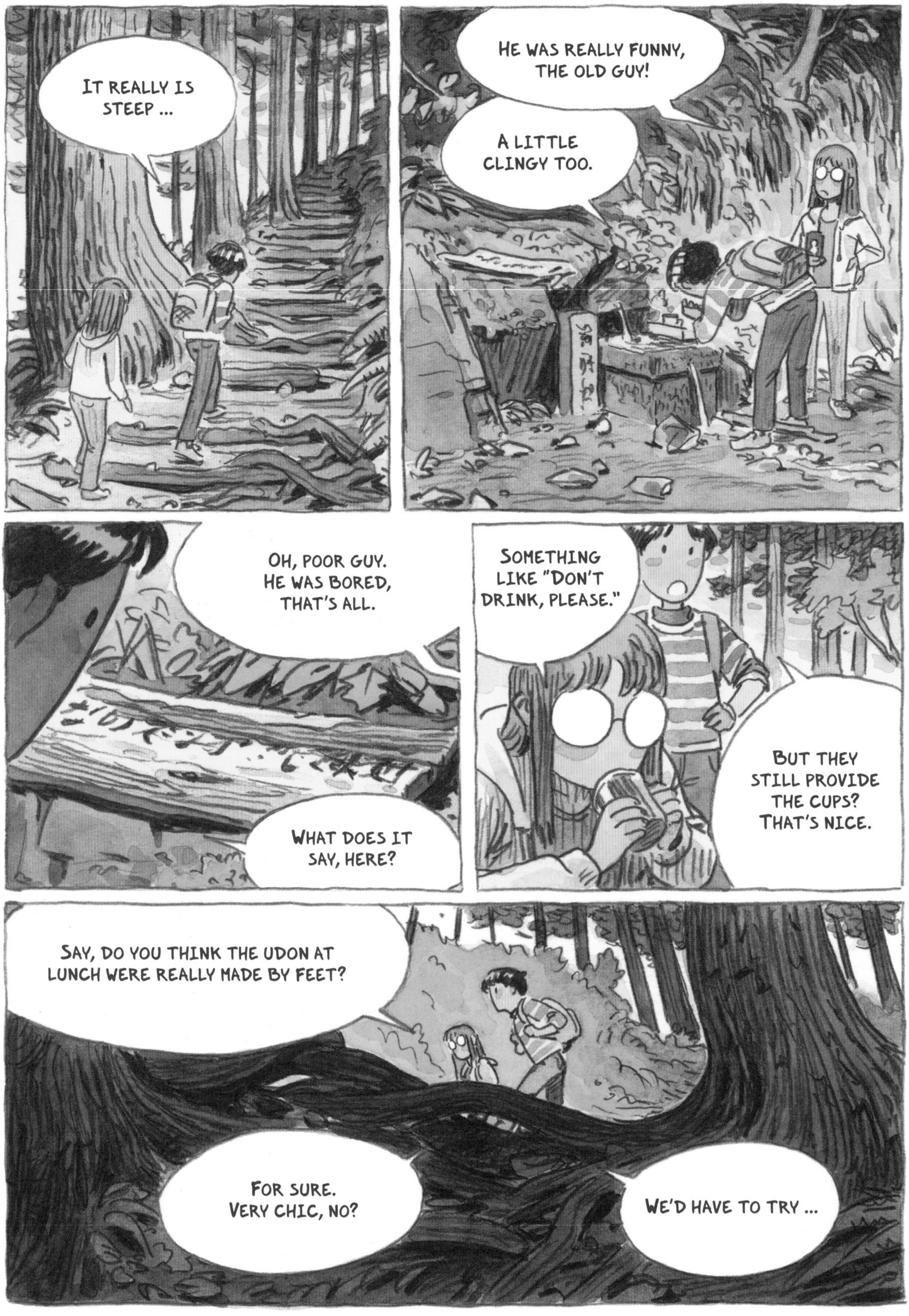
IT REALLY IS STEEP ...
HE WAS REALLY FUNNY, THE OLD GUY!
A LITTLE CLINGY TOO.
OH, POOR GUY. HE WAS BORED, THAT'S ALL.
WHAT DOES IT SAY, HERE?
SOMETHING LIKE "DON'T DRINK, PLEASE."
BUT THEY STILL PROVIDE THE CUPS? THAT'S NICE.
SAY, DO YOU THINK THE UDON AT LUNCH WERE REALLY MADE BY FEET?
FOR SURE. VERY CHIC, NO?
WE'D HAVE TO TRY ...

BRRR, STRANGE ATMOSPHERE.

IT'S GETTING DARK.

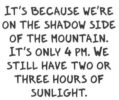

IT'S BECAUSE WE'RE ON THE SHADOW SIDE OF THE MOUNTAIN. IT'S ONLY 4 PM. WE STILL HAVE TWO OR THREE HOURS OF SUNLIGHT.

IF WE HURRY, WE CAN MANAGE.

BUT I'M POOPED!

WON'T WORRY. IF YOU WANT, WE'LL TAKE THE AERIAL TRAMWAY DOWN.

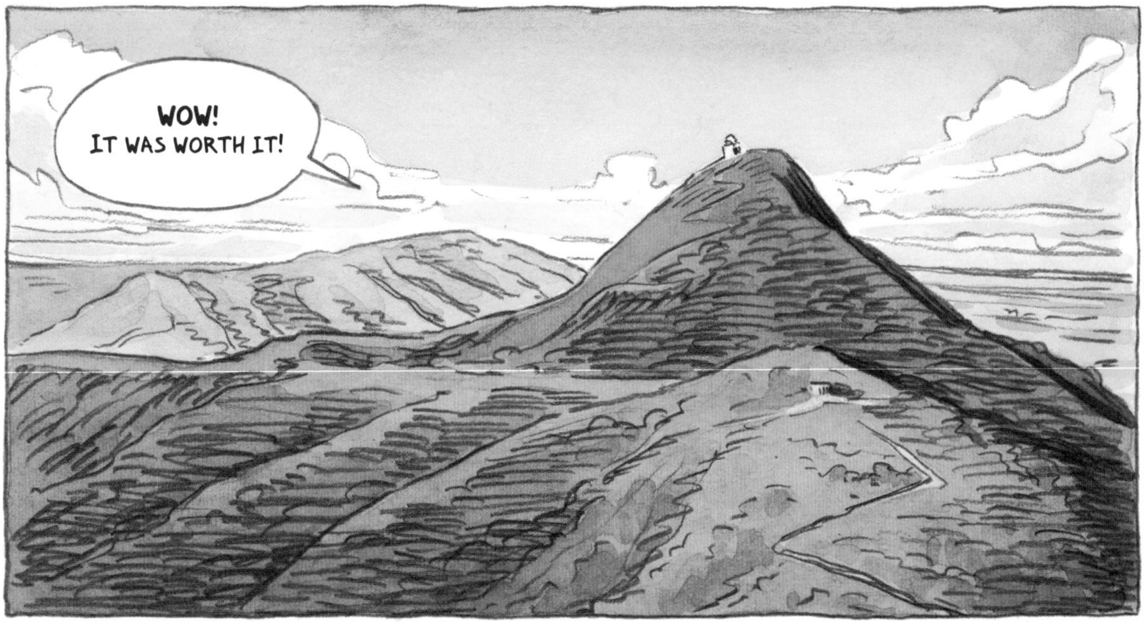
WOW!
IT WAS WORTH IT!

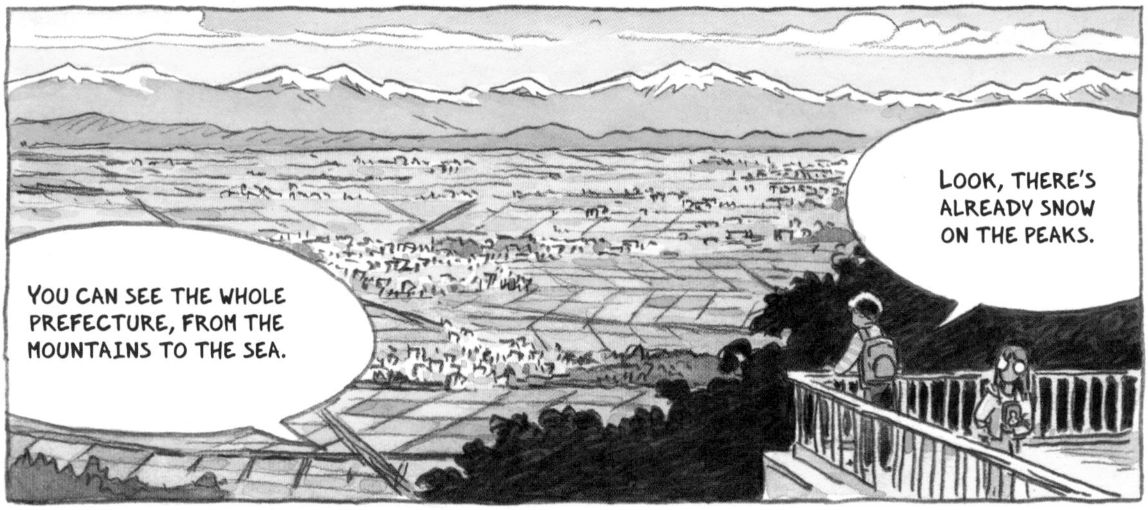
LOOK, THERE'S ALREADY SNOW ON THE PEAKS.
YOU CAN SEE THE WHOLE PREFECTURE, FROM THE MOUNTAINS TO THE SEA.

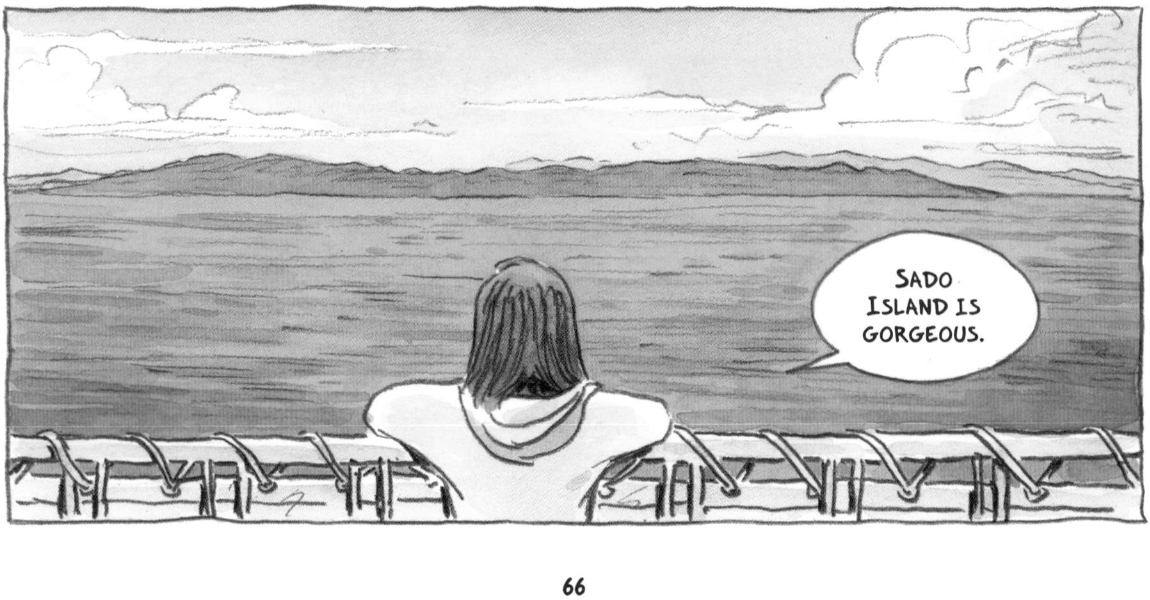
SADO ISLAND IS GORGEOUS.

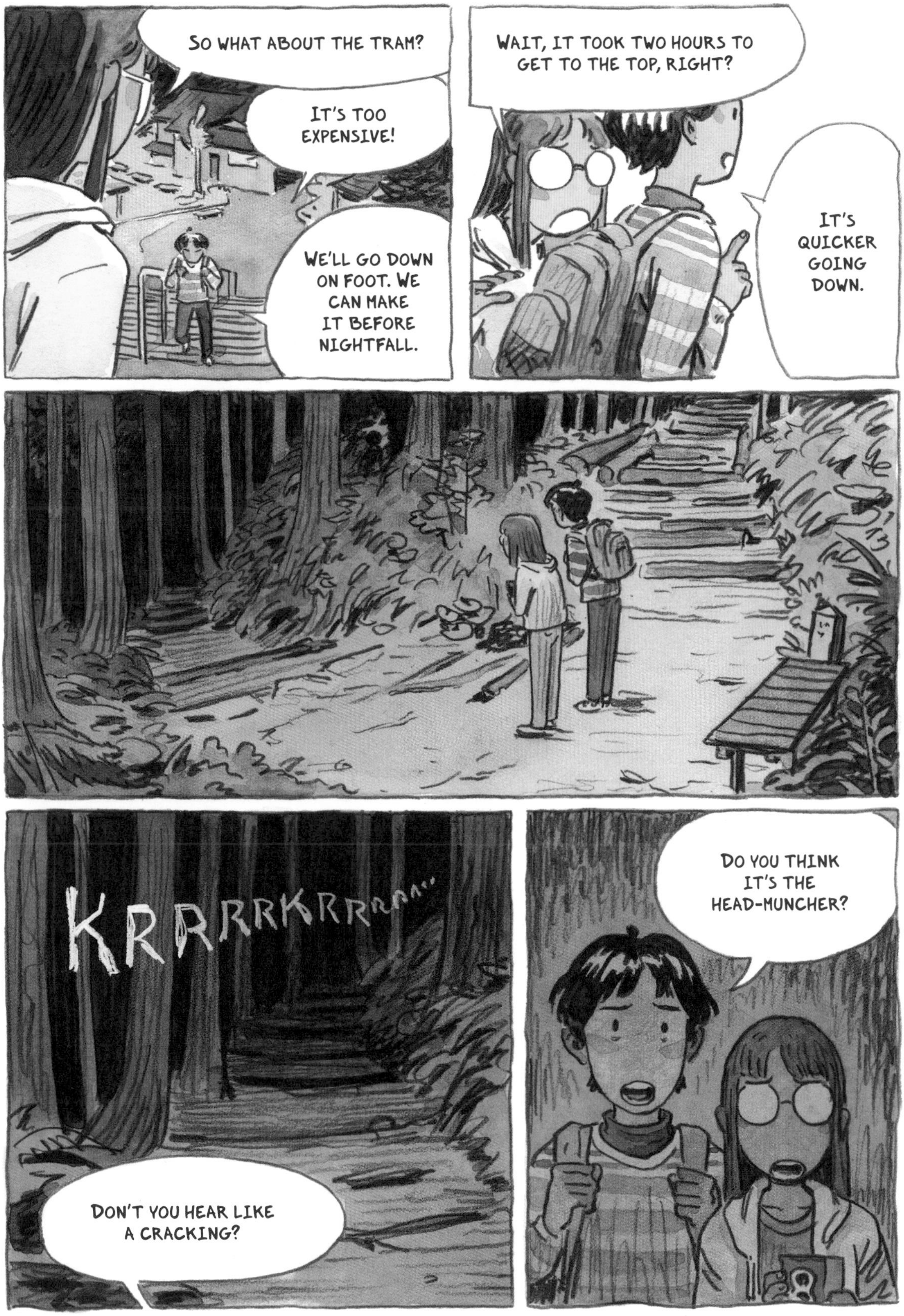
So what about the tram?
It's too expensive!
We'll go down on foot. We can make it before nightfall.
Wait, it took two hours to get to the top, right?
It's quicker going down.
KRRRRKRRrrr...
Don't you hear like a cracking?
Do you think it's the head-muncher?

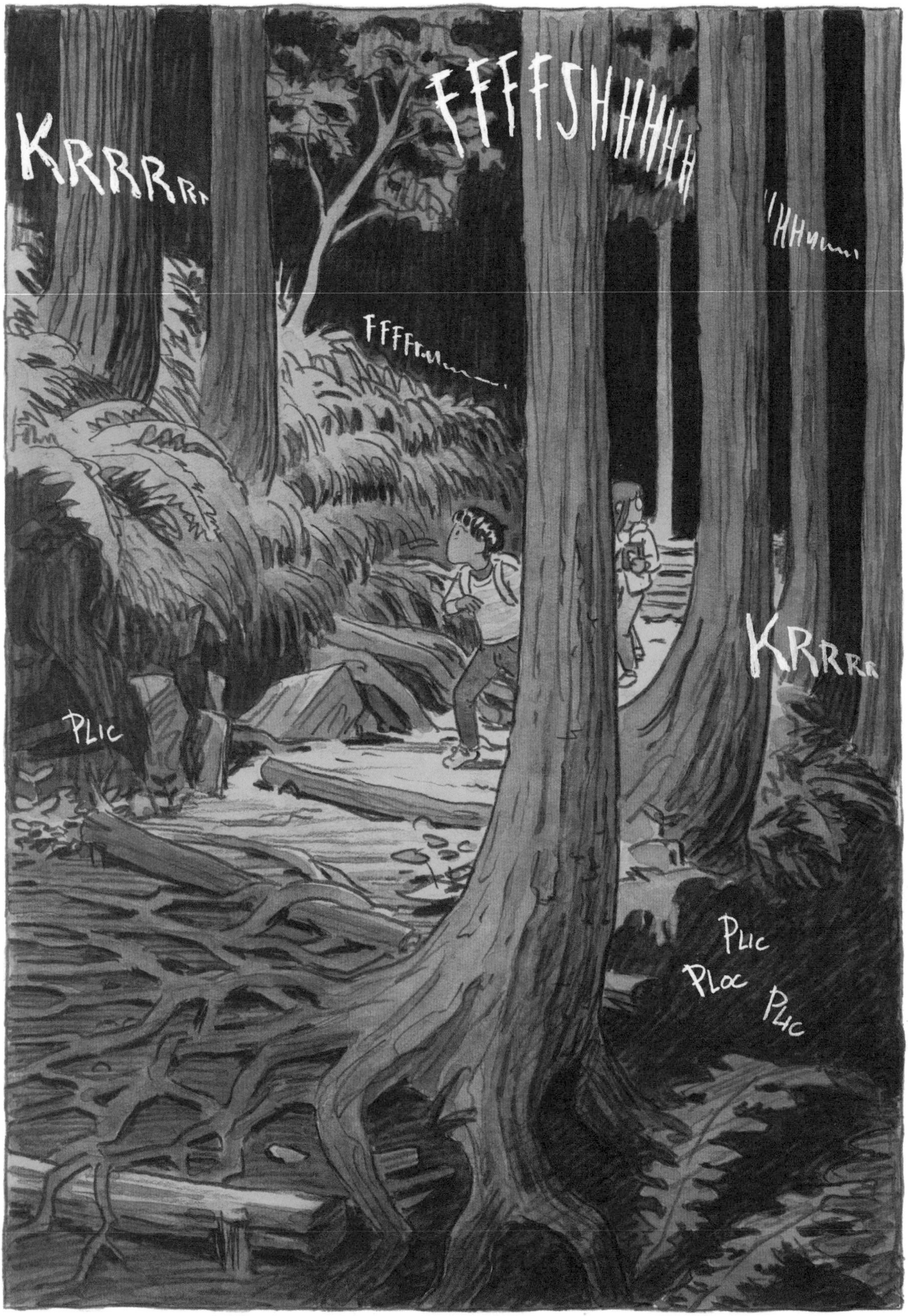
KRRRRrr
FFFFSHHHHHHHHHHHhhh...
FFFFrr...
PLIC
KRRRR
PLIC
PLOC
PLIC

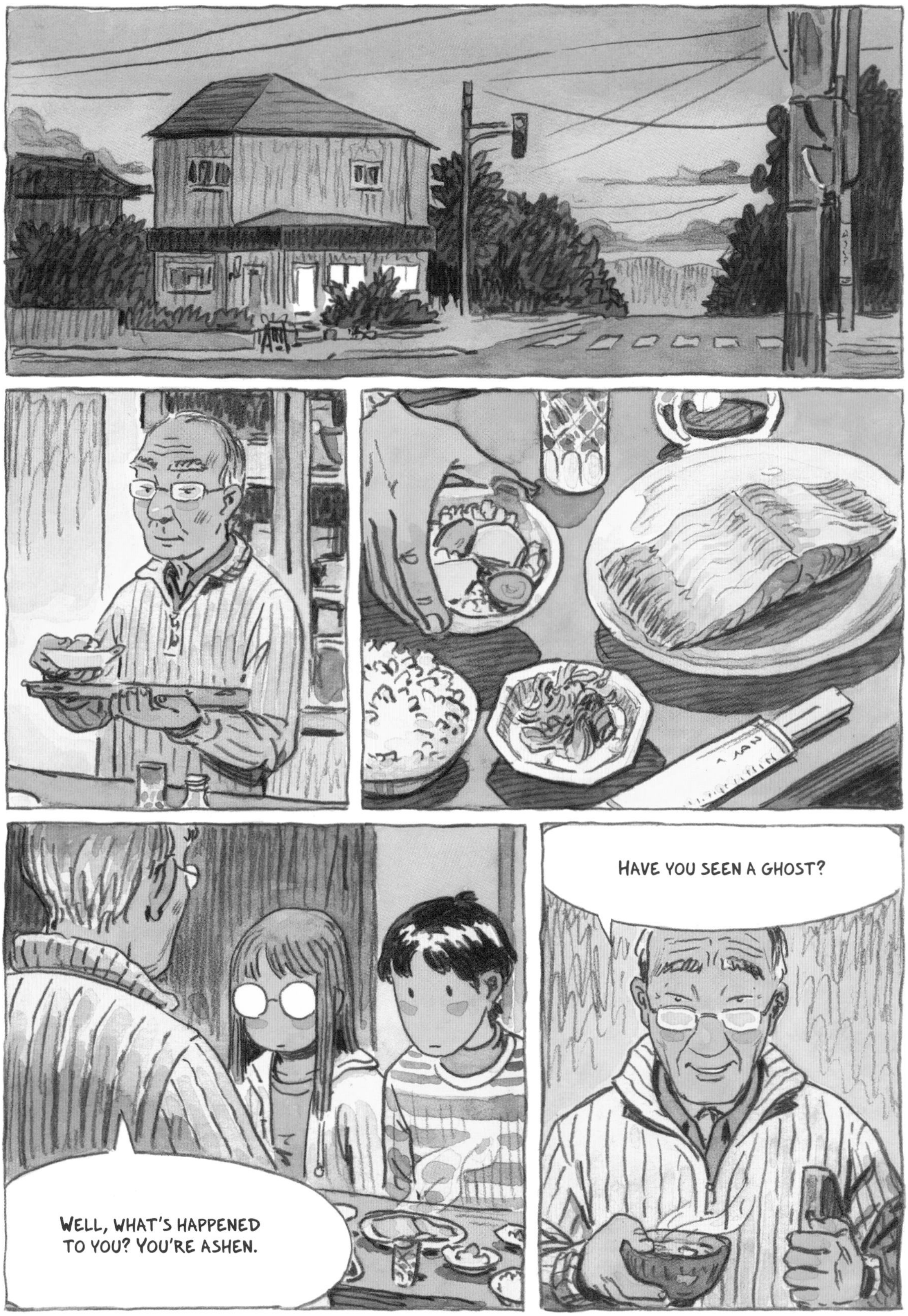
Well, what's happened to you? You're ashen.
Have you seen a ghost?

Photo 4/8

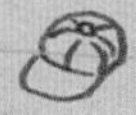

In front of the Temple
(old guy with a cap)

Yahiko
November 9, 2014
Sunny weather but
shot in the forest.

Settings:

Light 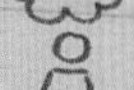
Distance 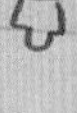

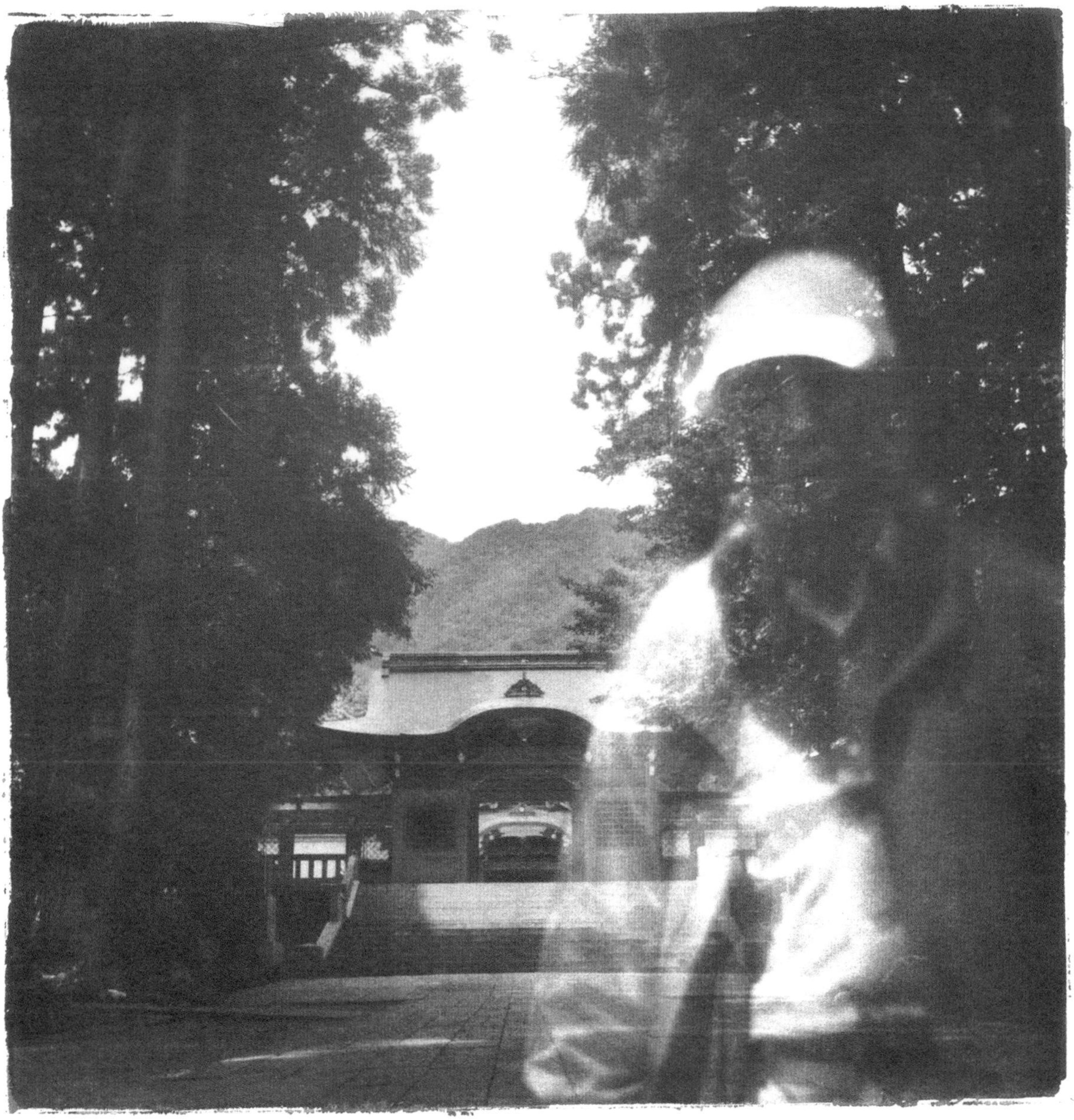

The two-faced town

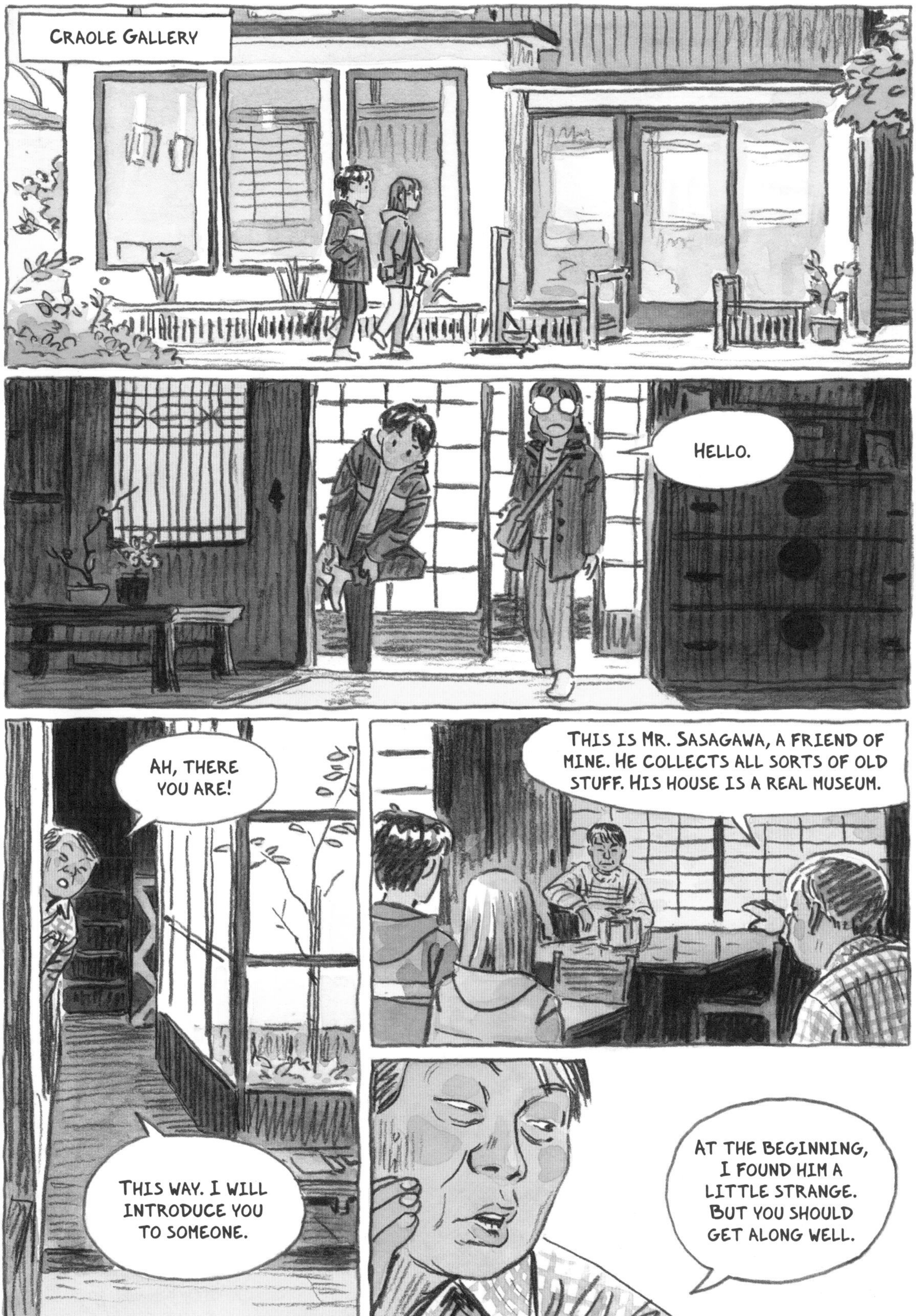
CRAOLE GALLERY
HELLO.
AH, THERE YOU ARE!
THIS WAY. I WILL INTRODUCE YOU TO SOMEONE.
THIS IS MR. SASAGAWA, A FRIEND OF MINE. HE COLLECTS ALL SORTS OF OLD STUFF. HIS HOUSE IS A REAL MUSEUM.
AT THE BEGINNING, I FOUND HIM A LITTLE STRANGE. BUT YOU SHOULD GET ALONG WELL.

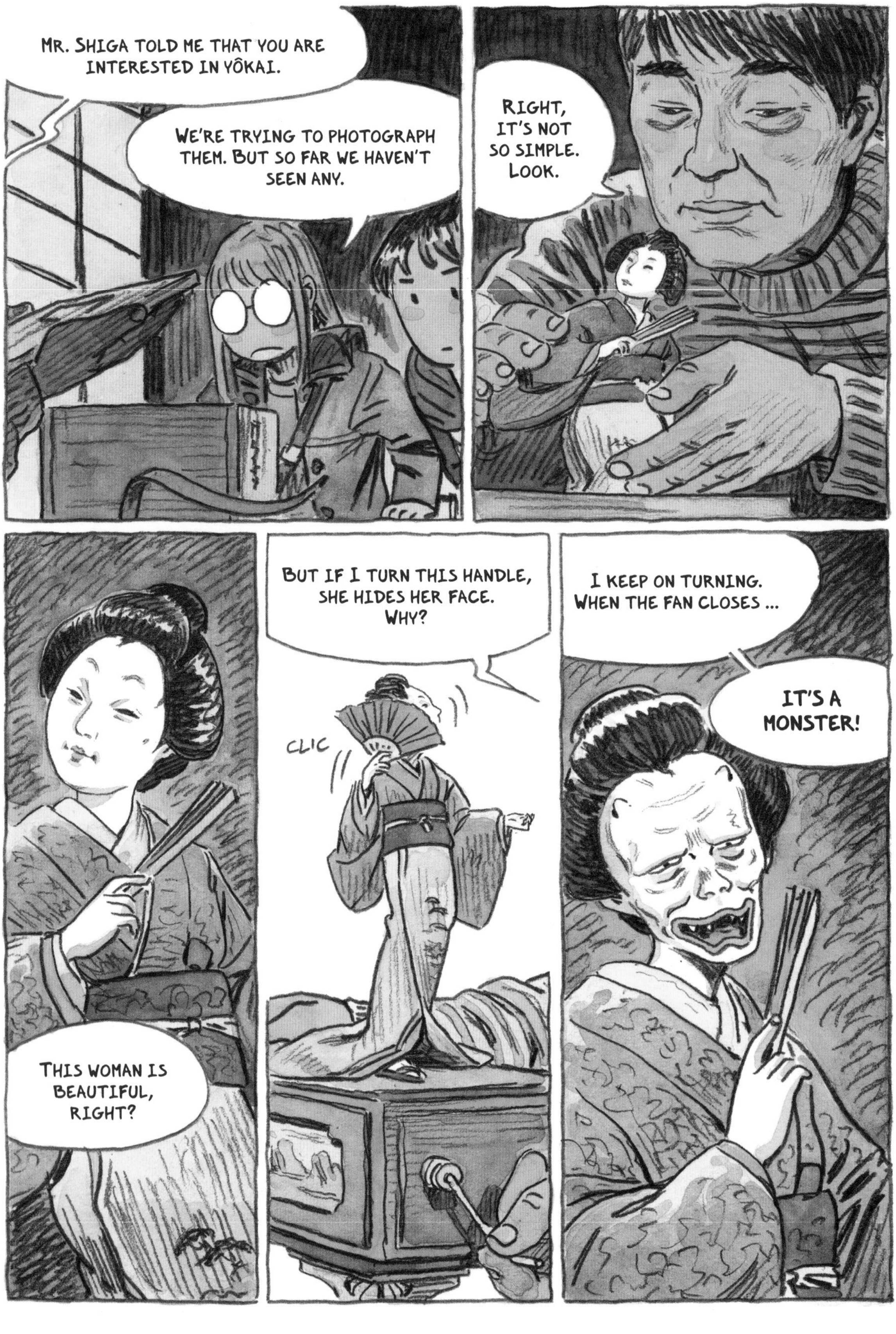
Mr. Shiga told me that you are interested in yôkai.
We're trying to photograph them. But so far we haven't seen any.
Right, it's not so simple. Look.
This woman is beautiful, right?
But if I turn this handle, she hides her face. Why?
CLIC
I keep on turning. When the fan closes ...
It's a monster!

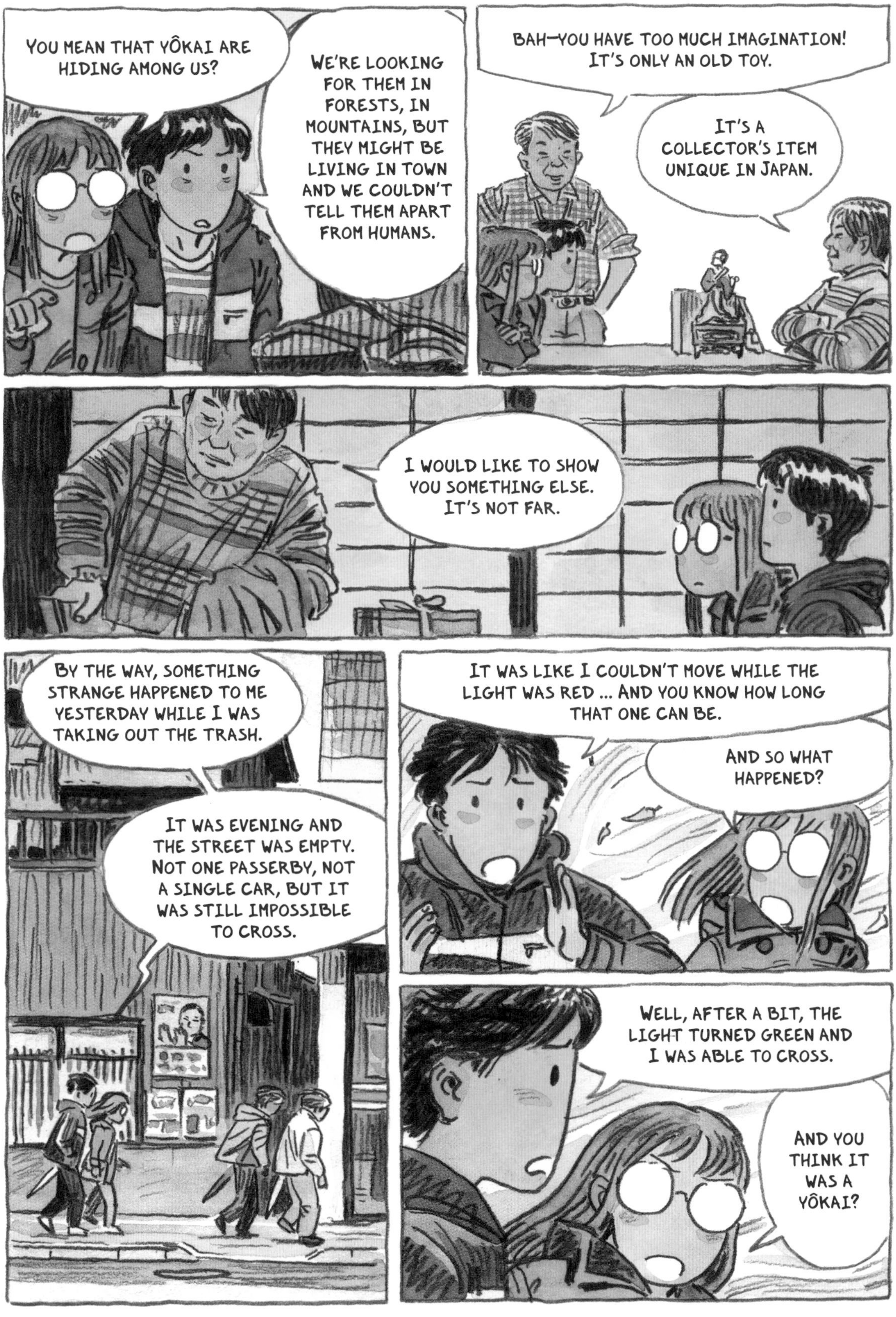
You mean that Yôkai are hiding among us?
We're looking for them in forests, in mountains, but they might be living in town and we couldn't tell them apart from humans.
Bah—you have too much imagination! It's only an old toy.
It's a collector's item unique in Japan.
I would like to show you something else. It's not far.
By the way, something strange happened to me yesterday while I was taking out the trash.
It was evening and the street was empty. Not one passerby, not a single car, but it was still impossible to cross.
It was like I couldn't move while the light was red ... And you know how long that one can be.
And so what happened?
Well, after a bit, the light turned green and I was able to cross.
And you think it was a Yôkai?

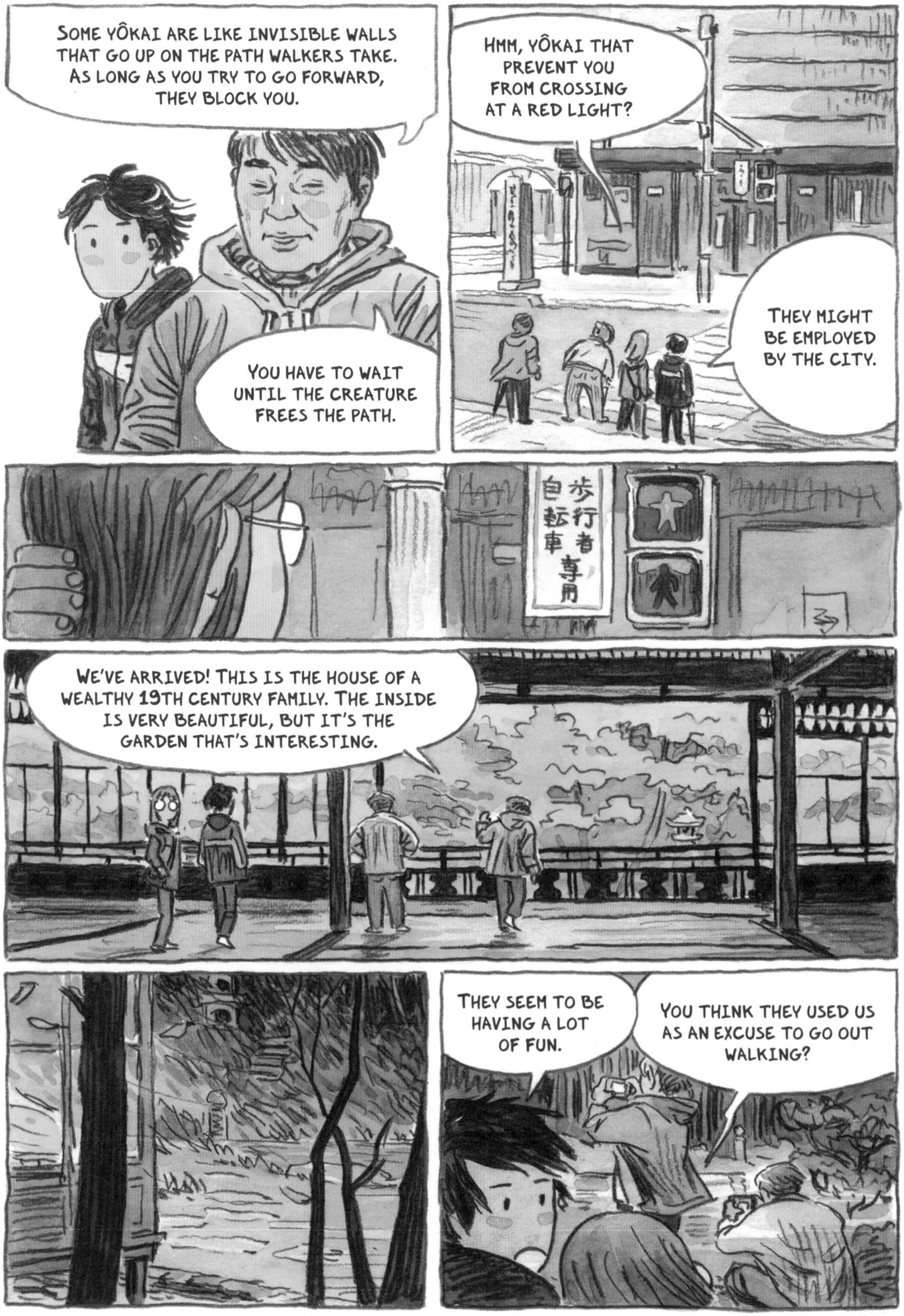
SOME YÔKAI ARE LIKE INVISIBLE WALLS THAT GO UP ON THE PATH WALKERS TAKE. AS LONG AS YOU TRY TO GO FORWARD, THEY BLOCK YOU.
YOU HAVE TO WAIT UNTIL THE CREATURE FREES THE PATH.
HMM, YÔKAI THAT PREVENT YOU FROM CROSSING AT A RED LIGHT?
THEY MIGHT BE EMPLOYED BY THE CITY.
自転車
歩行者専用
WE'VE ARRIVED! THIS IS THE HOUSE OF A WEALTHY 19TH CENTURY FAMILY. THE INSIDE IS VERY BEAUTIFUL, BUT IT'S THE GARDEN THAT'S INTERESTING.
THEY SEEM TO BE HAVING A LOT OF FUN.
YOU THINK THEY USED US AS AN EXCUSE TO GO OUT WALKING?

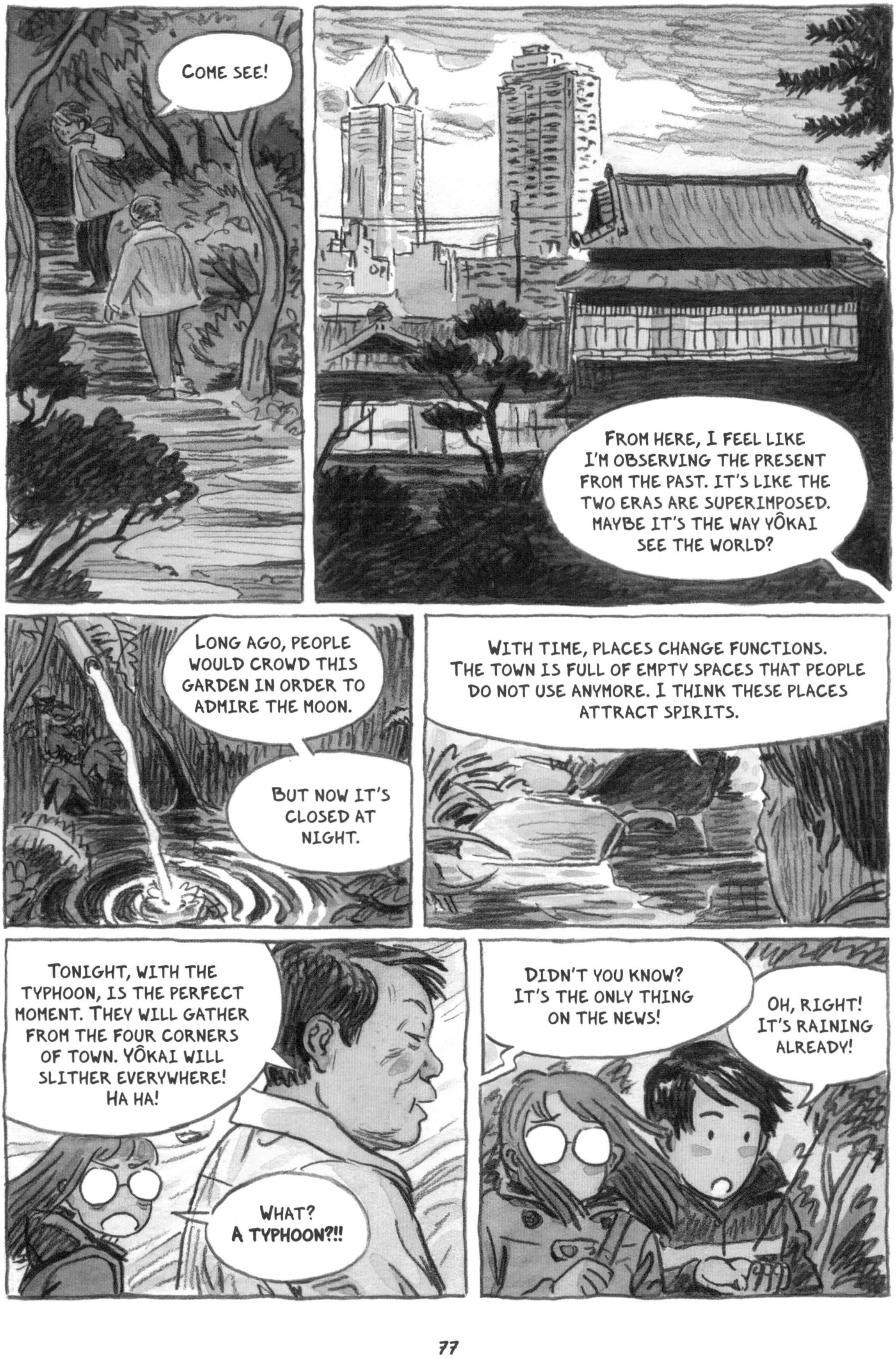
COME SEE!
FROM HERE, I FEEL LIKE I'M OBSERVING THE PRESENT FROM THE PAST. IT'S LIKE THE TWO ERAS ARE SUPERIMPOSED. MAYBE IT'S THE WAY YÔKAI SEE THE WORLD?
LONG AGO, PEOPLE WOULD CROWD THIS GARDEN IN ORDER TO ADMIRE THE MOON.
BUT NOW IT'S CLOSED AT NIGHT.
WITH TIME, PLACES CHANGE FUNCTIONS. THE TOWN IS FULL OF EMPTY SPACES THAT PEOPLE DO NOT USE ANYMORE. I THINK THESE PLACES ATTRACT SPIRITS.
TONIGHT, WITH THE TYPHOON, IS THE PERFECT MOMENT. THEY WILL GATHER FROM THE FOUR CORNERS OF TOWN. YÔKAI WILL SLITHER EVERYWHERE! HA HA!
WHAT? A TYPHOON?!!
DIDN'T YOU KNOW? IT'S THE ONLY THING ON THE NEWS!
OH, RIGHT! IT'S RAINING ALREADY!

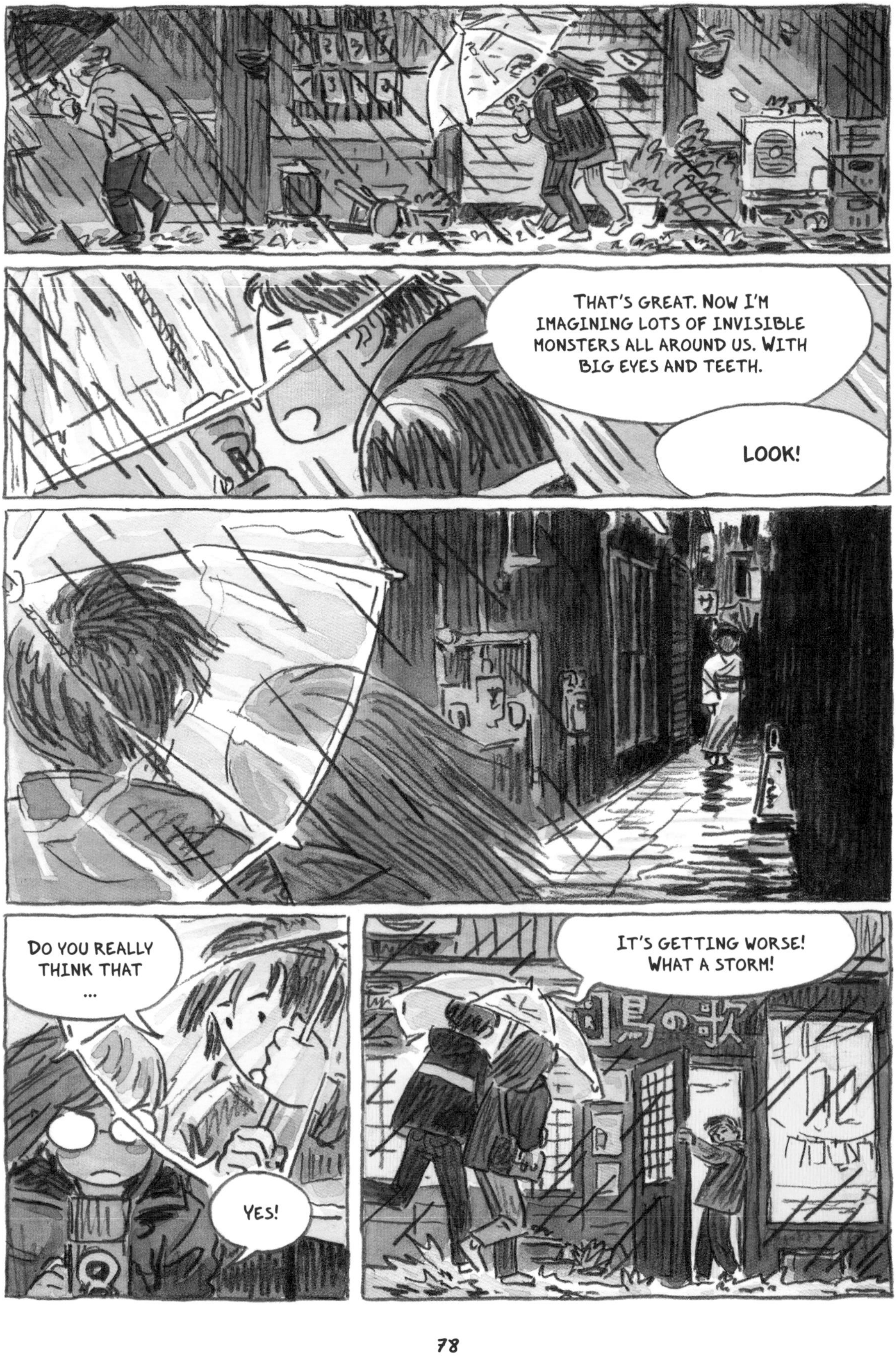
THAT'S GREAT. NOW I'M IMAGINING LOTS OF INVISIBLE MONSTERS ALL AROUND US. WITH BIG EYES AND TEETH.
LOOK!
DO YOU REALLY THINK THAT ...
YES!
IT'S GETTING WORSE! WHAT A STORM!

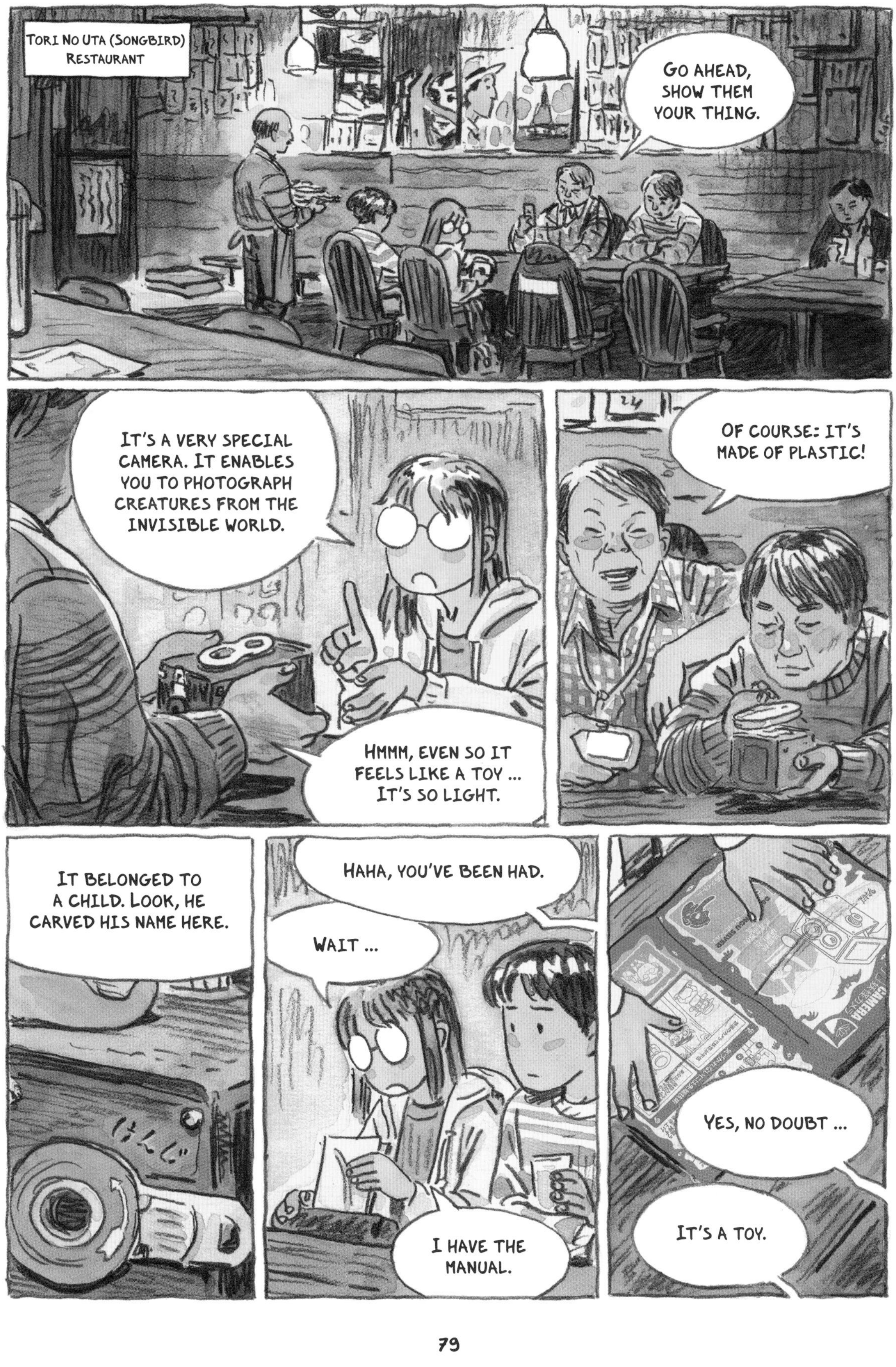
Tori No Uta (Songbird) Restaurant
Go ahead, show them your thing.
It's a very special camera. It enables you to photograph creatures from the invisible world.
Hmmm, even so it feels like a toy ... It's so light.
Of course: it's made of plastic!
It belonged to a child. Look, he carved his name here.
けんじ
Haha, you've been had.
Wait ...
I have the manual.
Yes, no doubt ...
It's a toy.

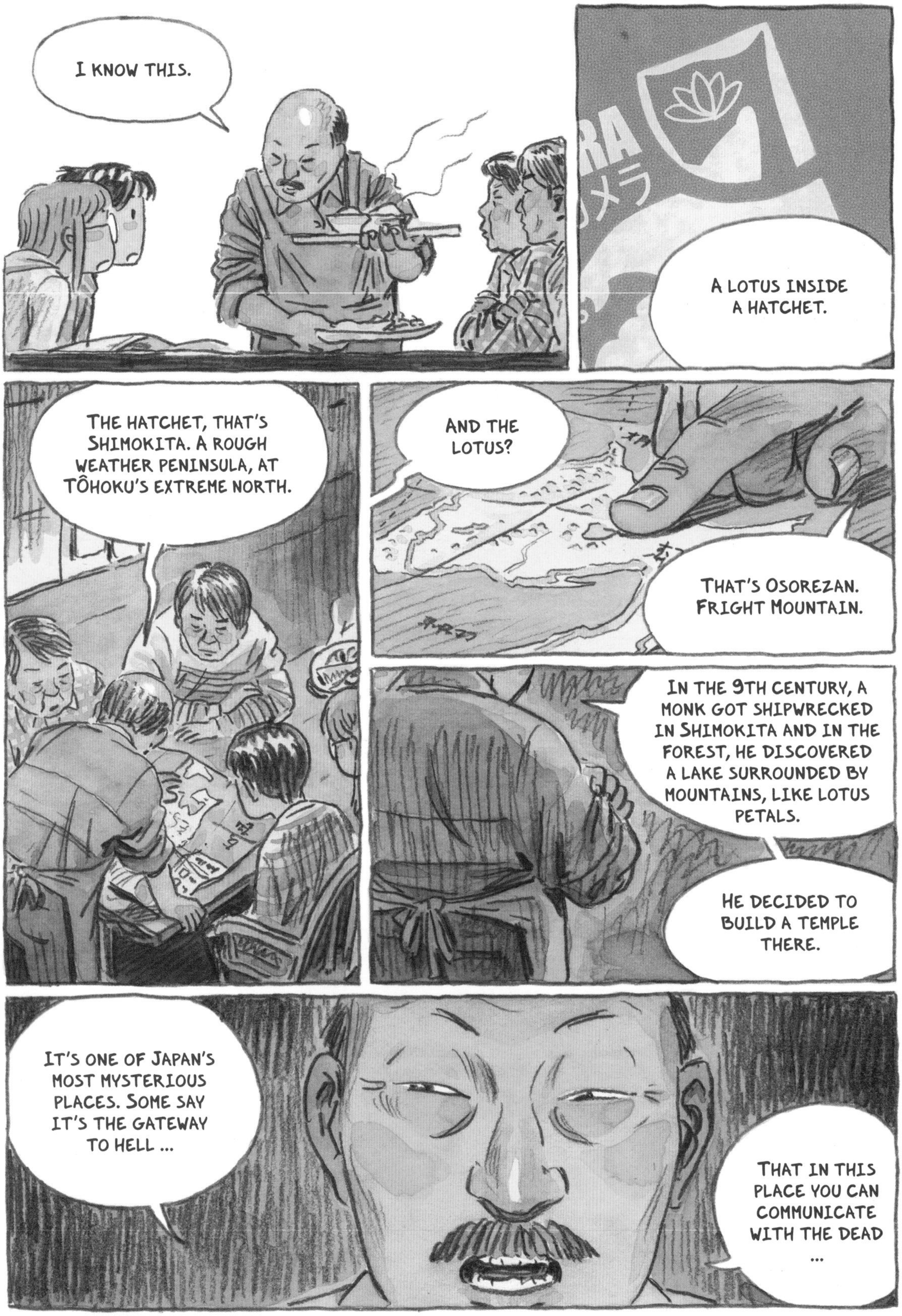
I KNOW THIS.
A LOTUS INSIDE A HATCHET.
THE HATCHET, THAT'S SHIMOKITA. A ROUGH WEATHER PENINSULA, AT TÔHOKU'S EXTREME NORTH.
AND THE LOTUS?
THAT'S OSOREZAN. FRIGHT MOUNTAIN.
IN THE 9TH CENTURY, A MONK GOT SHIPWRECKED IN SHIMOKITA AND IN THE FOREST, HE DISCOVERED A LAKE SURROUNDED BY MOUNTAINS, LIKE LOTUS PETALS.
HE DECIDED TO BUILD A TEMPLE THERE.
IT'S ONE OF JAPAN'S MOST MYSTERIOUS PLACES. SOME SAY IT'S THE GATEWAY TO HELL ...
THAT IN THIS PLACE YOU CAN COMMUNICATE WITH THE DEAD ...

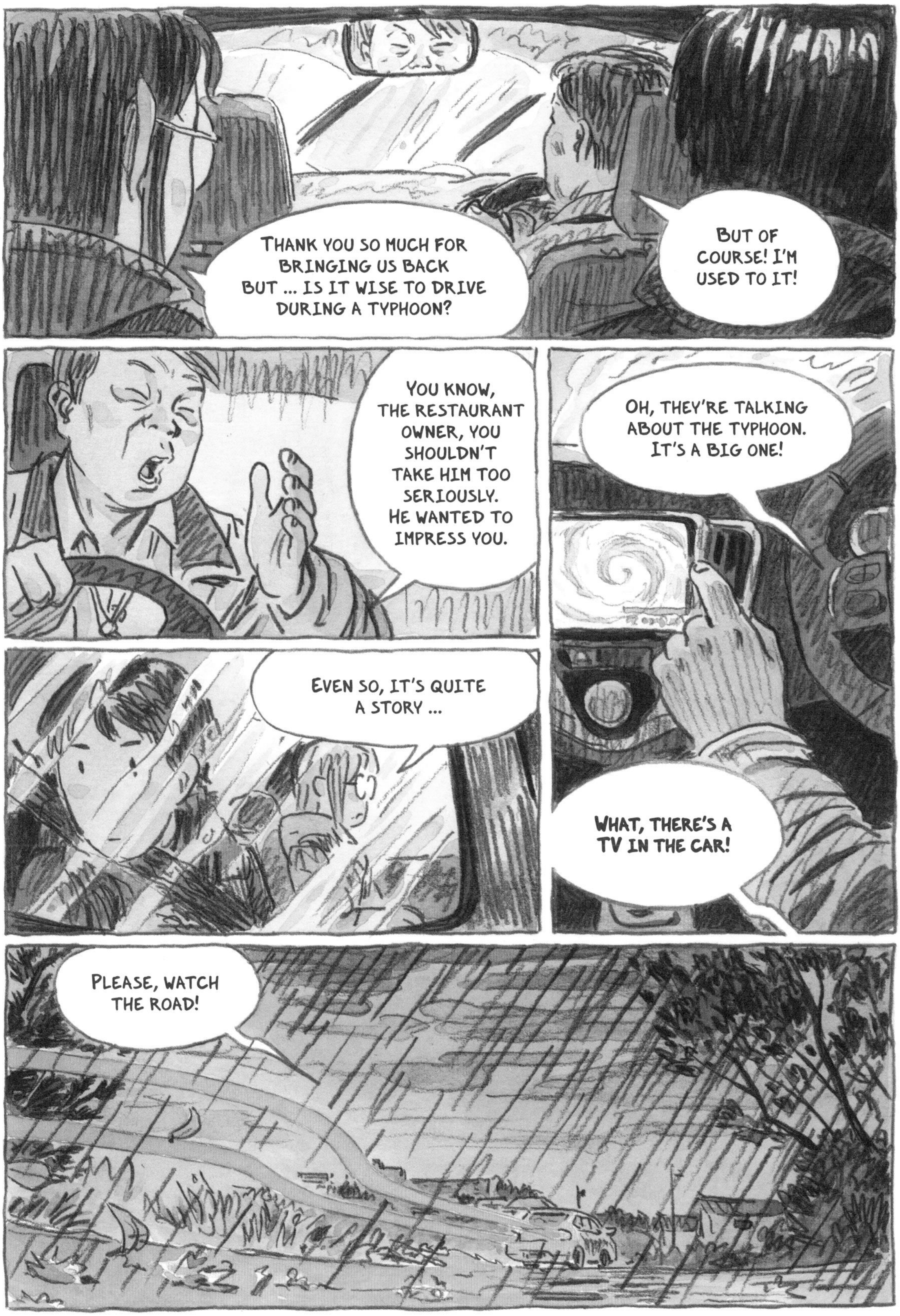
THANK YOU SO MUCH FOR BRINGING US BACK BUT ... IS IT WISE TO DRIVE DURING A TYPHOON?
BUT OF COURSE! I'M USED TO IT!
YOU KNOW, THE RESTAURANT OWNER, YOU SHOULDN'T TAKE HIM TOO SERIOUSLY. HE WANTED TO IMPRESS YOU.
OH, THEY'RE TALKING ABOUT THE TYPHOON. IT'S A BIG ONE!
EVEN SO, IT'S QUITE A STORY ...
WHAT, THERE'S A TV IN THE CAR!
PLEASE, WATCH THE ROAD!

Lady in an alley

Niigata
Old city Furumachi
November 20, 2014
Rotten weather in the evening
(typhoon!)

Settings:
Light
Distance

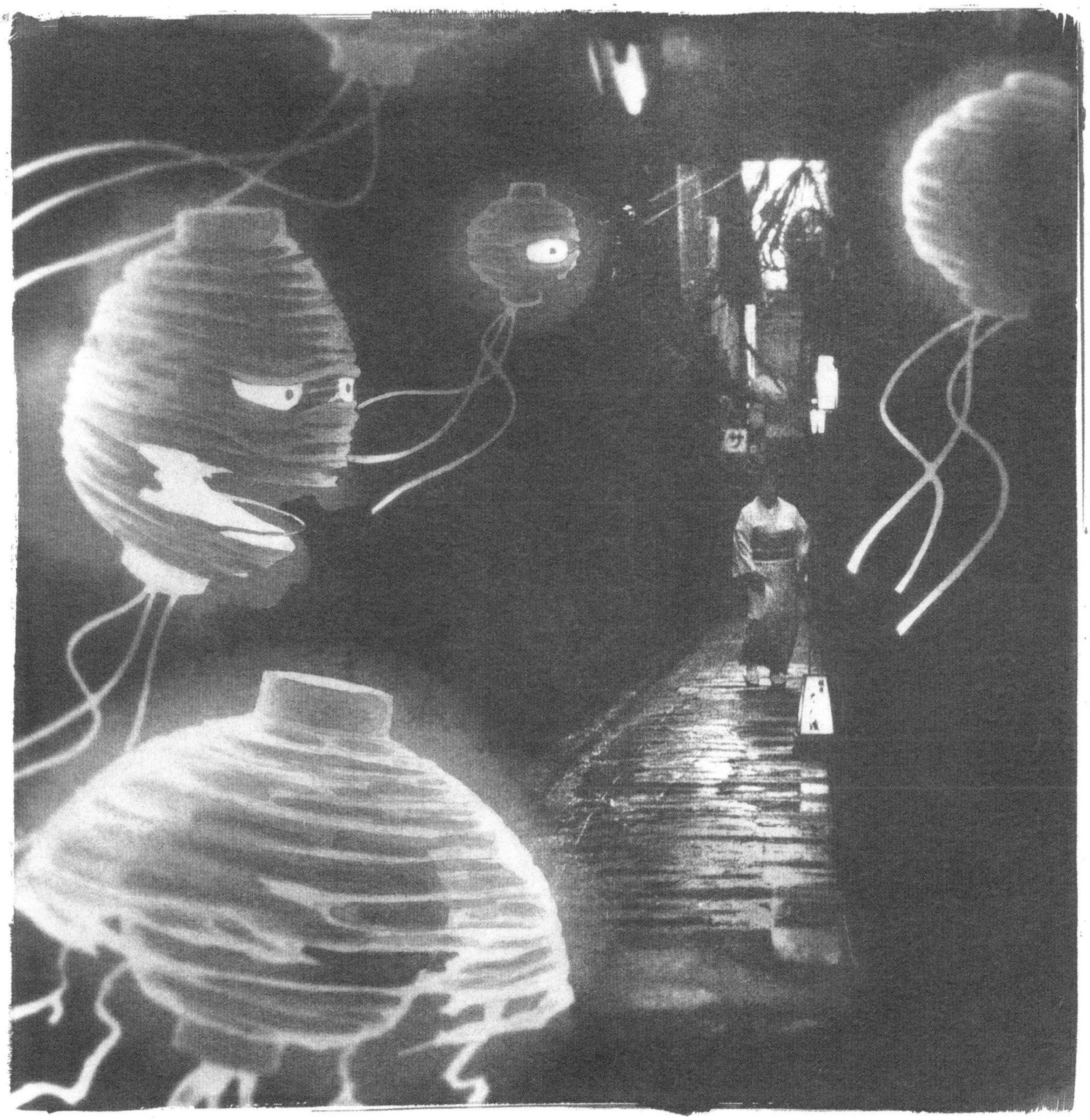

6
Uncertain horizon

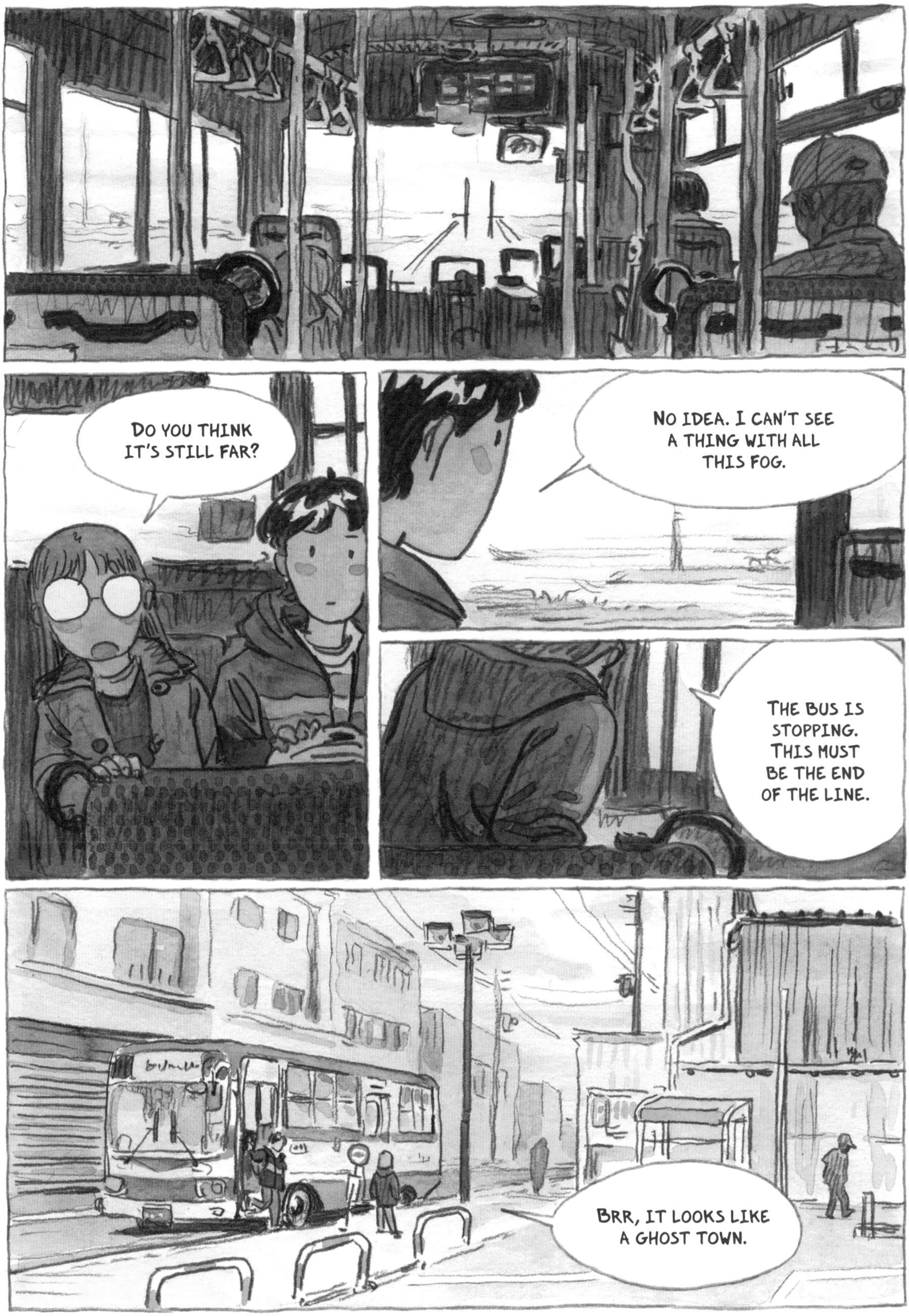
Do you think it's still far?
No idea. I can't see a thing with all this fog.
The bus is stopping. This must be the end of the line.
Brr, it looks like a ghost town.

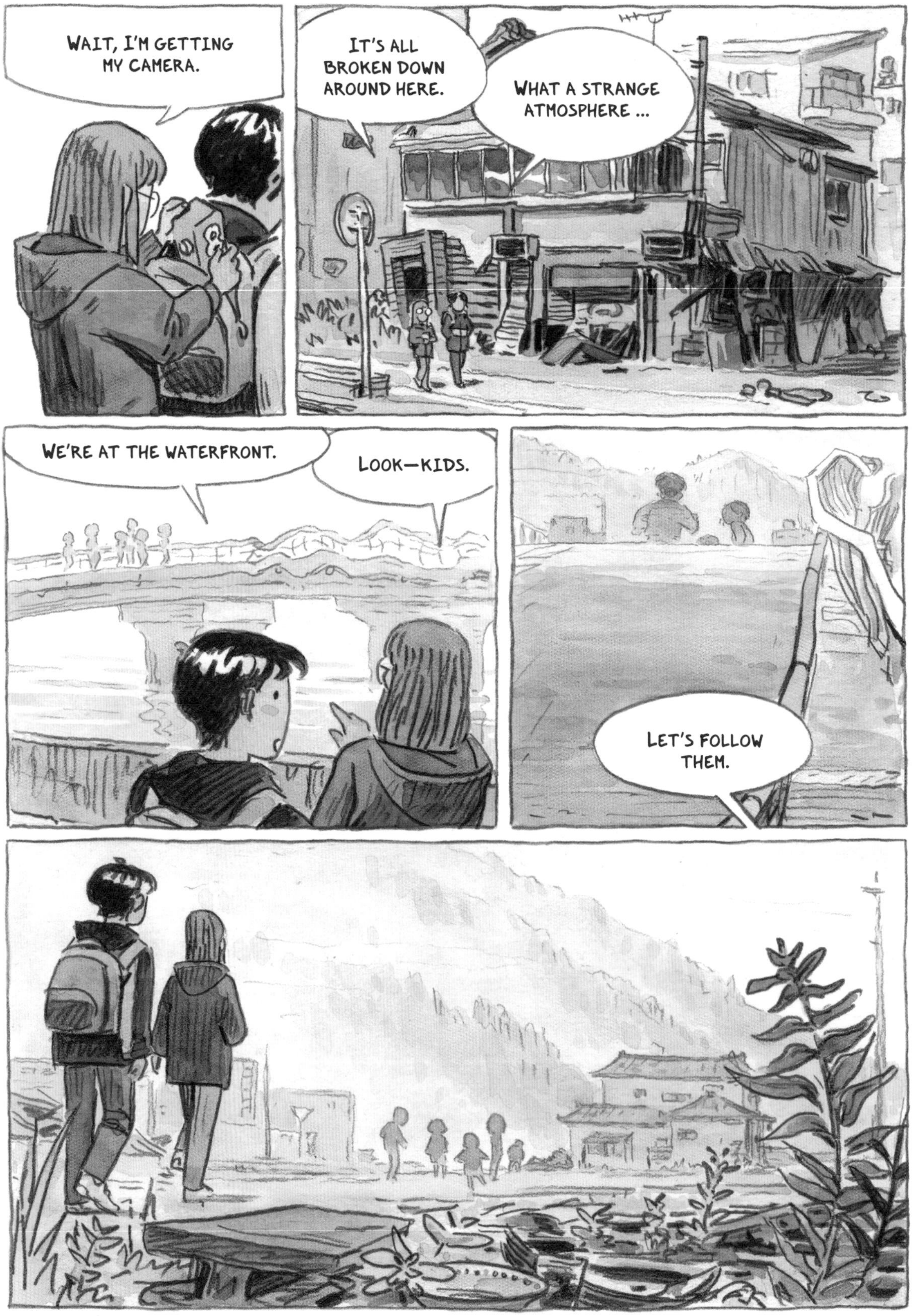
WAIT, I'M GETTING MY CAMERA.
IT'S ALL BROKEN DOWN AROUND HERE.
WHAT A STRANGE ATMOSPHERE ...
WE'RE AT THE WATERFRONT.
LOOK—KIDS.
LET'S FOLLOW THEM.

THEY'VE DISAPPEARED.

LOOK AROUND THE HOUSE. I'LL HAVE A LOOK NEAR THE WATER.

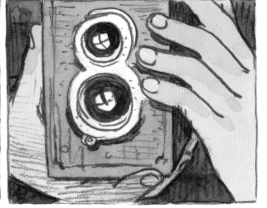

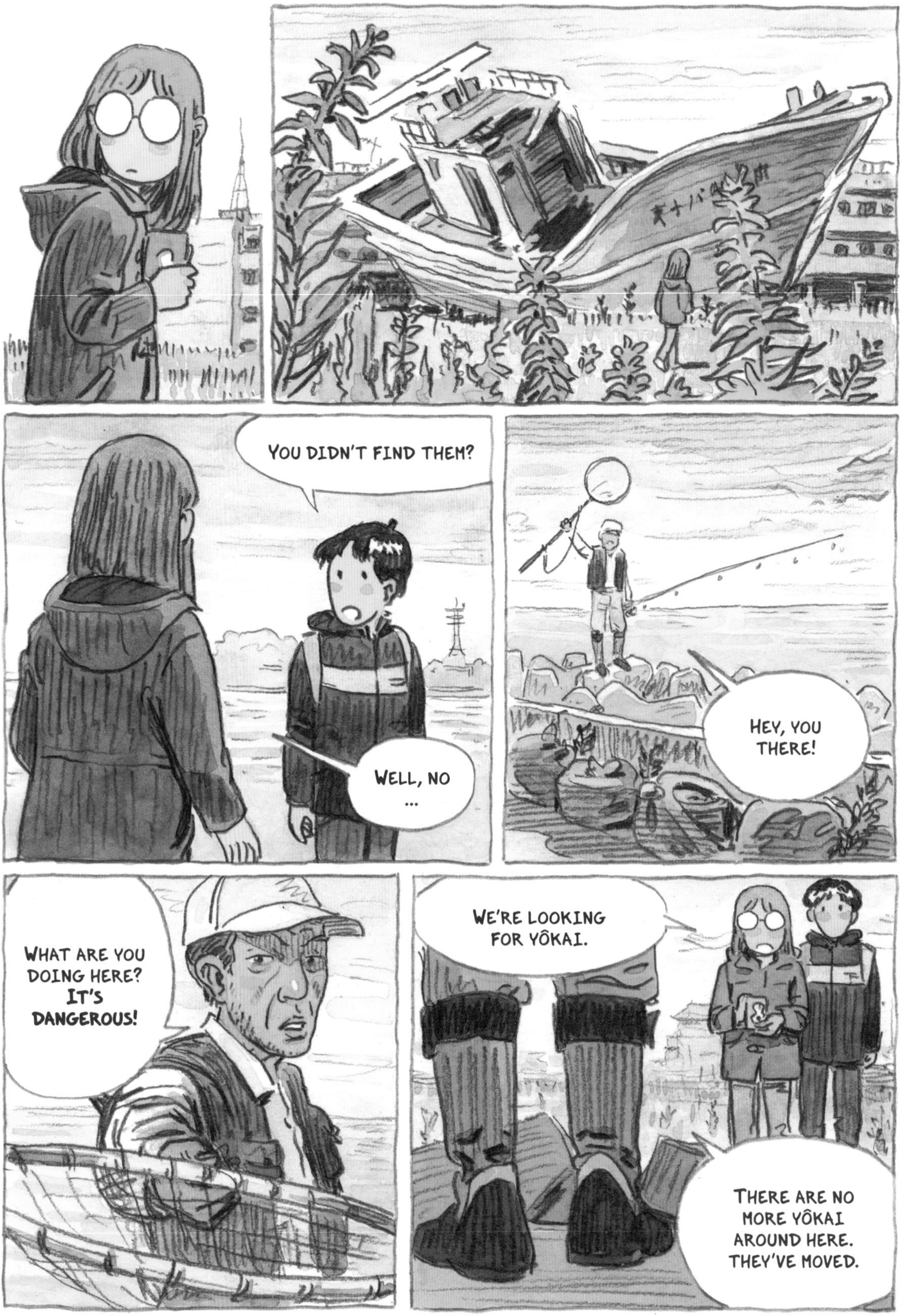

YOU DIDN'T FIND THEM?
WELL, NO ...
HEY, YOU THERE!
WHAT ARE YOU DOING HERE? IT'S DANGEROUS!
WE'RE LOOKING FOR YÔKAI.
THERE ARE NO MORE YÔKAI AROUND HERE. THEY'VE MOVED.

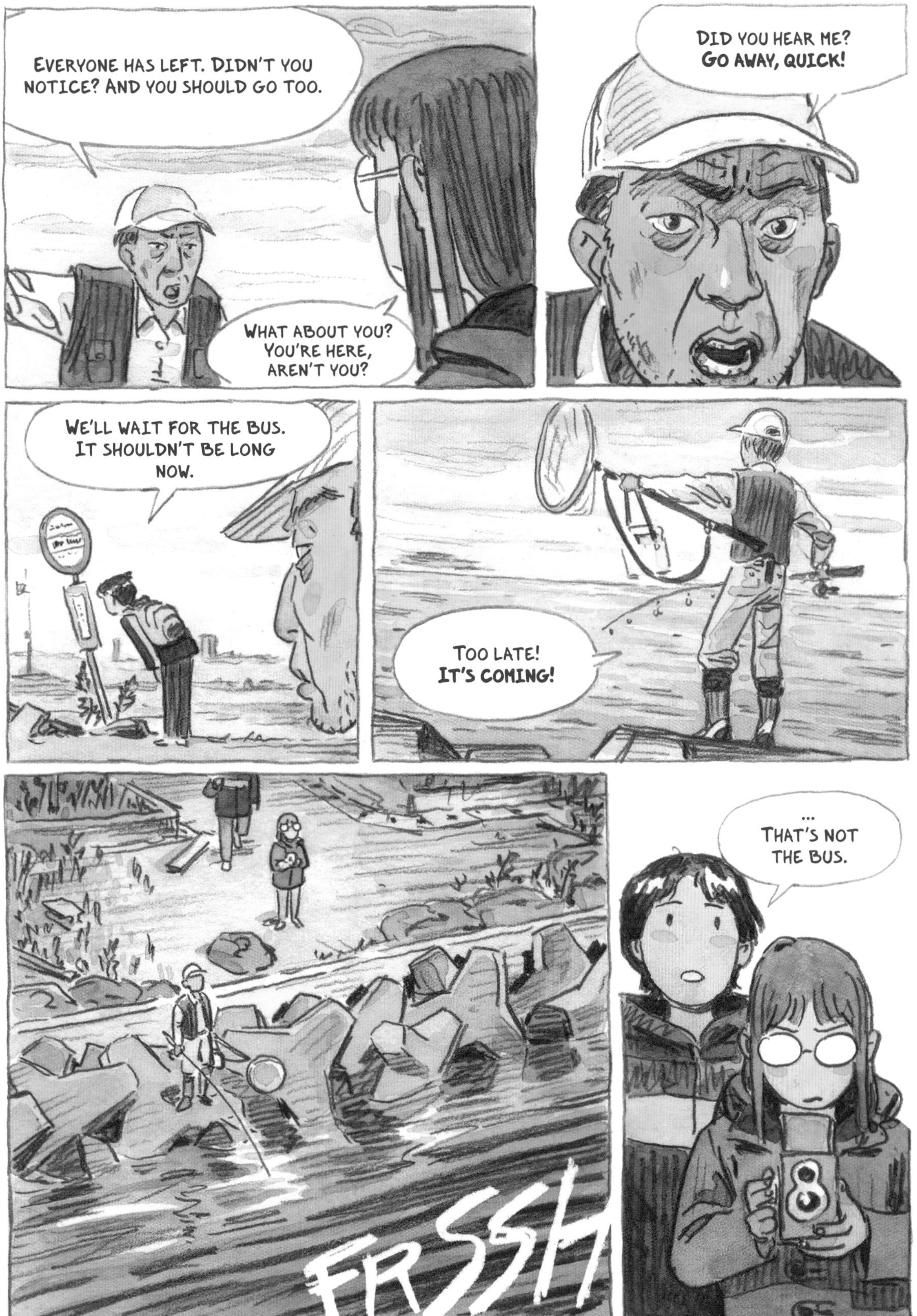
EVERYONE HAS LEFT. DIDN'T YOU NOTICE? AND YOU SHOULD GO TOO.
WHAT ABOUT YOU? YOU'RE HERE, AREN'T YOU?
DID YOU HEAR ME? GO AWAY, QUICK!
WE'LL WAIT FOR THE BUS. IT SHOULDN'T BE LONG NOW.
TOO LATE! IT'S COMING!
FRSSH
... THAT'S NOT THE BUS.

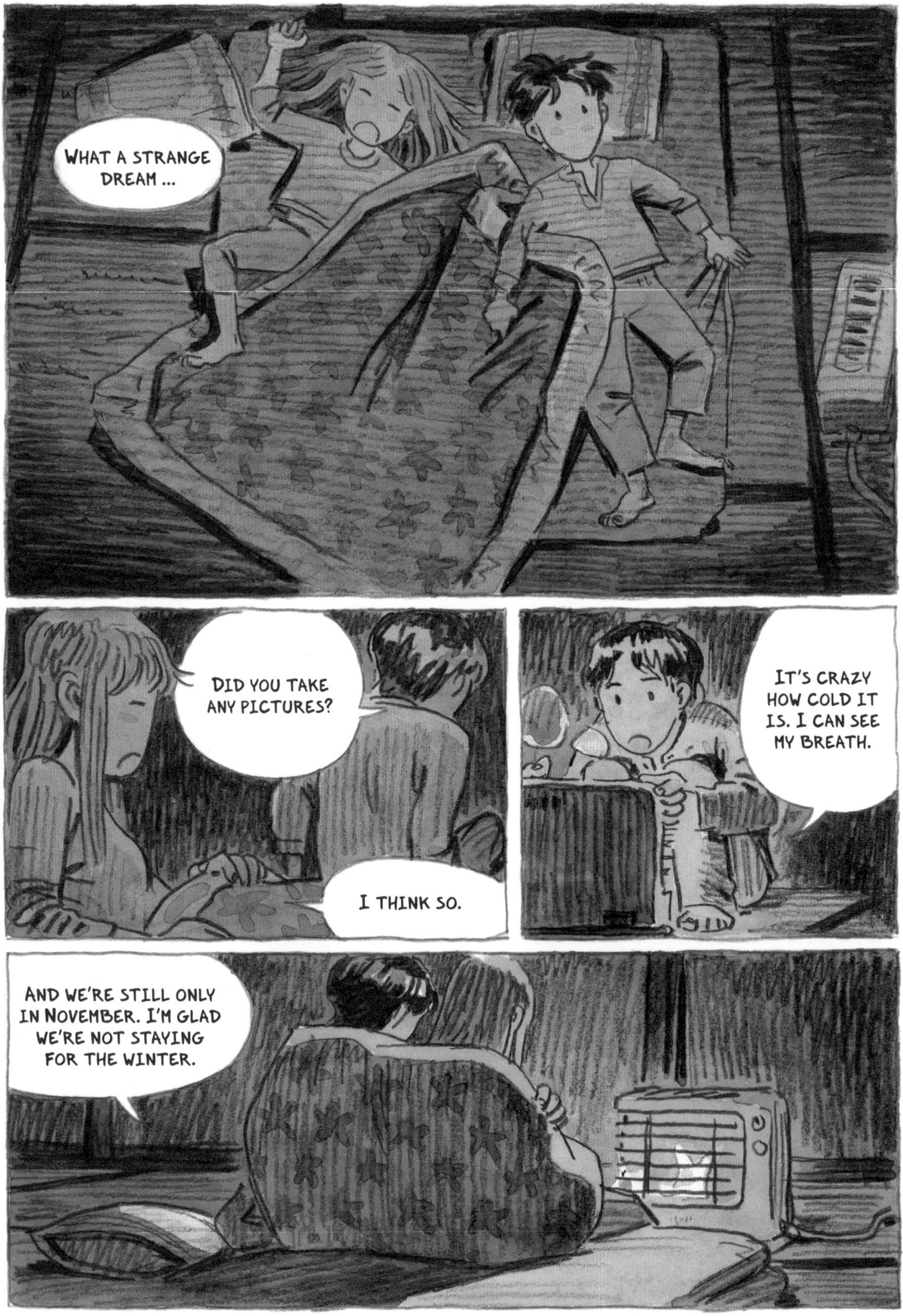
WHAT A STRANGE DREAM ...
DID YOU TAKE ANY PICTURES?
I THINK SO.
IT'S CRAZY HOW COLD IT IS. I CAN SEE MY BREATH.
AND WE'RE STILL ONLY IN NOVEMBER. I'M GLAD WE'RE NOT STAYING FOR THE WINTER.

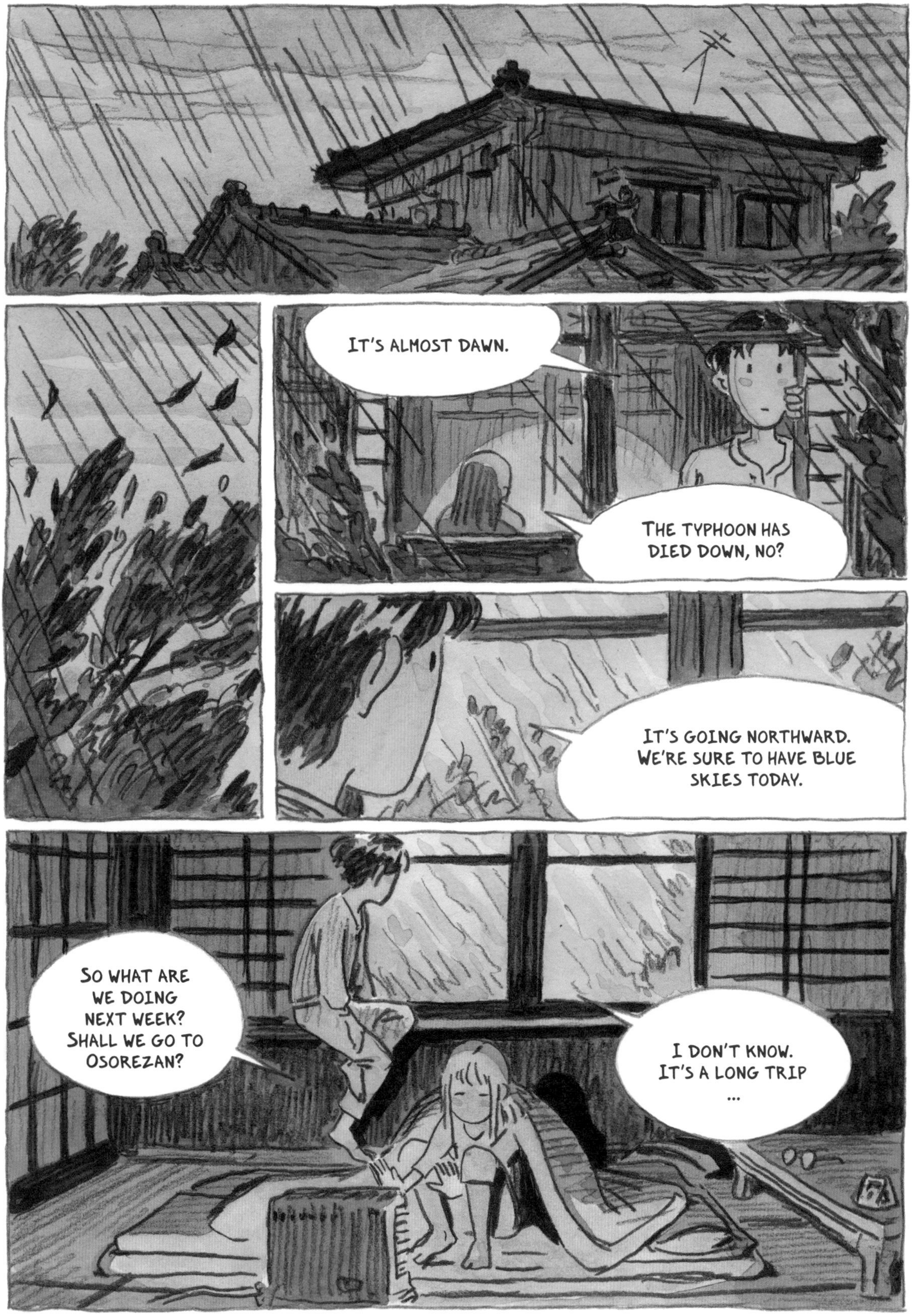

IT'S ALMOST DAWN.
THE TYPHOON HAS DIED DOWN, NO?
IT'S GOING NORTHWARD. WE'RE SURE TO HAVE BLUE SKIES TODAY.
SO WHAT ARE WE DOING NEXT WEEK? SHALL WE GO TO OSOREZAN?
I DON'T KNOW. IT'S A LONG TRIP ...

Dream
(aquatic monster)

A seaside city
Night of November 20, 2014
Foggy weather

Settings:

Light

Distance

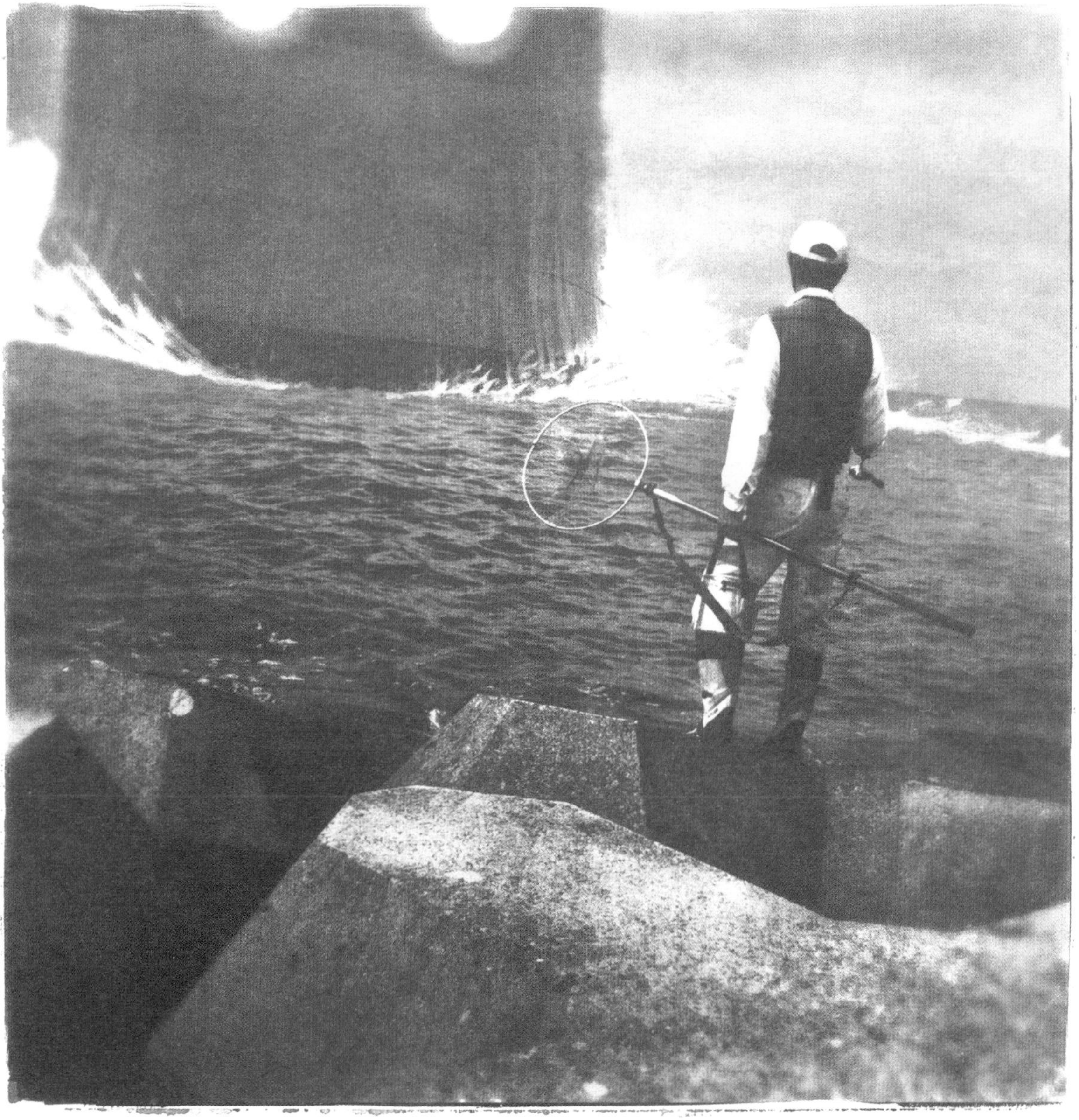

7

Jizō's sleeve

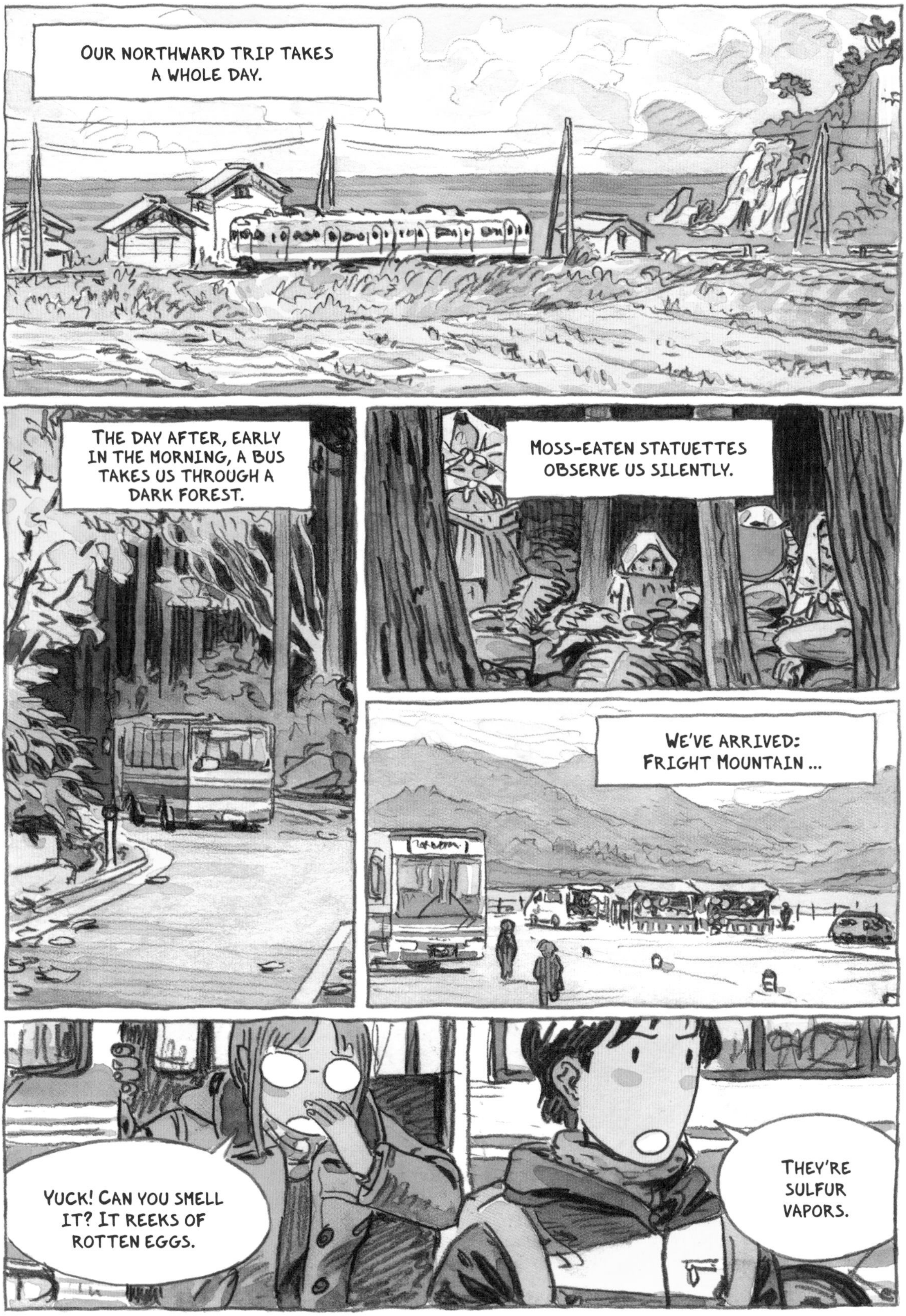
OUR NORTHWARD TRIP TAKES A WHOLE DAY.
THE DAY AFTER, EARLY IN THE MORNING, A BUS TAKES US THROUGH A DARK FOREST.
MOSS-EATEN STATUETTES OBSERVE US SILENTLY.
WE'VE ARRIVED: FRIGHT MOUNTAIN ...
YUCK! CAN YOU SMELL IT? IT REEKS OF ROTTEN EGGS.
THEY'RE SULFUR VAPORS.

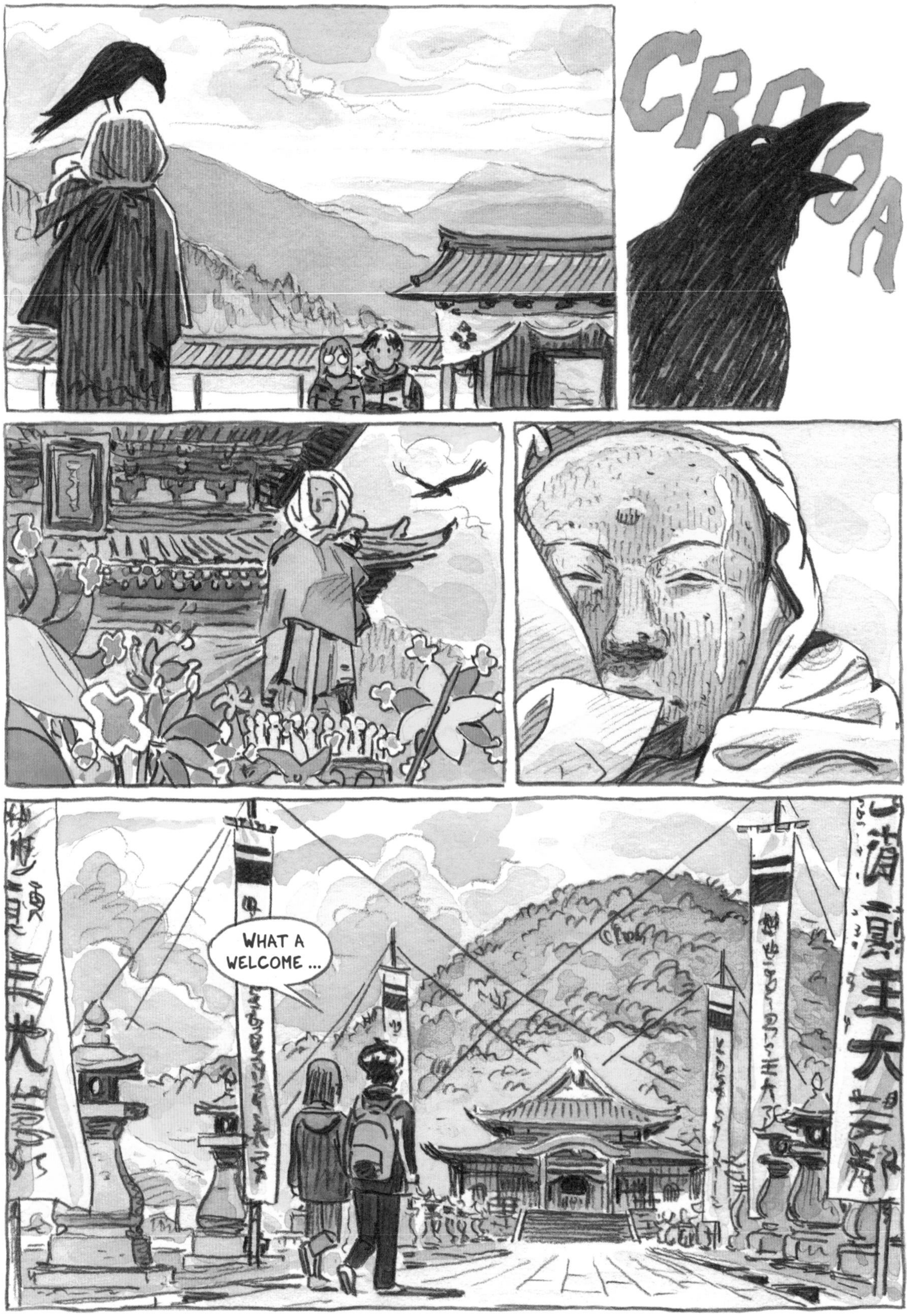
CROOA
WHAT A WELCOME ...

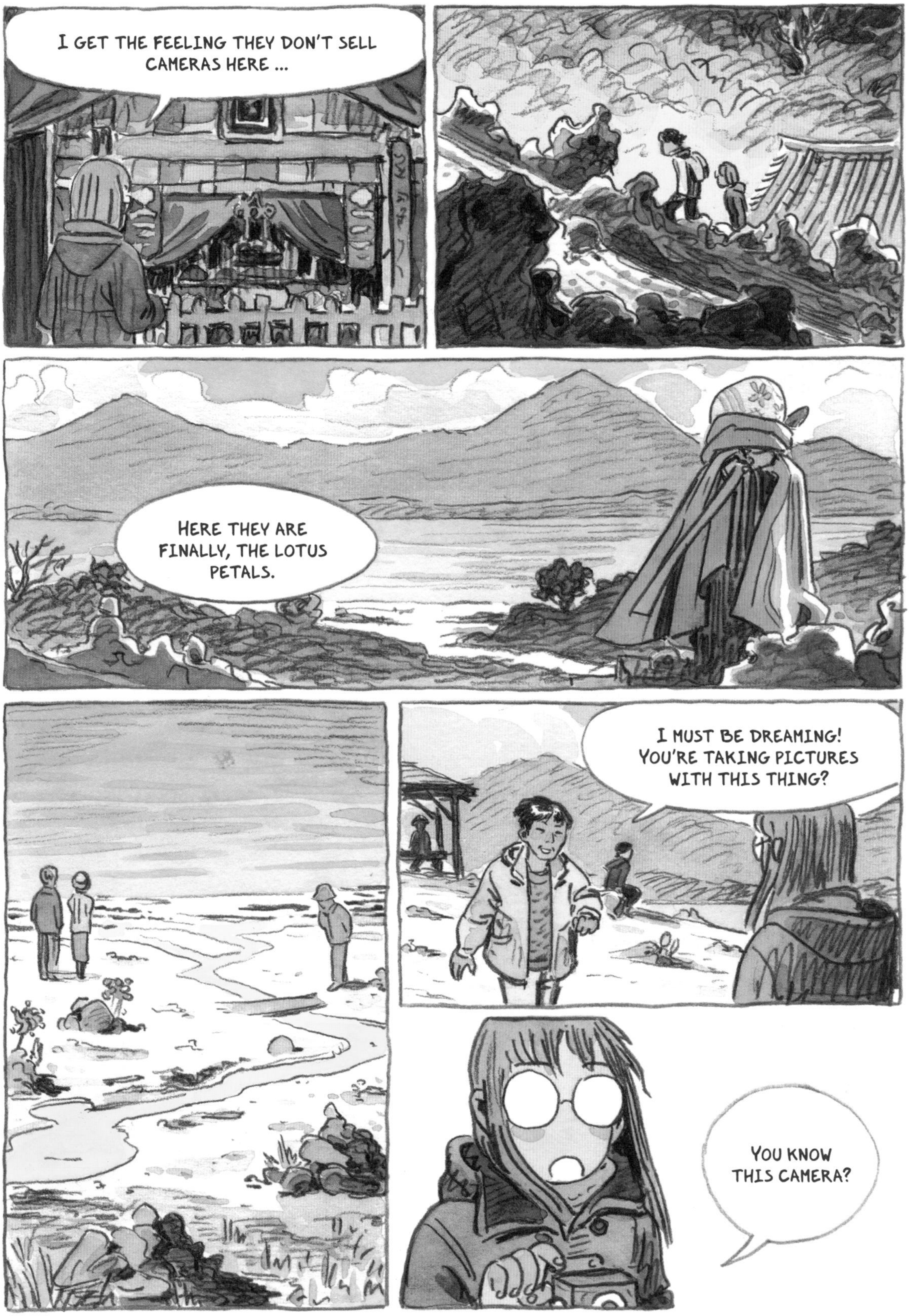
I GET THE FEELING THEY DON'T SELL CAMERAS HERE ...
HERE THEY ARE FINALLY, THE LOTUS PETALS.
I MUST BE DREAMING! YOU'RE TAKING PICTURES WITH THIS THING?
YOU KNOW THIS CAMERA?

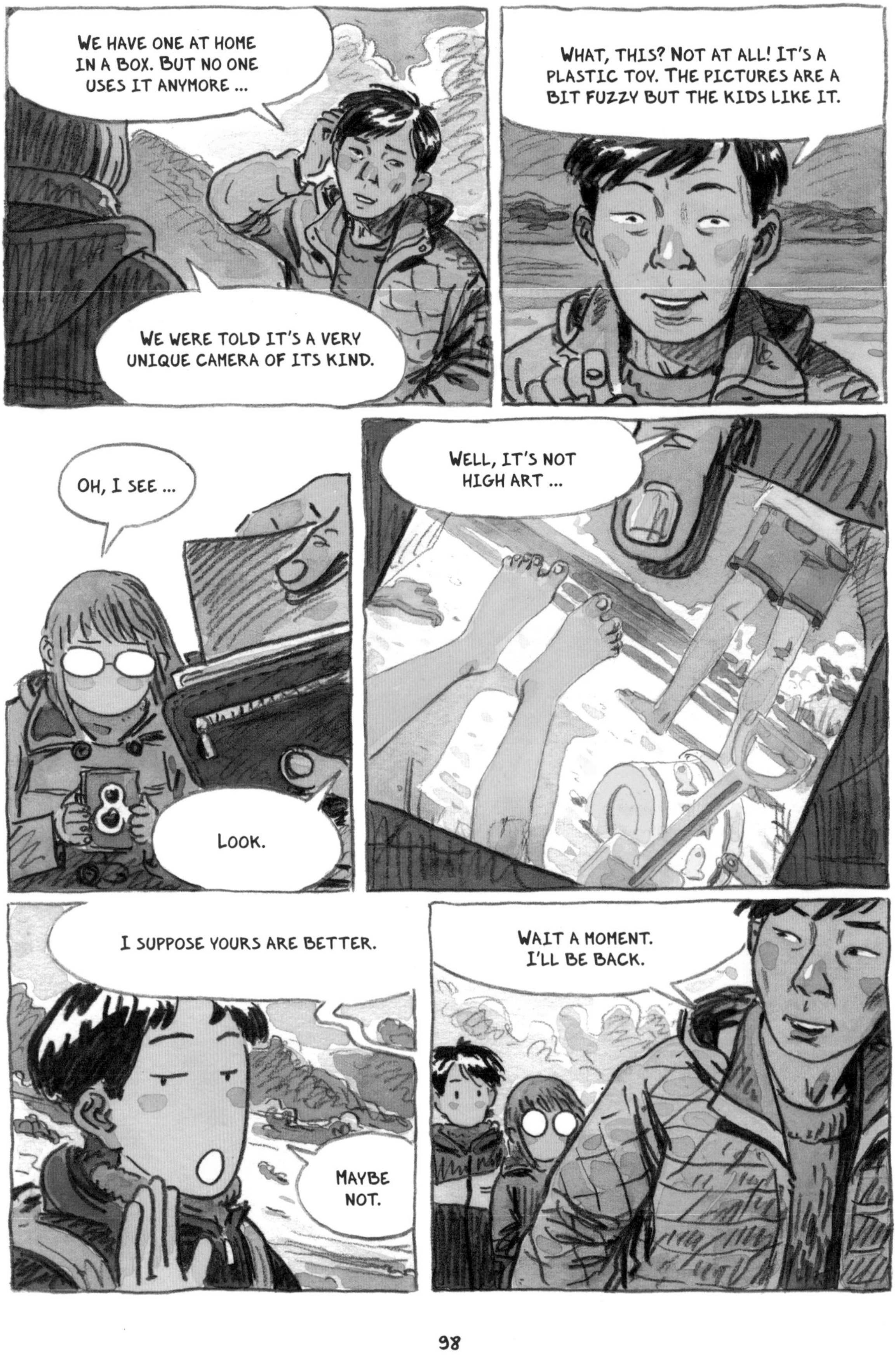
WE HAVE ONE AT HOME IN A BOX. BUT NO ONE USES IT ANYMORE ...
WE WERE TOLD IT'S A VERY UNIQUE CAMERA OF ITS KIND.
WHAT, THIS? NOT AT ALL! IT'S A PLASTIC TOY. THE PICTURES ARE A BIT FUZZY BUT THE KIDS LIKE IT.
OH, I SEE ...
LOOK.
WELL, IT'S NOT HIGH ART ...
I SUPPOSE YOURS ARE BETTER.
MAYBE NOT.
WAIT A MOMENT. I'LL BE BACK.

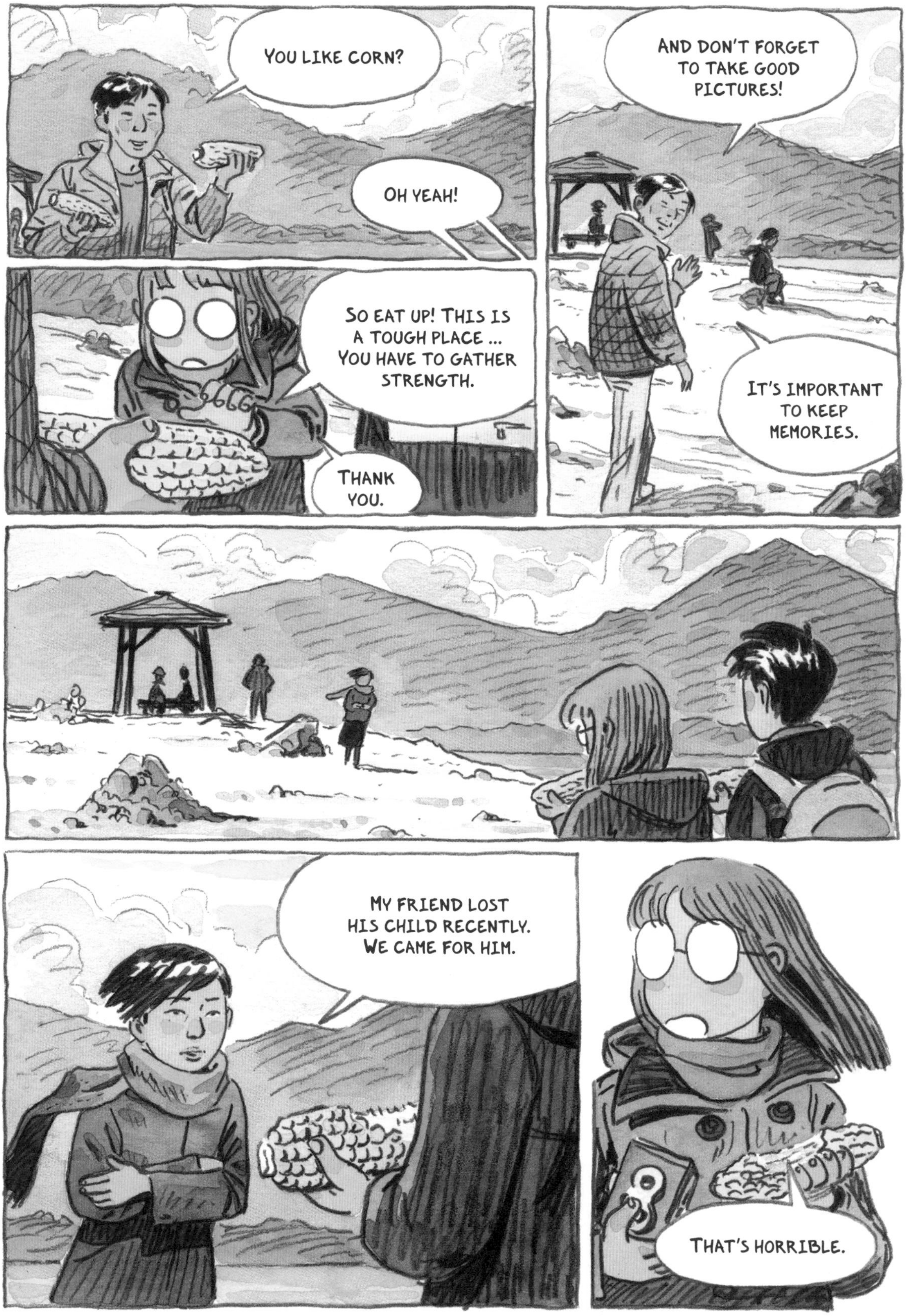

YOU LIKE CORN?
OH YEAH!
AND DON'T FORGET TO TAKE GOOD PICTURES!
SO EAT UP! THIS IS A TOUGH PLACE ... YOU HAVE TO GATHER STRENGTH.
THANK YOU.
IT'S IMPORTANT TO KEEP MEMORIES.
MY FRIEND LOST HIS CHILD RECENTLY. WE CAME FOR HIM.
THAT'S HORRIBLE.

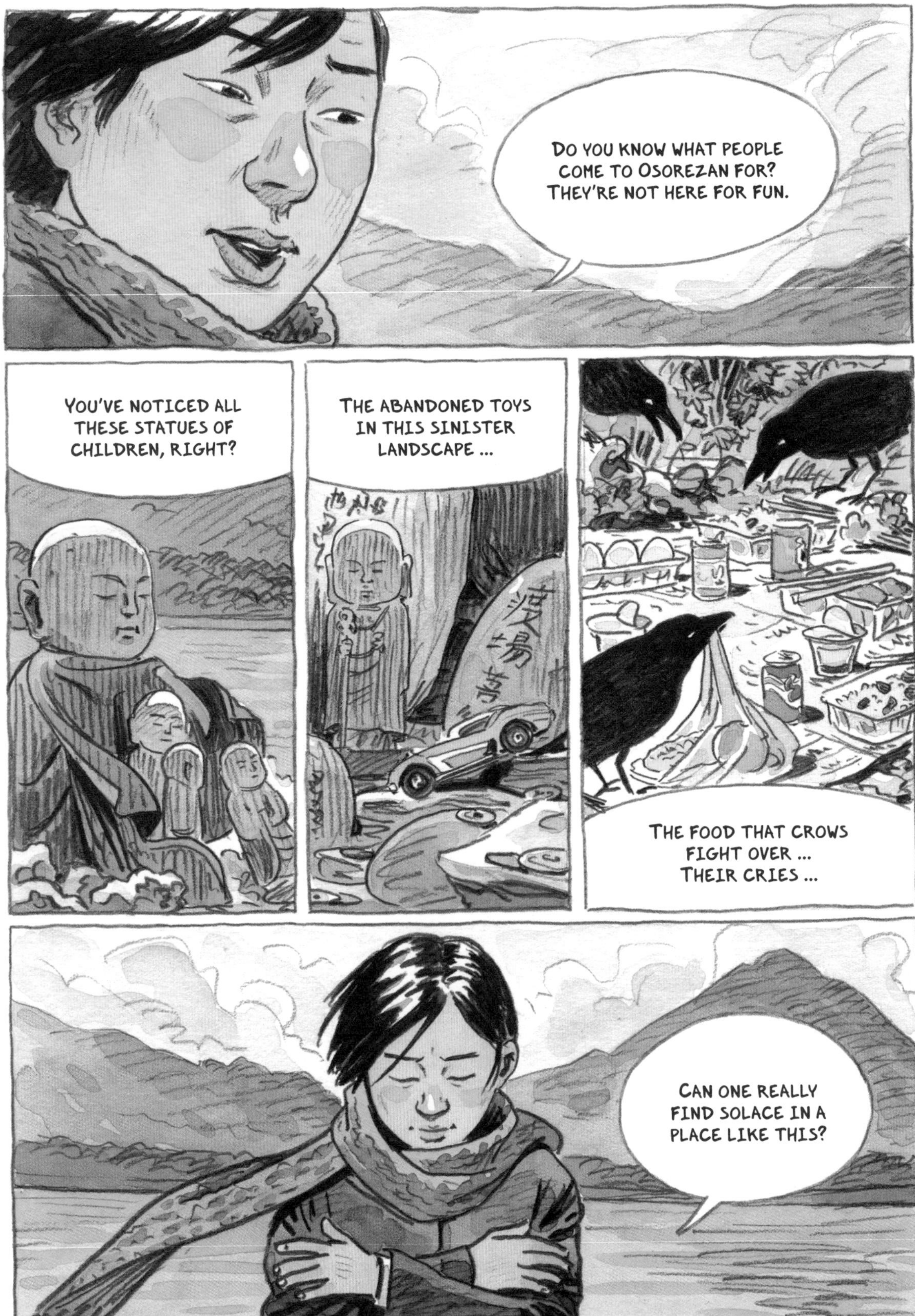
Do you know what people come to Osorezan for? They're not here for fun.
You've noticed all these statues of children, right?
The abandoned toys in this sinister landscape ...
The food that crows fight over ... Their cries ...
Can one really find solace in a place like this?

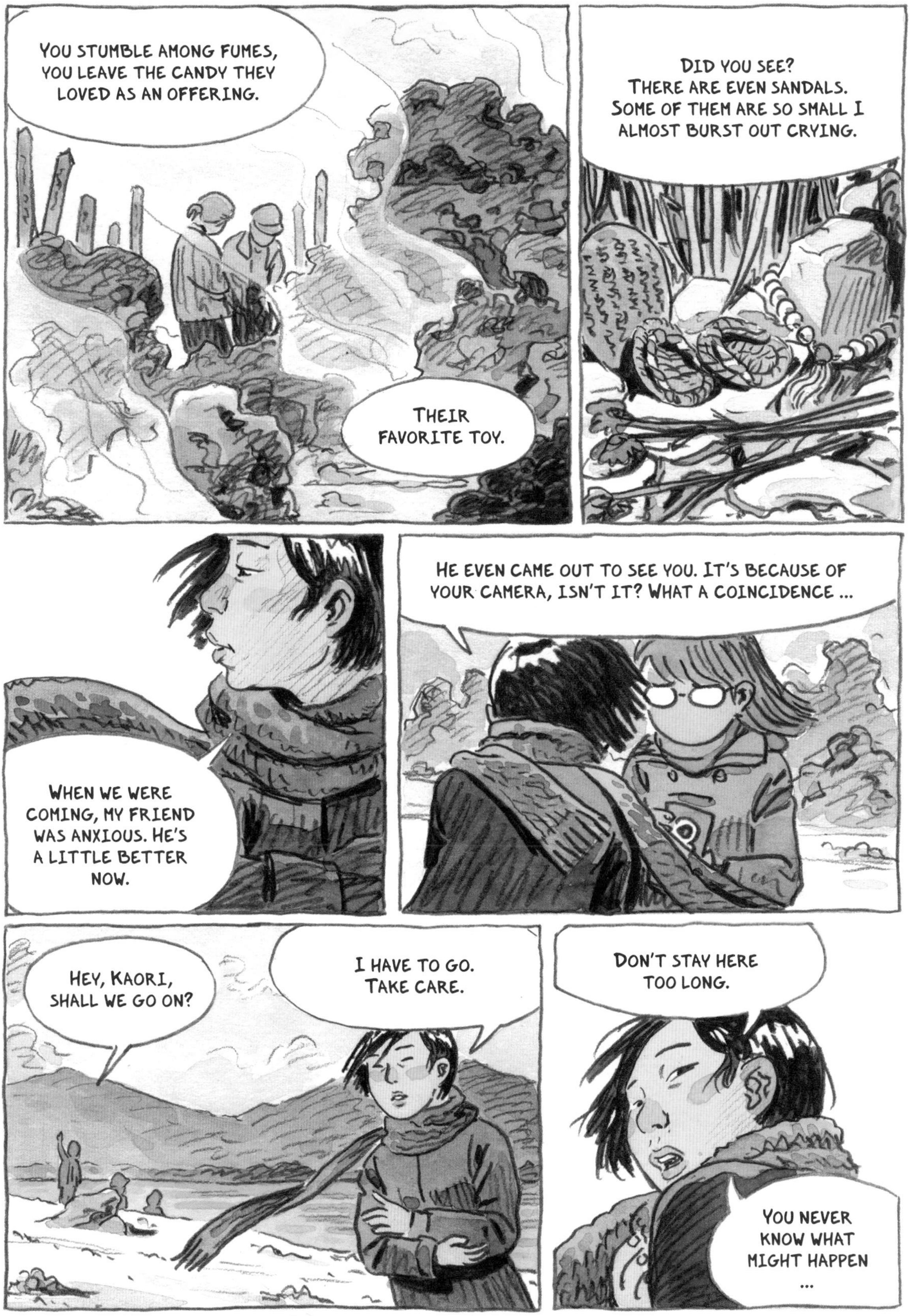
YOU STUMBLE AMONG FUMES, YOU LEAVE THE CANDY THEY LOVED AS AN OFFERING.
THEIR FAVORITE TOY.
DID YOU SEE? THERE ARE EVEN SANDALS. SOME OF THEM ARE SO SMALL I ALMOST BURST OUT CRYING.
WHEN WE WERE COMING, MY FRIEND WAS ANXIOUS. HE'S A LITTLE BETTER NOW.
HE EVEN CAME OUT TO SEE YOU. IT'S BECAUSE OF YOUR CAMERA, ISN'T IT? WHAT A COINCIDENCE ...
HEY, KAORI, SHALL WE GO ON?
I HAVE TO GO. TAKE CARE.
DON'T STAY HERE TOO LONG.
YOU NEVER KNOW WHAT MIGHT HAPPEN ...

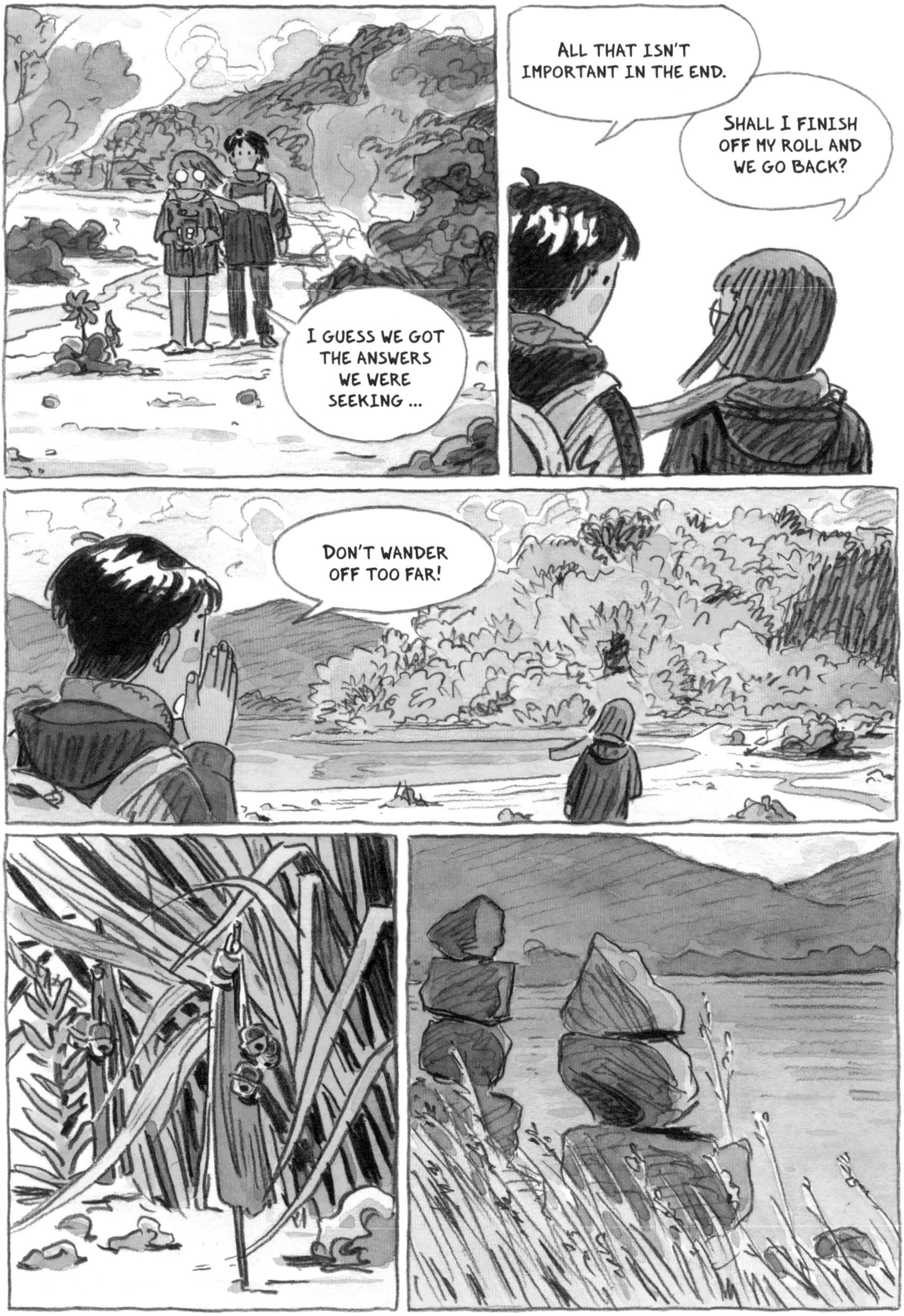
I GUESS WE GOT THE ANSWERS WE WERE SEEKING ...
ALL THAT ISN'T IMPORTANT IN THE END.
SHALL I FINISH OFF MY ROLL AND WE GO BACK?
DON'T WANDER OFF TOO FAR!

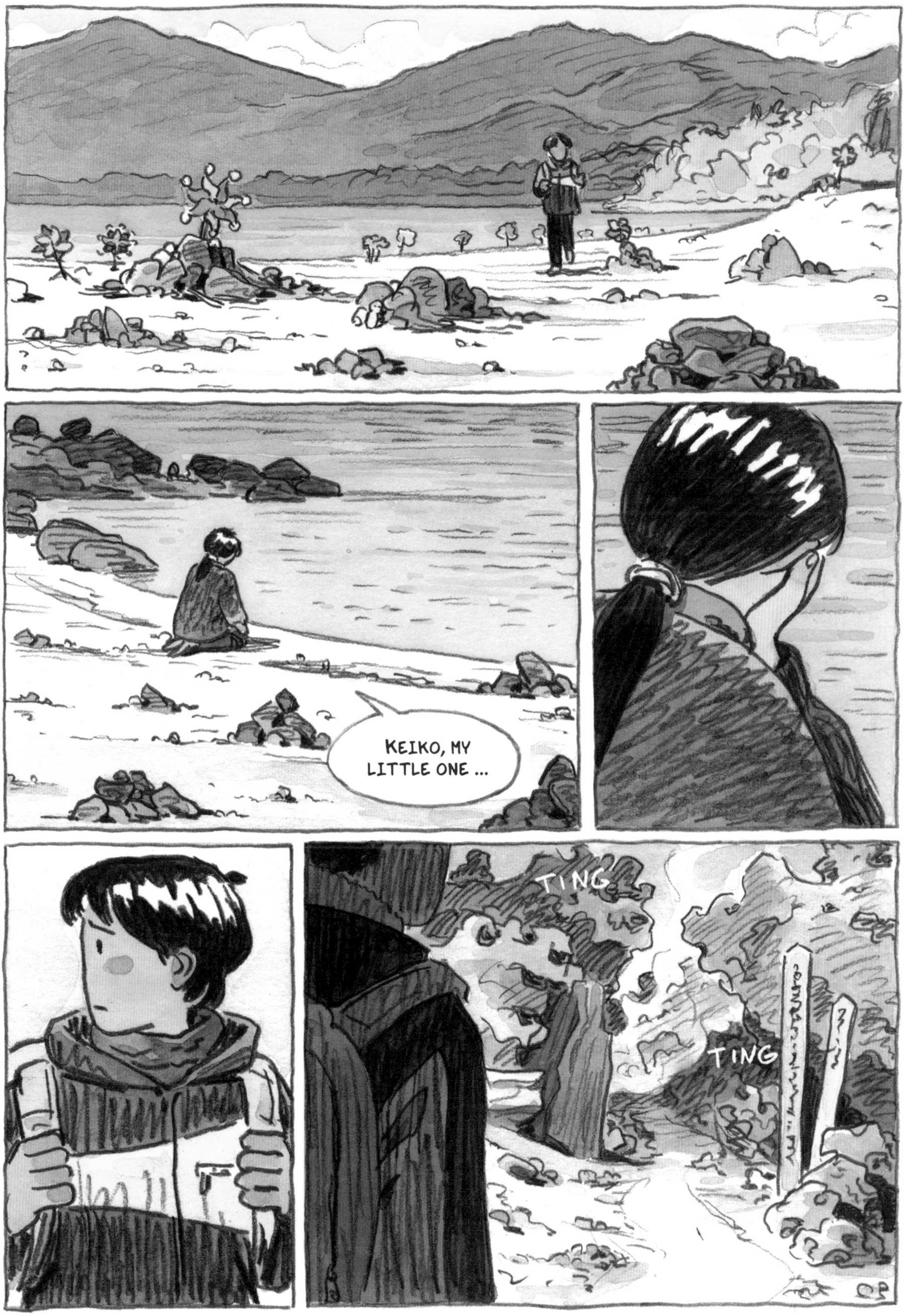
KEIKO, MY LITTLE ONE ...
TING
TING

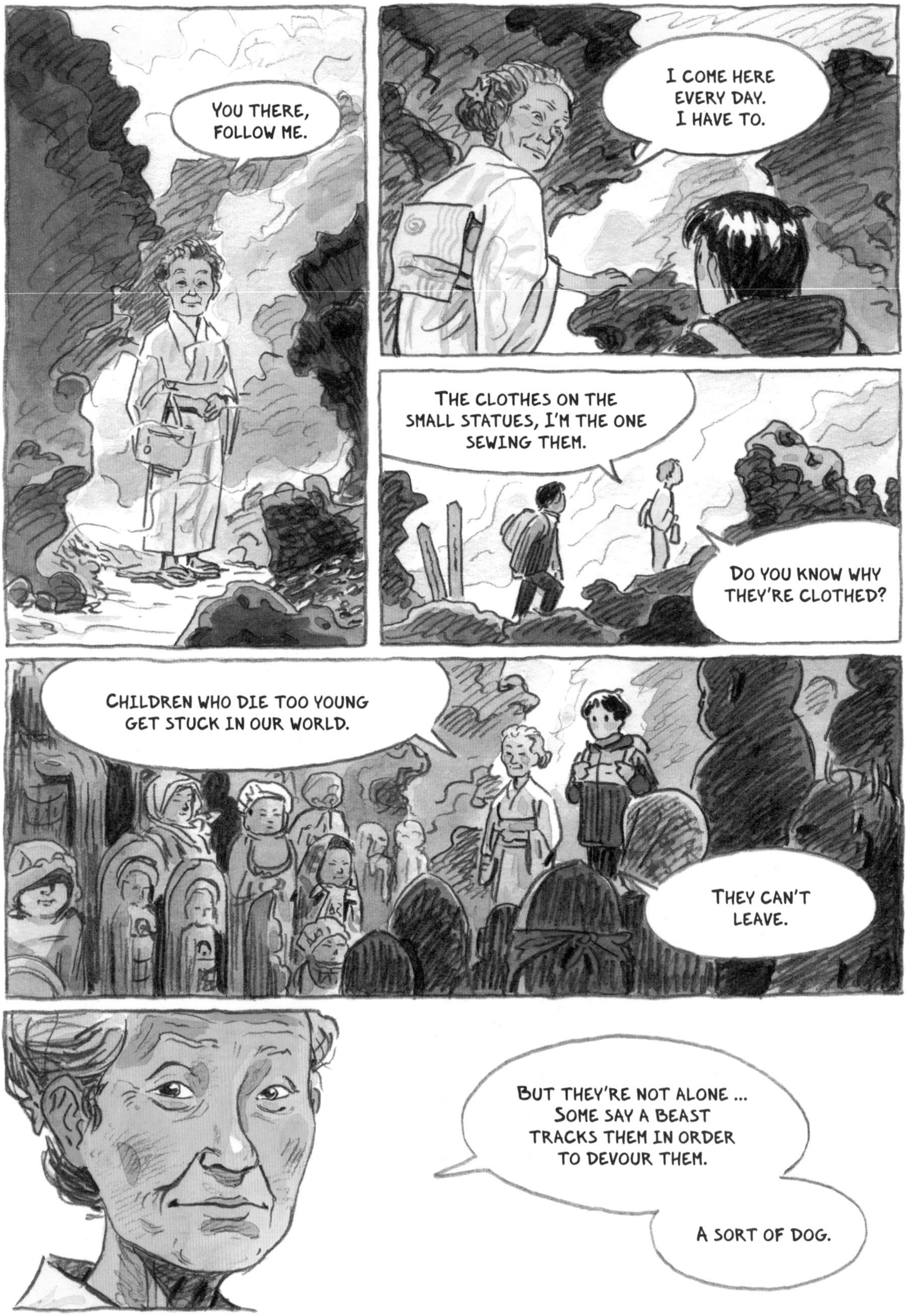
YOU THERE, FOLLOW ME.
I COME HERE EVERY DAY. I HAVE TO.
THE CLOTHES ON THE SMALL STATUES, I'M THE ONE SEWING THEM.
DO YOU KNOW WHY THEY'RE CLOTHED?
CHILDREN WHO DIE TOO YOUNG GET STUCK IN OUR WORLD.
THEY CAN'T LEAVE.
BUT THEY'RE NOT ALONE ... SOME SAY A BEAST TRACKS THEM IN ORDER TO DEVOUR THEM.
A SORT OF DOG.

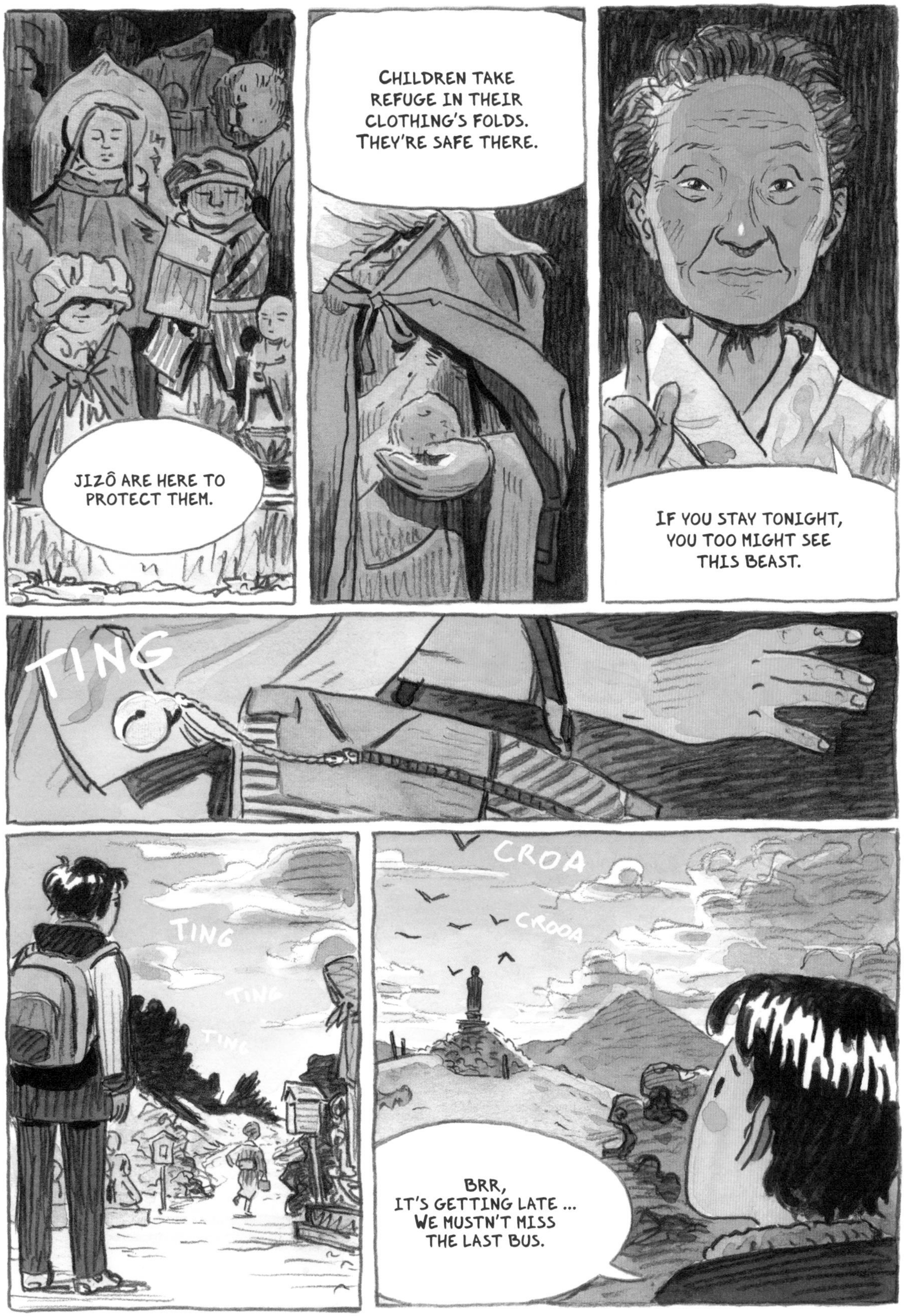
JIZÔ ARE HERE TO PROTECT THEM.
CHILDREN TAKE REFUGE IN THEIR CLOTHING'S FOLDS. THEY'RE SAFE THERE.
IF YOU STAY TONIGHT, YOU TOO MIGHT SEE THIS BEAST.
TING
TING
TING
TING
CROA
CROOA
BRR, IT'S GETTING LATE ... WE MUSTN'T MISS THE LAST BUS.

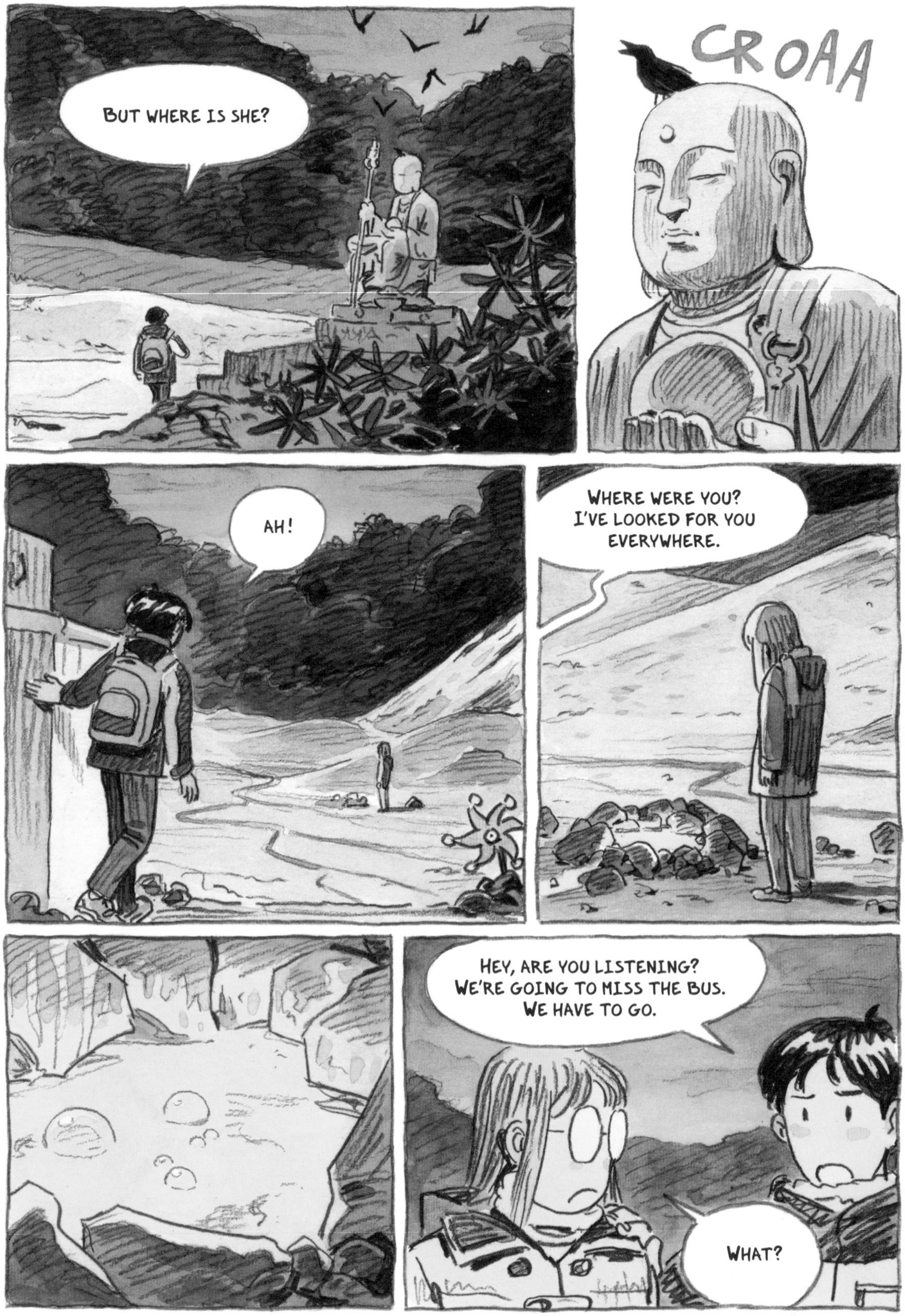
But where is she?
CROAA
Ah!
Where were you? I've looked for you everywhere.
Hey, are you listening? We're going to miss the bus. We have to go.
What?

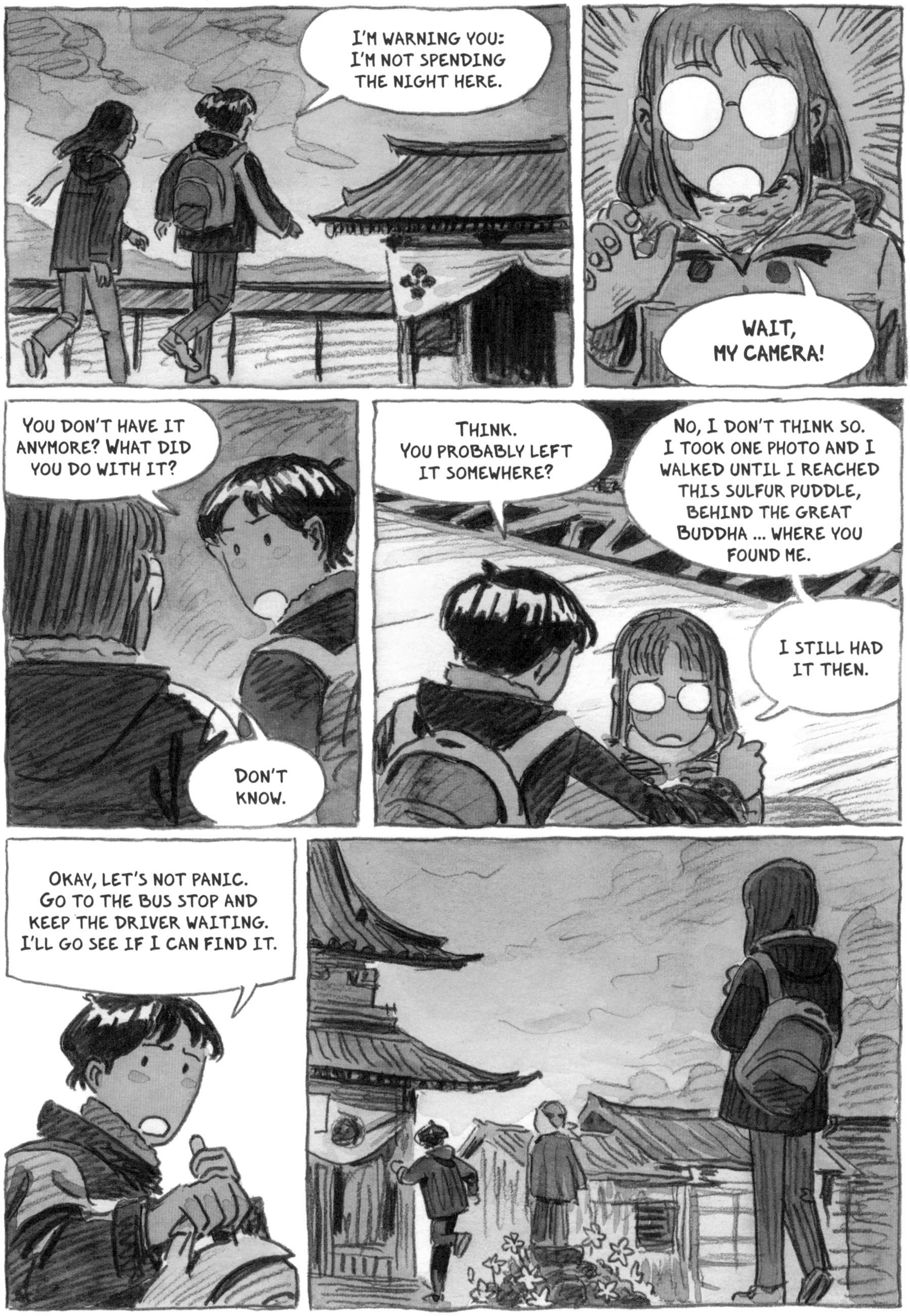

I'M WARNING YOU: I'M NOT SPENDING THE NIGHT HERE.
WAIT, MY CAMERA!
YOU DON'T HAVE IT ANYMORE? WHAT DID YOU DO WITH IT?
DON'T KNOW.
THINK. YOU PROBABLY LEFT IT SOMEWHERE?
NO, I DON'T THINK SO. I TOOK ONE PHOTO AND I WALKED UNTIL I REACHED THIS SULFUR PUDDLE, BEHIND THE GREAT BUDDHA ... WHERE YOU FOUND ME.
I STILL HAD IT THEN.
OKAY, LET'S NOT PANIC. GO TO THE BUS STOP AND KEEP THE DRIVER WAITING. I'LL GO SEE IF I CAN FIND IT.

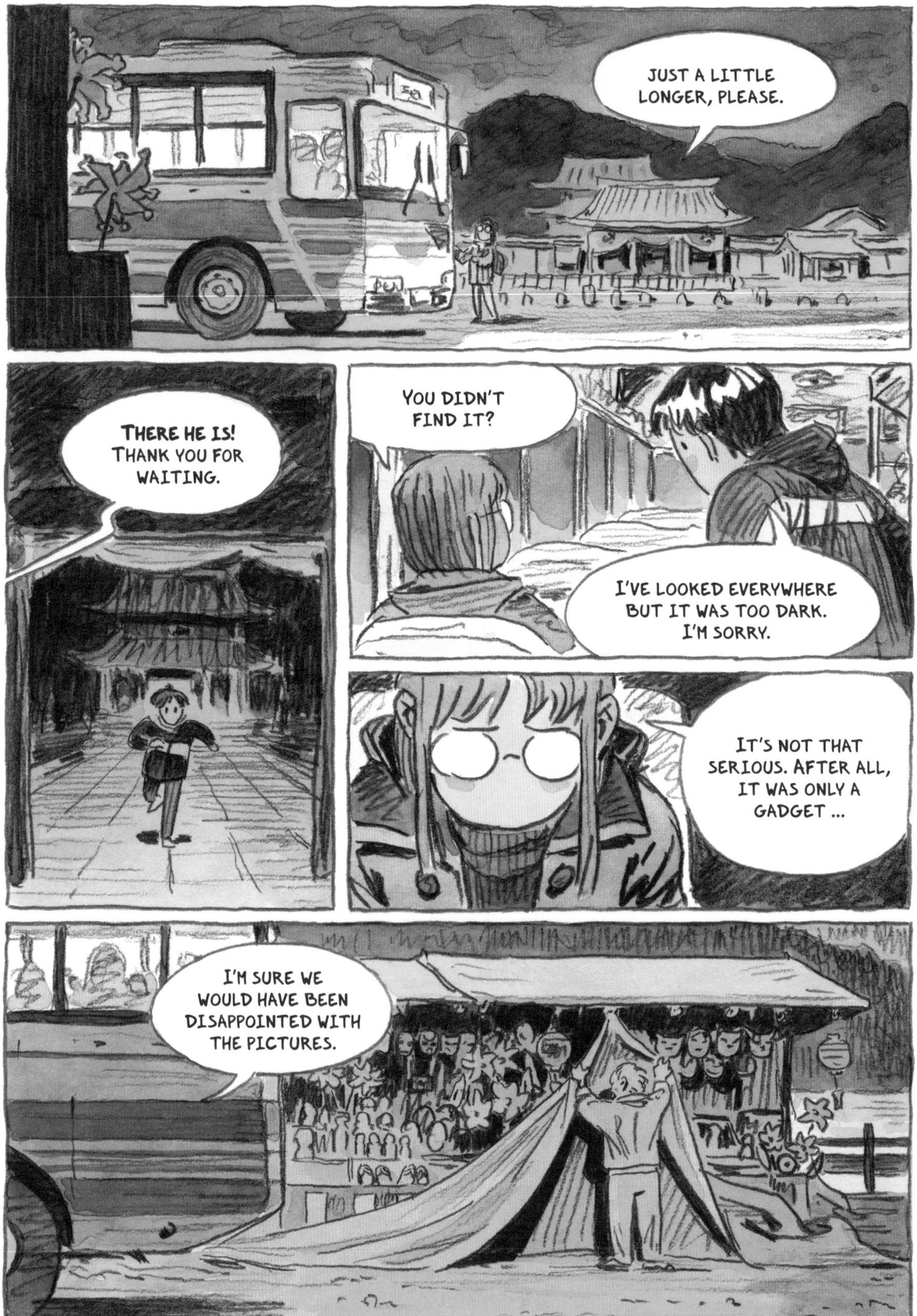
JUST A LITTLE LONGER, PLEASE.
THERE HE IS! THANK YOU FOR WAITING.
YOU DIDN'T FIND IT?
I'VE LOOKED EVERYWHERE BUT IT WAS TOO DARK. I'M SORRY.
IT'S NOT THAT SERIOUS. AFTER ALL, IT WAS ONLY A GADGET ...
I'M SURE WE WOULD HAVE BEEN DISAPPOINTED WITH THE PICTURES.

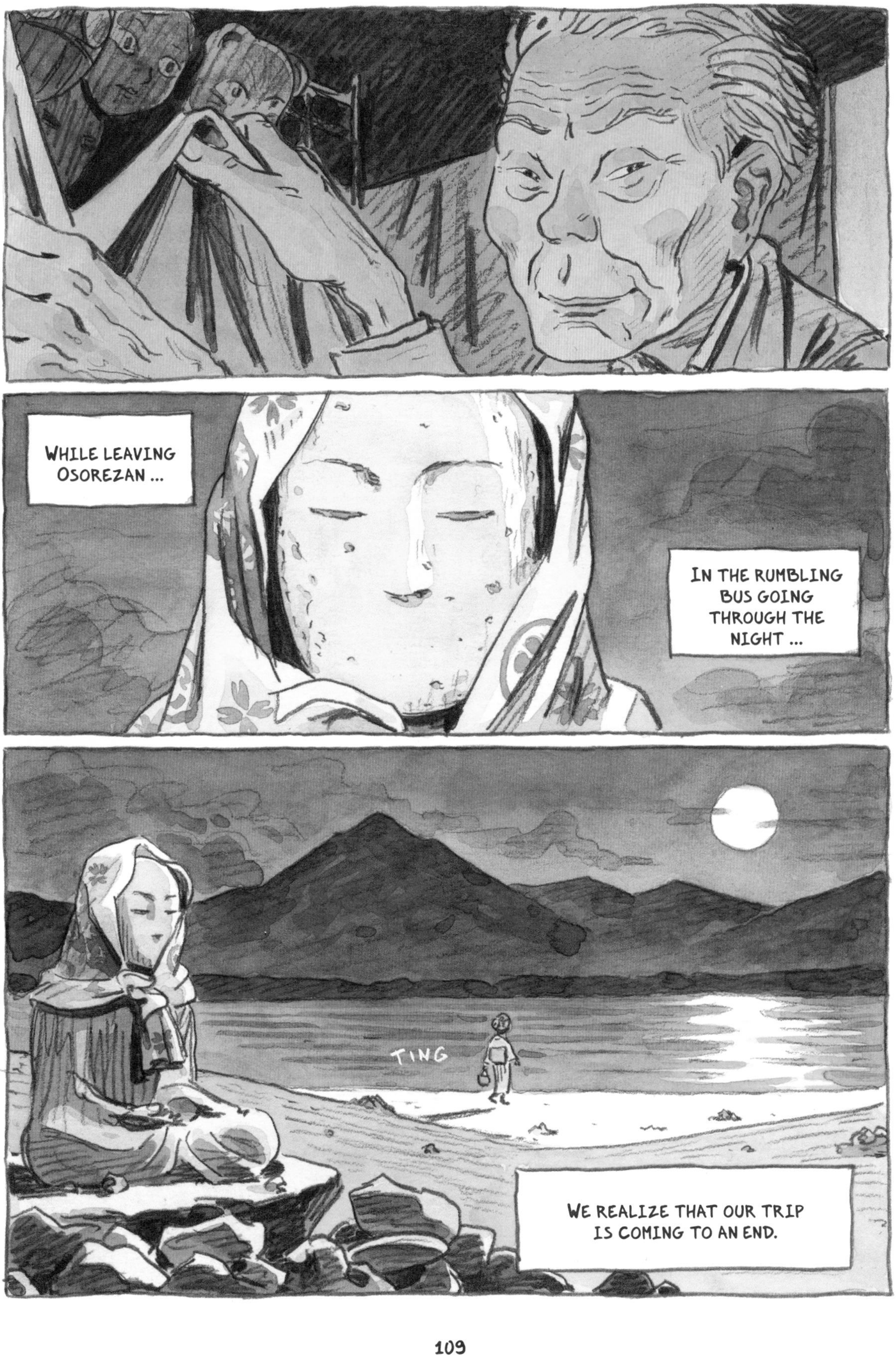
WHILE LEAVING OSOREZAN ...
IN THE RUMBLING BUS GOING THROUGH THE NIGHT ...
TING
WE REALIZE THAT OUR TRIP IS COMING TO AN END.

Fright Mountain
(silhouettes)

Osorezan
November 26, 2014
Overcast weather

Settings:

Light
Distance

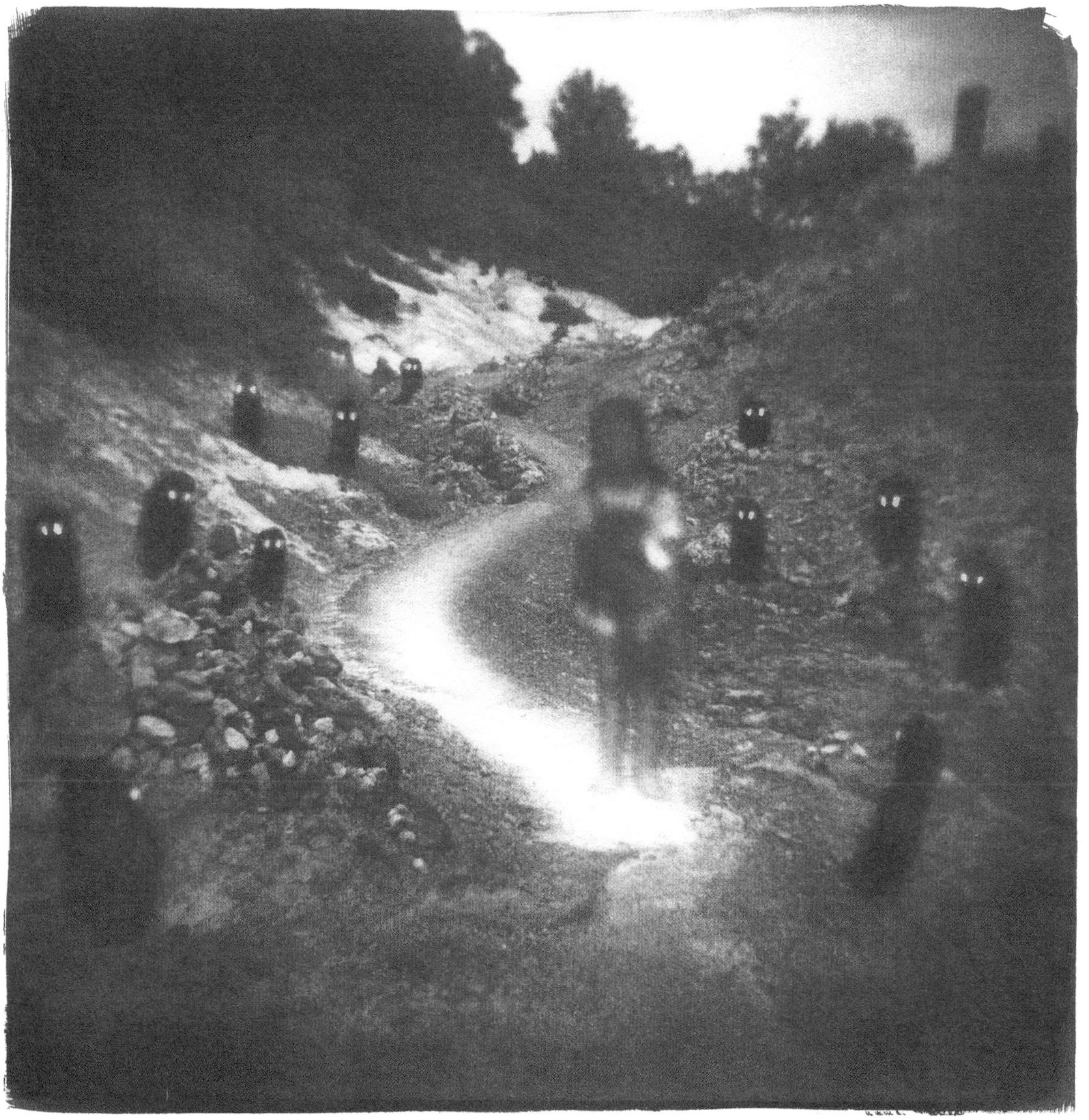

SHORTLY AFTER WE LEFT, SNOW BEGAN FALLING ON NIIGATA. IN THE PLANE THAT'S TAKING US BACK TO FRANCE, I THINK OF THE LONG, HARSH WINTER THAT'S JUST BEGINNING FOR THOSE WHO LIVE THERE.

OVER THERE, THE FROZEN WINDS BLOW MERCILESSLY, SEEPING INTO EVERY HOUSE.

MEMORIES OF THESE PAST FEW MONTHS COLLIDE INSIDE MY HEAD.

OUR LAST MEAL AT MARGUTTA. WE'RE GLAD TO SEE MS. KOJIMA AGAIN.

YOU'VE GOTTEN FAT, CECILE.

WELL, WHOSE FAULT IS THAT?

THESE MOTHS ARE MAKING HOLES IN MY PRETTY CLOTHES, THE BRATS.

[LITTLE] SAD, BUT WE'RE [GLAD] [NOT] TO LEAVE.

AT TORII NO UTA: A KEN TAKAKURA TRIBUTE EVENING (DIED LAST MONTH). THE BOSS SHOWS THE YAKUSA MOVIES THAT MADE HIM FAMOUS. EVERYONE IN THE ROOM IS OLD, BUT THEY SING THOSE SONGS WITH THE HEARTS OF KIDS.

A DRUNKEN MONK OFFERS ME A WEIRD BRACELET.

GOODBYES WITH MR. SHIGA ARE SHORT AND HE GOES BACK TO WATCH THE MOVIES.

TOO MOVED TO DRIVE US BACK THIS TIME?

BAH!

WHEN I LOST MY CAMERA, I HAD THE FEELING OF COMING OUT OF A DREAM.

NOW EVEN MORE, FLYING ABOVE SIBERIA, OUR TRIP SEEMS SO FAR AWAY, ALMOST UNREAL.

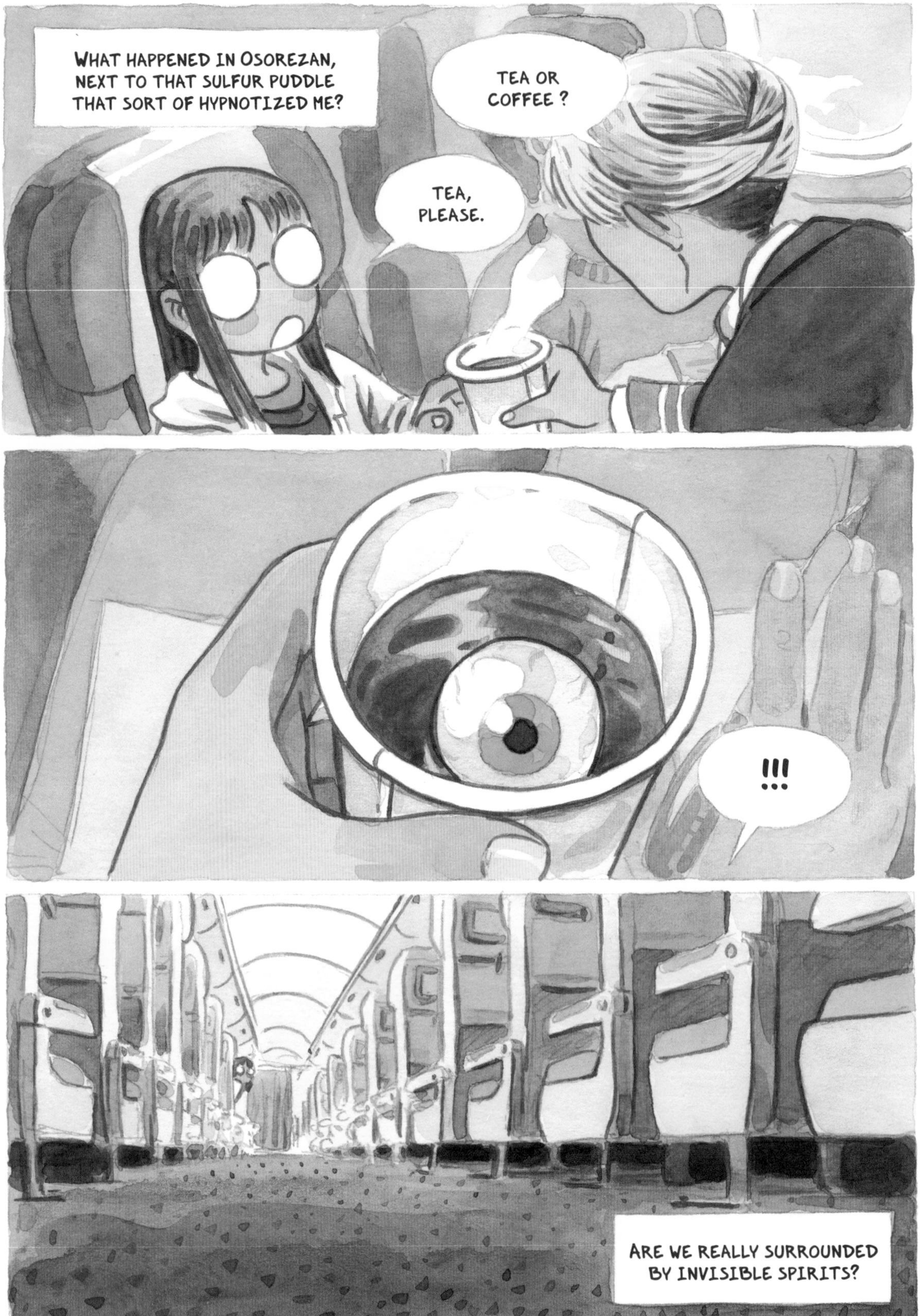
WHAT HAPPENED IN OSOREZAN, NEXT TO THAT SULFUR PUDDLE THAT SORT OF HYPNOTIZED ME?
TEA OR COFFEE ?
TEA, PLEASE.
!!!
...
ARE WE REALLY SURROUNDED BY INVISIBLE SPIRITS?

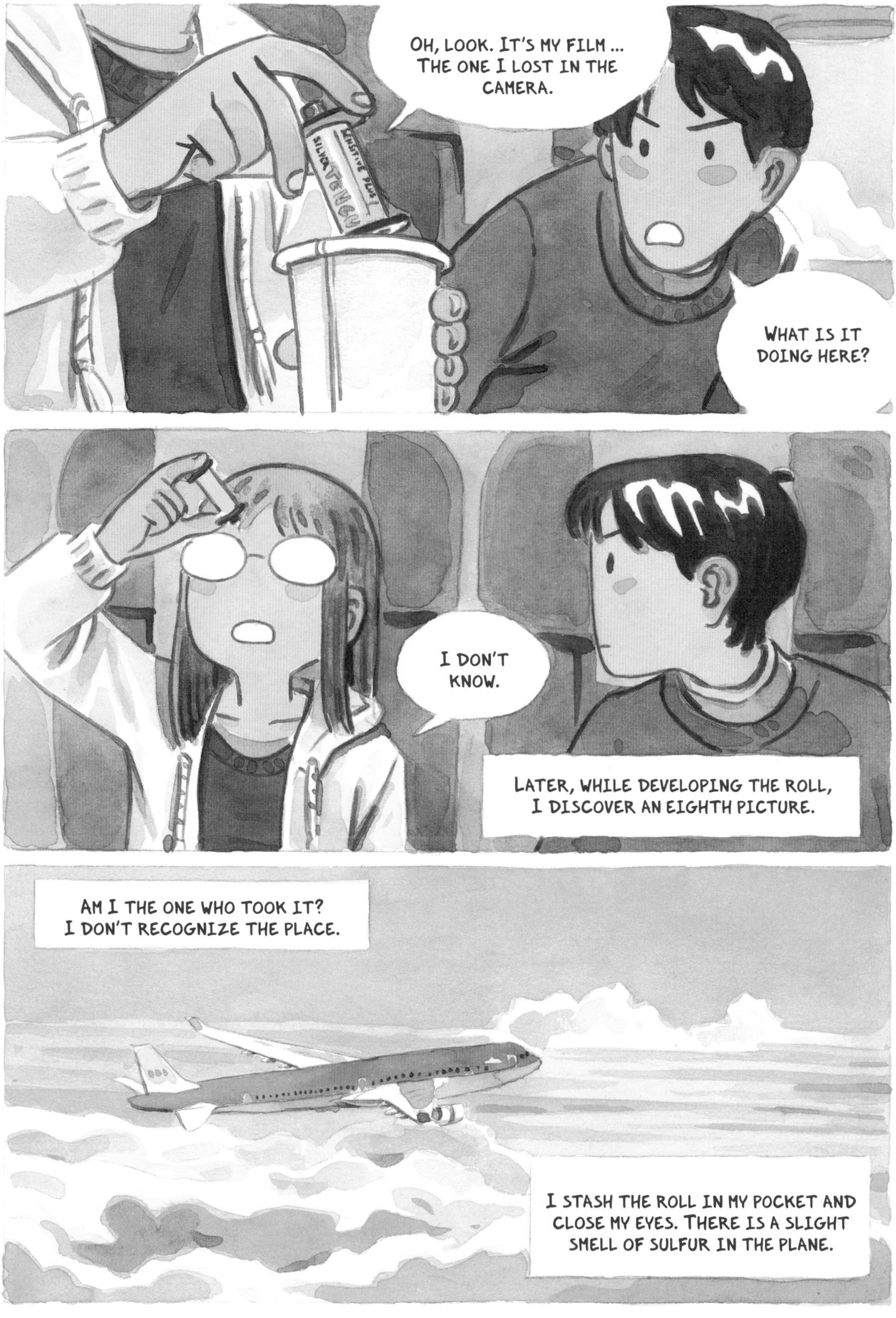

OH, LOOK. IT'S MY FILM ...
THE ONE I LOST IN THE CAMERA.
WHAT IS IT DOING HERE?
I DON'T KNOW.
LATER, WHILE DEVELOPING THE ROLL, I DISCOVER AN EIGHTH PICTURE.
AM I THE ONE WHO TOOK IT? I DON'T RECOGNIZE THE PLACE.
I STASH THE ROLL IN MY POCKET AND CLOSE MY EYES. THERE IS A SLIGHT SMELL OF SULFUR IN THE PLANE.

Photo 8/8

The other world
(mystery picture)

Unknown place
Date id.

Settings:

?

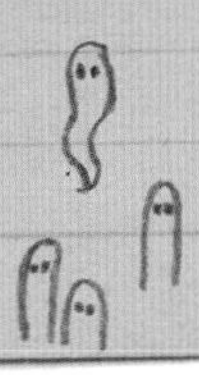

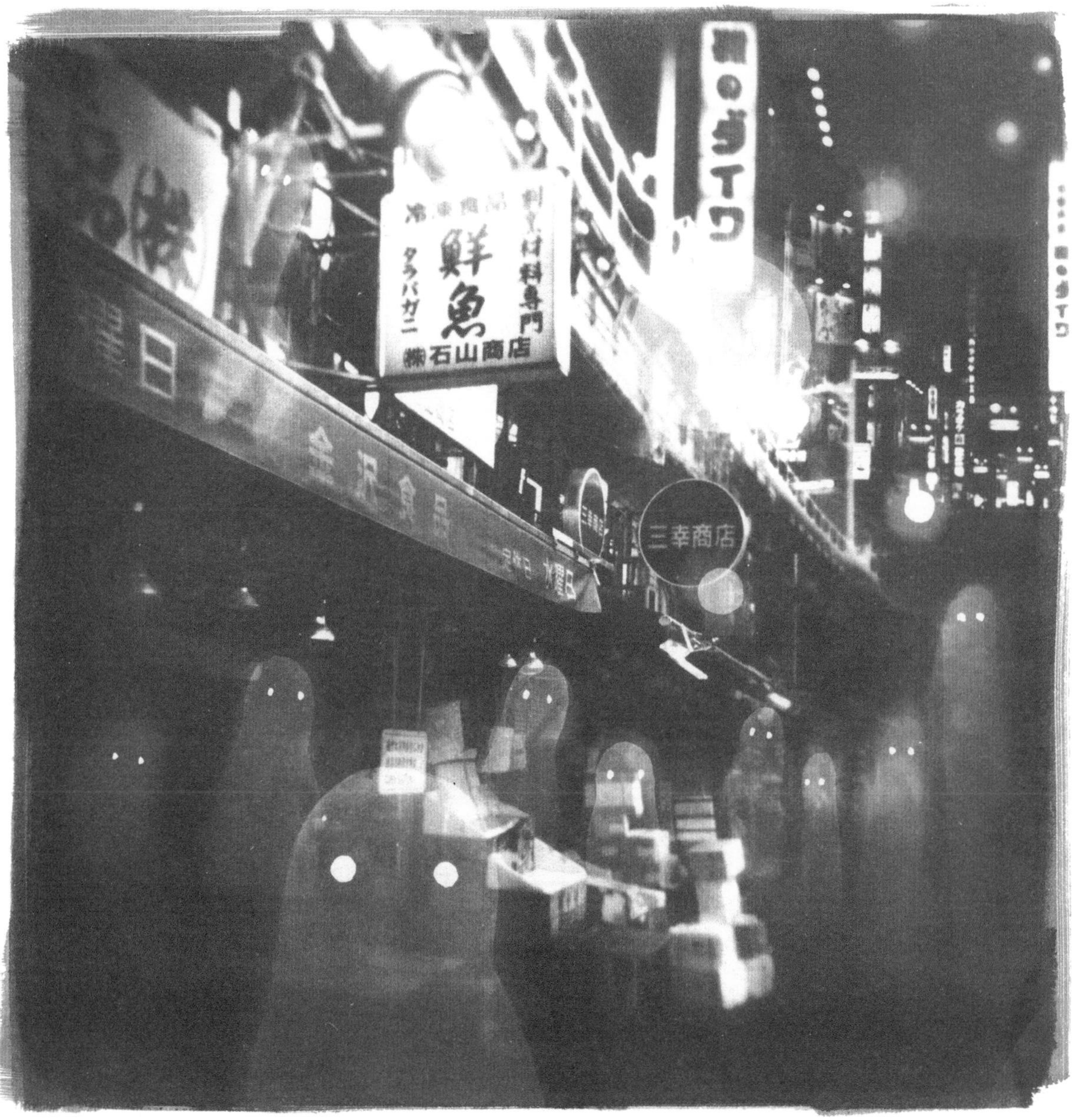
鮮魚
タラバガニ
㈱石山商店
金沢食品
水曜日
三幸商店

Yōkai Hunter's Notebook

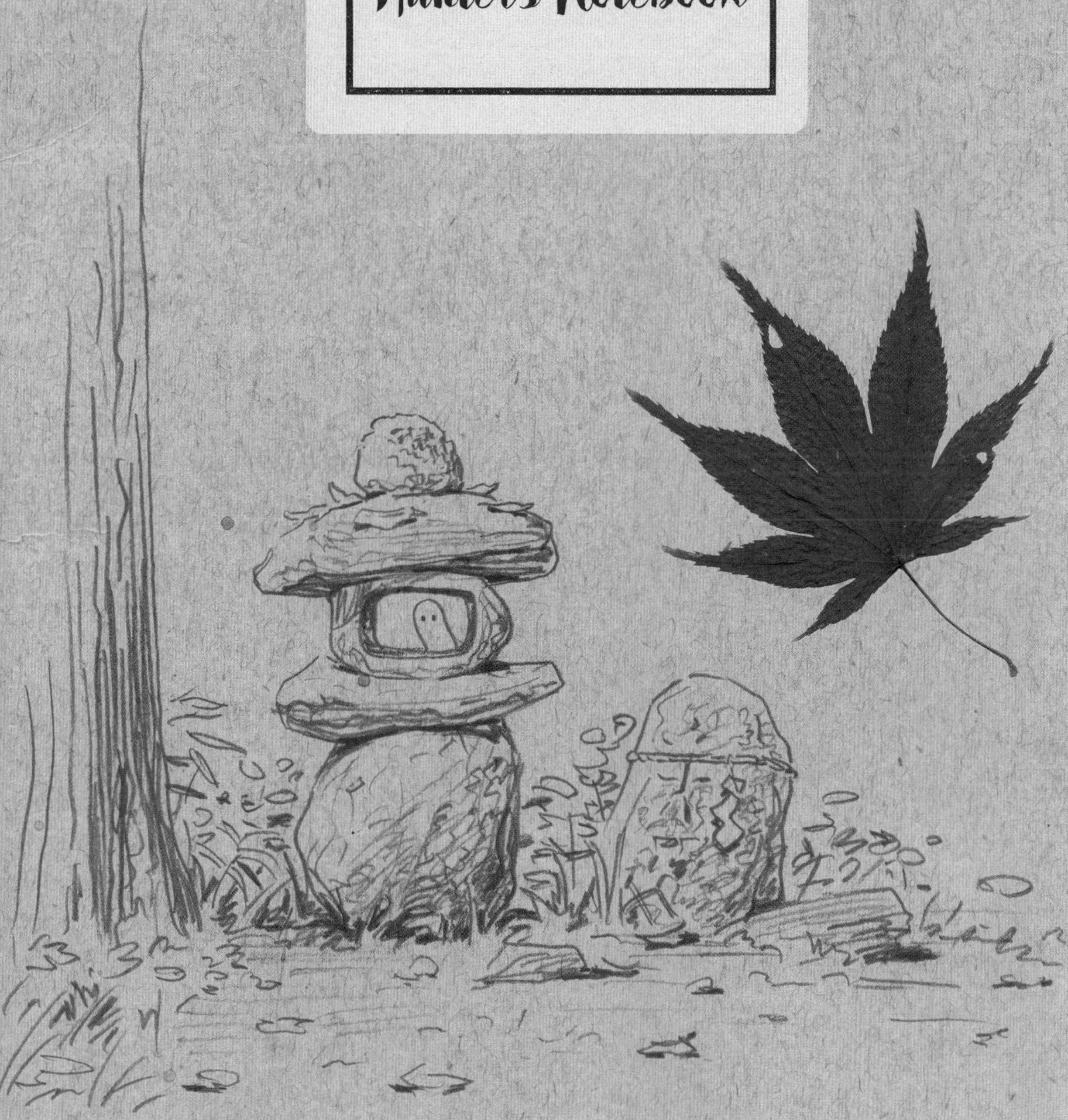

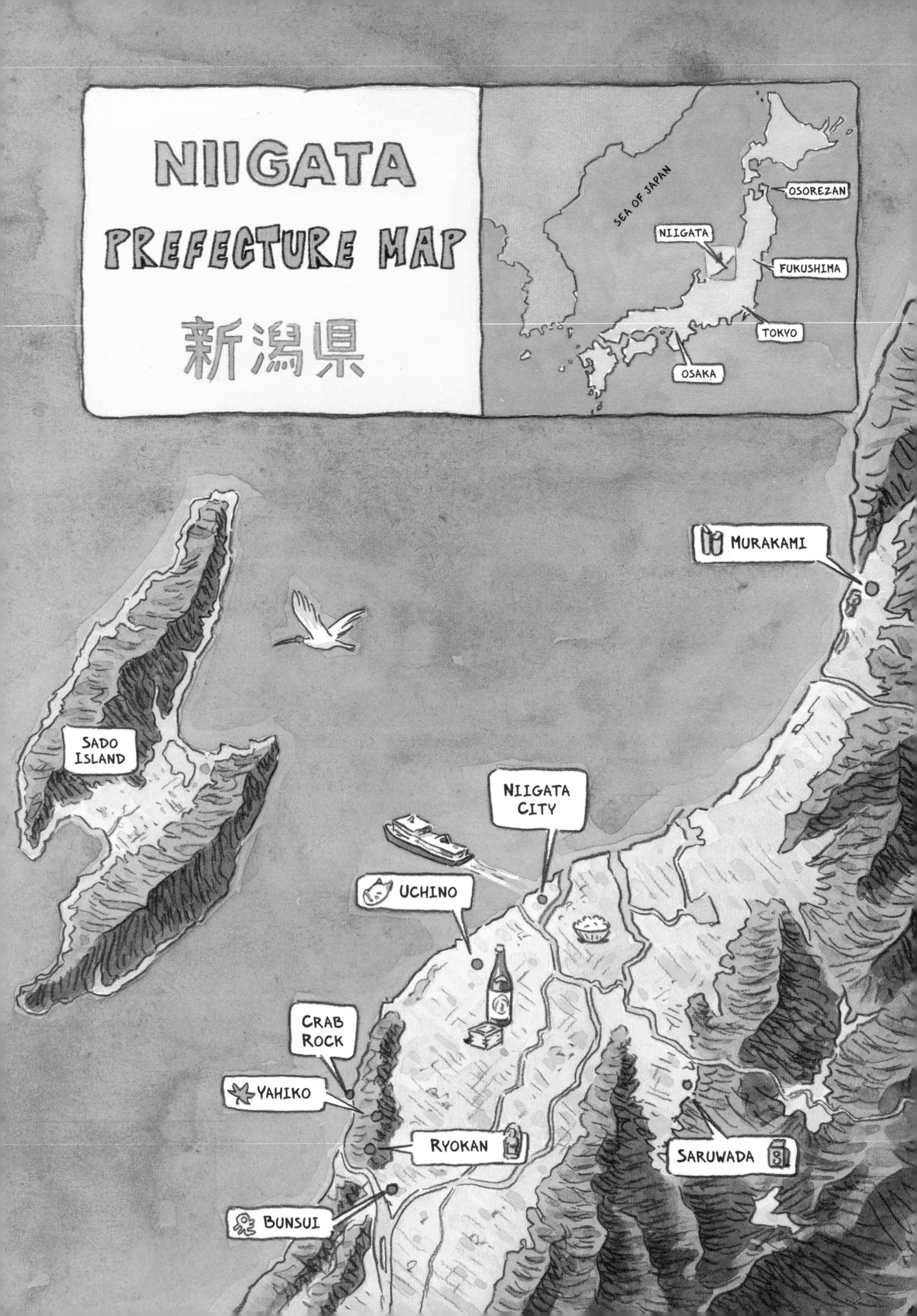
NIIGATA
PREFECTURE MAP
新潟県
SEA OF JAPAN
OSOREZAN
NIIGATA
FUKUSHIMA
TOKYO
OSAKA
MURAKAMI
SADO ISLAND
NIIGATA CITY
UCHINO
CRAB ROCK
YAHIKO
RYOKAN
SARUWADA
BUNSUI

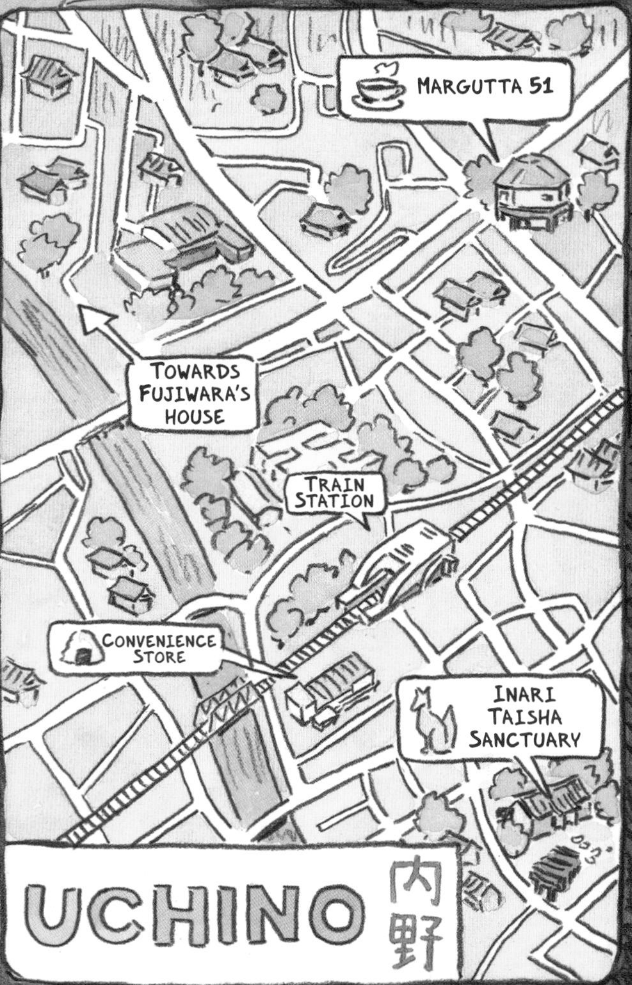
Margutta 51
Towards Fujiwara's House
Train Station
Convenience Store
Inari Taisha Sanctuary
UCHINO 内野

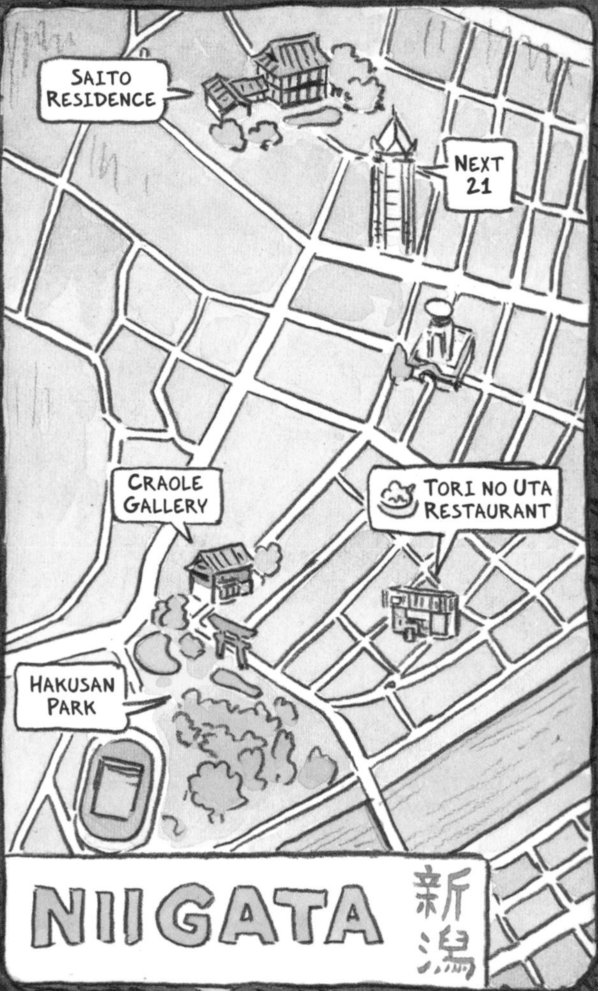
Saito Residence
Next 21
Craole Gallery
Tori no Uta Restaurant
Hakusan Park
NIIGATA 新潟

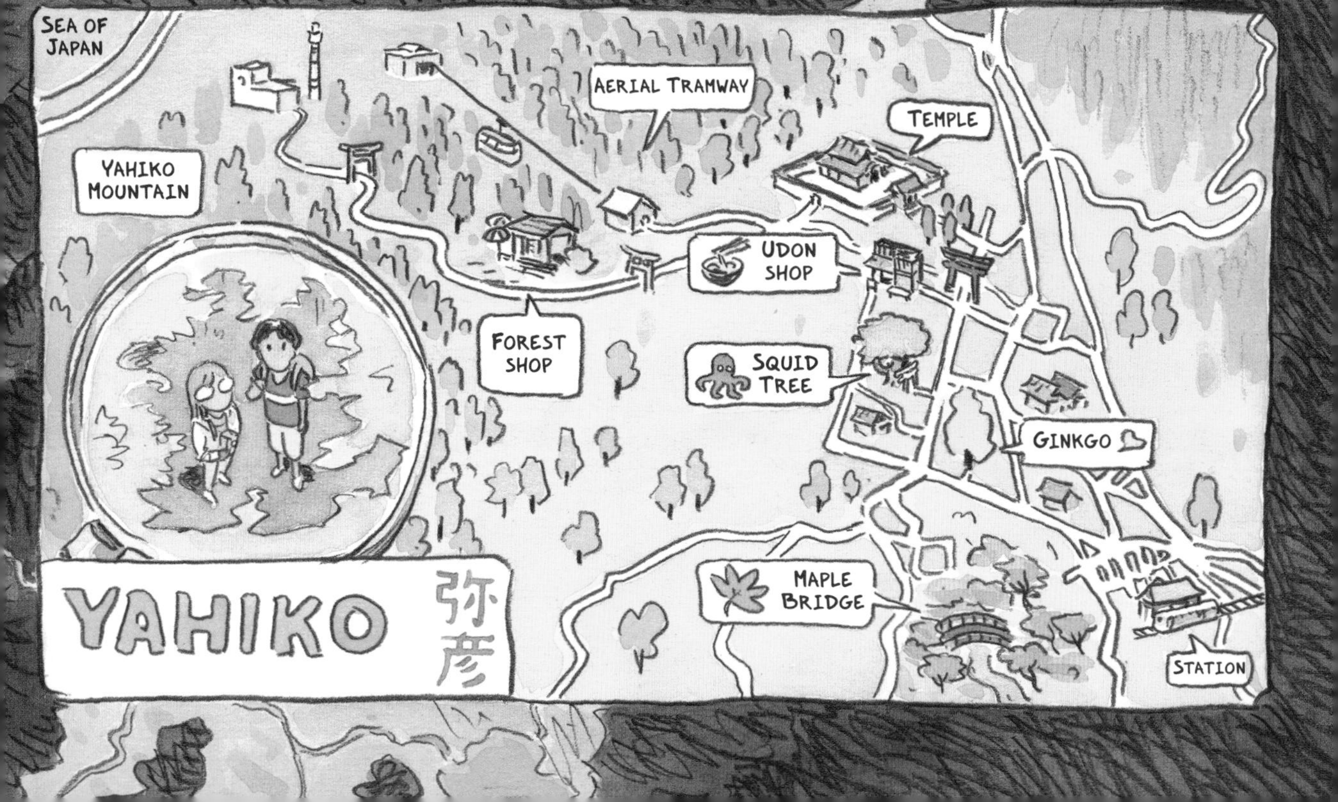
Sea of Japan
Aerial Tramway
Temple
Yahiko Mountain
Udon Shop
Forest Shop
Squid Tree
Ginkgo
Maple Bridge
Station
YAHIKO 弥彦

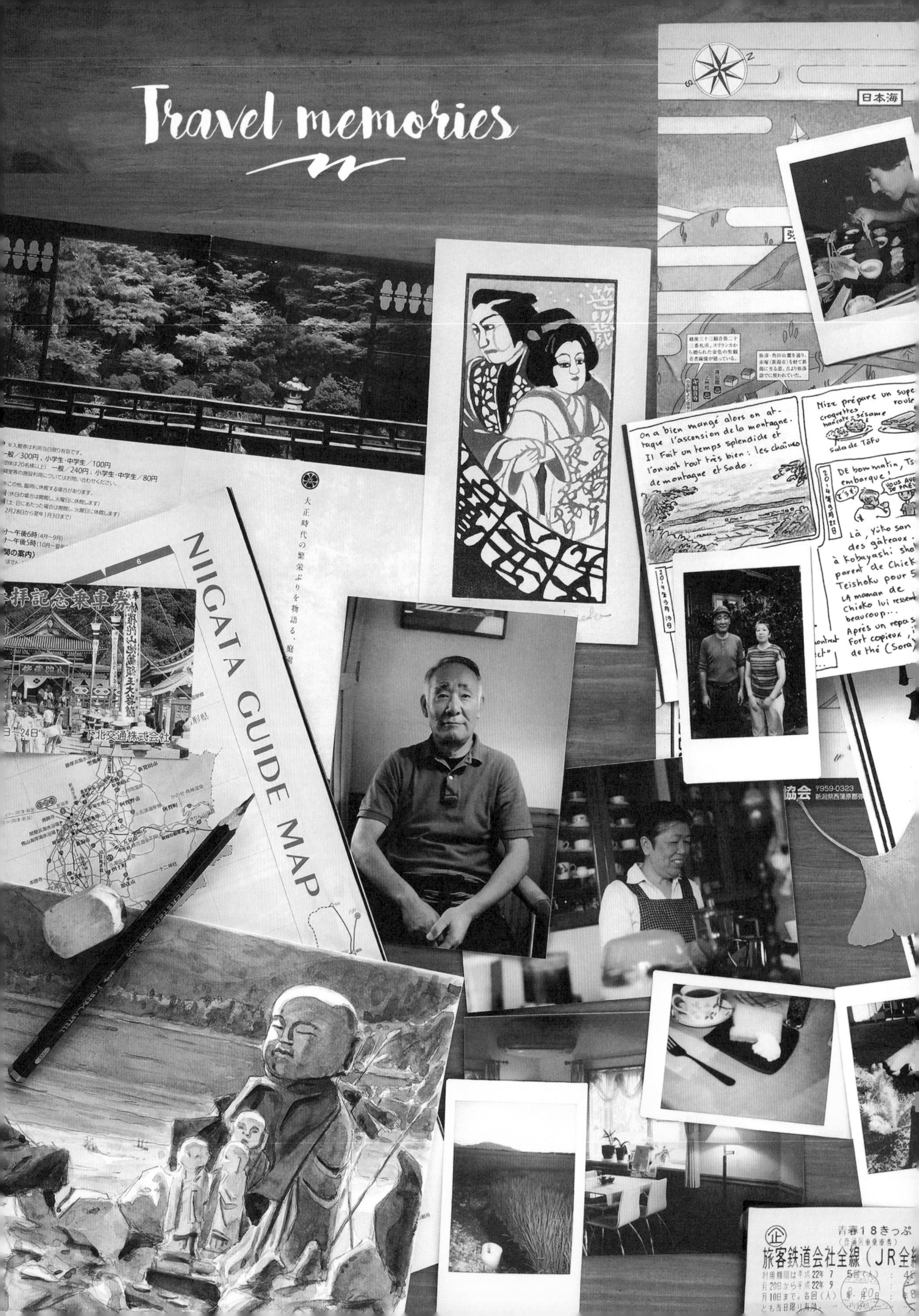

Travel memories
日本海
NIIGATA GUIDE MAP
大正時代の繁栄ぶりを物語る、
下北交通株式会社
On a bien mangé alors on attaque l'ascension de la montagne. Il fait un temps splendide et l'on voit tout très bien : les chaînes de montagne et Sado.
Mize prépare un super
croquettes
sésame
Salade de Tôfu
Là, Yûko san
des gâteaux.
à Kobayashi sho
parent de Chick
Teishoku pour 5
La maman de Chiko lui ressemble beaucoup...
Après un repas fort copieux,
de thé (Sora)
〒959-0323
新潟県西蒲原郡
青春18きっぷ
旅客鉄道会社全線（JR全

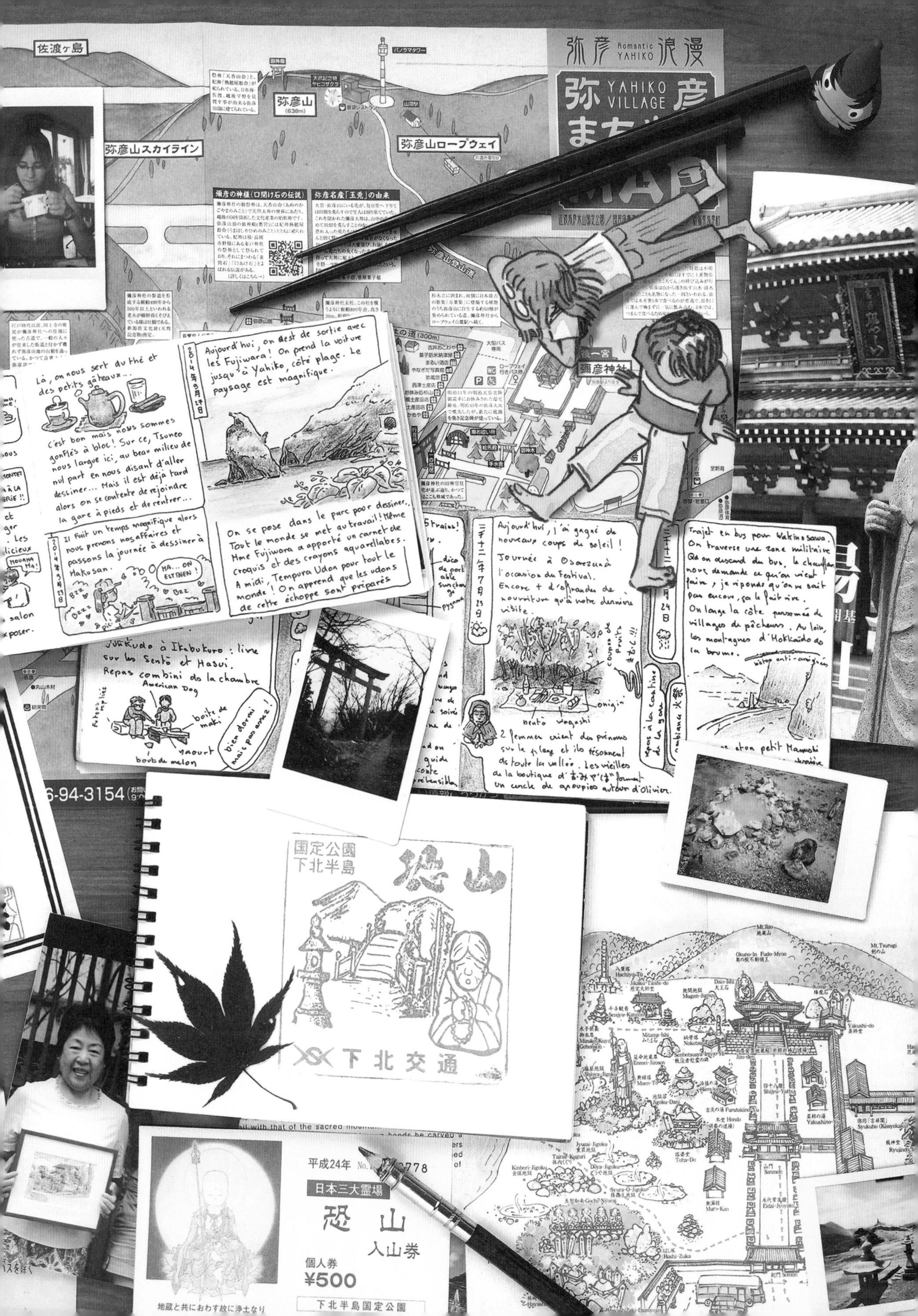

佐渡ヶ島
弥彦山
(638m)
弥彦山スカイライン
弥彦山ロープウェイ
パノラマタワー
弥彦 Romantic YAHIKO 浪漫
弥彦 YAHIKO VILLAGE
彌彦神社
Aujourd'hui, on est de sortie avec les Fujiwara ! On prend la voiture jusqu'à Yahiko, côté plage. Le paysage est magnifique.
2014年9月27日
Là, on nous sert du thé et des petits gâteaux...
C'est bon mais nous sommes gonflés à bloc ! Sur ce, Tsuneo nous largue ici, au beau milieu de nul part en nous disant d'aller dessiner... Mais il est déjà tard alors on se contente de rejoindre la gare à pieds et de rentrer...
Il fait un temps magnifique alors nous prenons nos affaires et passons la journée à dessiner à Hakusan.
2014年9月28日
MA... ON EST BIEN !
On se pose dans le parc pour dessiner. Tout le monde se met au travail ! Même Mme Fujiwara a apporté un carnet de croquis et des crayons aquarellables. A midi, Tempura Udon pour tout le monde ! On apprend que les udons de cette échoppe sont préparés
Repas combini ds la chambre
American Dog
boite de maki
yaourt
bouts de melon
Aujourd'hui, j'ai gagné de nouveaux coups de soleil !
Journée à Osorezan à l'occasion du Festival.
Encore + d'offrandes de nourriture qu'à notre dernière visite.
onigiri
bento
wagashi
2 femmes crient des prénoms sur la plage et ils résonnent de toute la vallée. Les vieilles de la boutique d'おみやげ forment un cercle de groupies autour d'Olivier.
repas à la cantine de la gare
Trajet en bus pour Wakinosawa. On traverse une zone militaire. Qd on descend du bus, le chauffeur nous demande ce qu'on vient faire, je réponds qu'on ne sait pas encore, ça le fait rire. On longe la côte parsemée de villages de pêcheurs. Au loin, les montagnes d'Hokkaido ds la brume.
-94-3154
国定公園
下北半島
恐山
下北交通
平成24年 No.
日本三大霊場
恐山
入山券
個人券
¥500
下北半島国定公園
地蔵と共におわす故に浄土なり
Mt.Jizo
地蔵山
Mt.Tsurugi
剣の山
Sanmon
山門

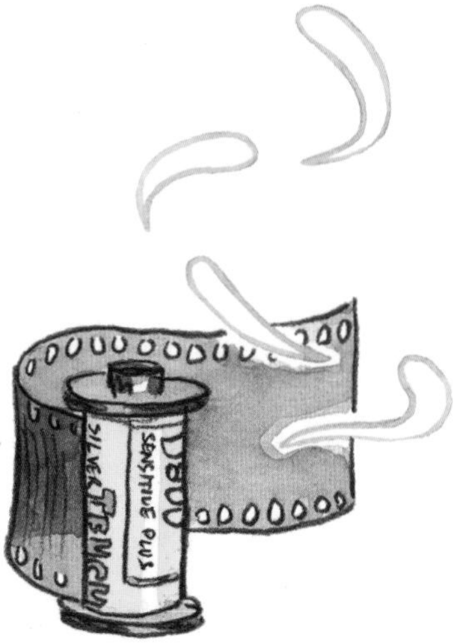
D800
SENSITIVE PLUS

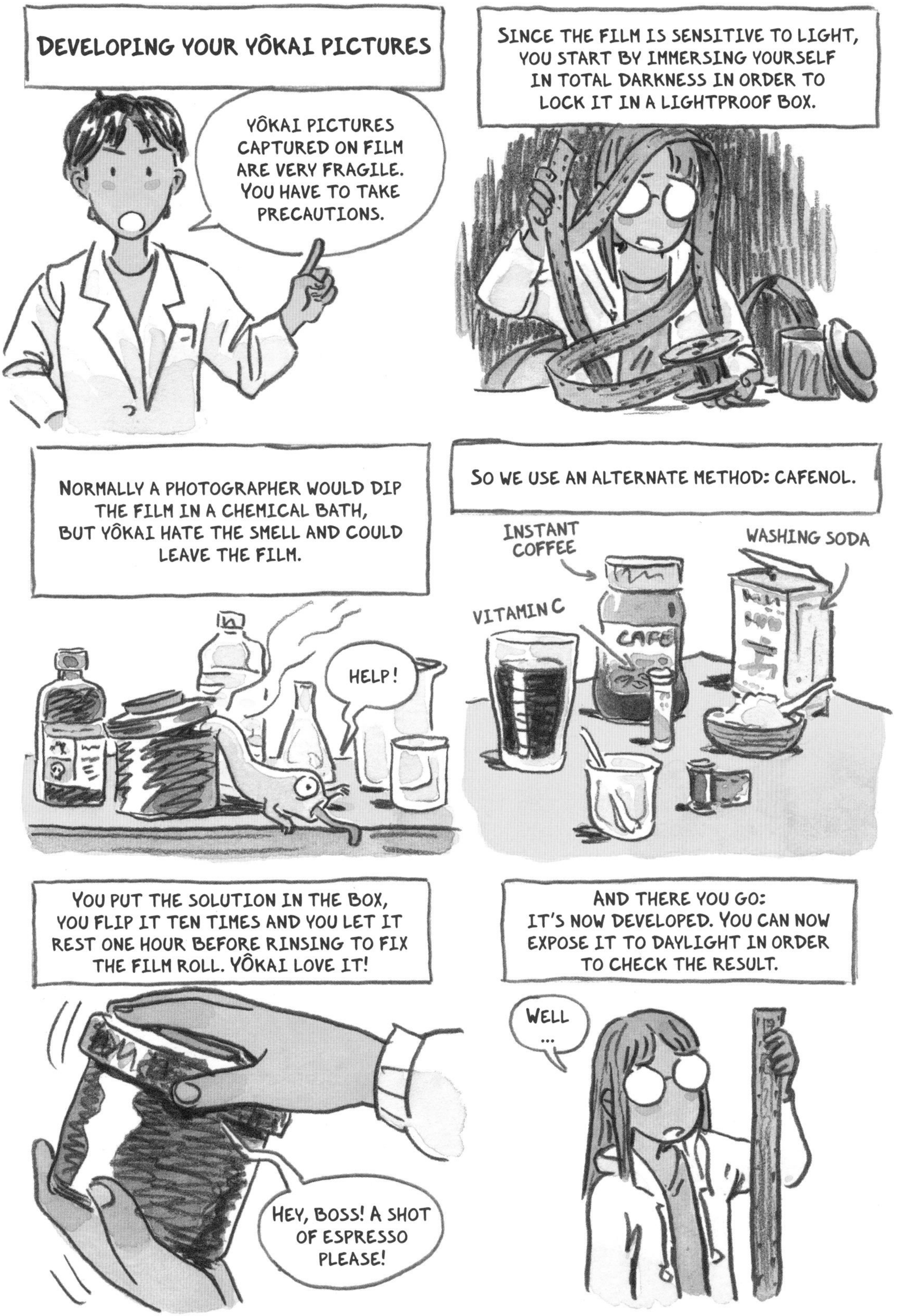
DEVELOPING YOUR YÔKAI PICTURES
YÔKAI PICTURES CAPTURED ON FILM ARE VERY FRAGILE. YOU HAVE TO TAKE PRECAUTIONS.
SINCE THE FILM IS SENSITIVE TO LIGHT, YOU START BY IMMERSING YOURSELF IN TOTAL DARKNESS IN ORDER TO LOCK IT IN A LIGHTPROOF BOX.
NORMALLY A PHOTOGRAPHER WOULD DIP THE FILM IN A CHEMICAL BATH, BUT YÔKAI HATE THE SMELL AND COULD LEAVE THE FILM.
HELP!
SO WE USE AN ALTERNATE METHOD: CAFENOL.
INSTANT COFFEE
WASHING SODA
VITAMIN C
CAFE
YOU PUT THE SOLUTION IN THE BOX, YOU FLIP IT TEN TIMES AND YOU LET IT REST ONE HOUR BEFORE RINSING TO FIX THE FILM ROLL. YÔKAI LOVE IT!
HEY, BOSS! A SHOT OF ESPRESSO PLEASE!
AND THERE YOU GO: IT'S NOW DEVELOPED. YOU CAN NOW EXPOSE IT TO DAYLIGHT IN ORDER TO CHECK THE RESULT.
WELL ...

PRINTING

As for the printing step, the problem is the same: you cannot use a normal enlarger.

Yôkai are sensitive to electric light. It would erase their image from the picture.

So we use a very ancient method, the cyanotype. It dates back to the origins of photography and enables us to print directly using sunlight.

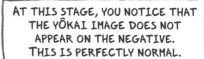
JOHN HERSCHEL 1842

You start by scanning the negative in order to print in large format on a transparency.

At this stage, you notice that the yôkai image does not appear on the negative. This is perfectly normal.

Sheltered from sunlight, you prepare a mixture made up of iron salt solution, potassium ferricyanide and distilled water ...

You carefully cover the sheet with this solution and you let it dry in total darkness.

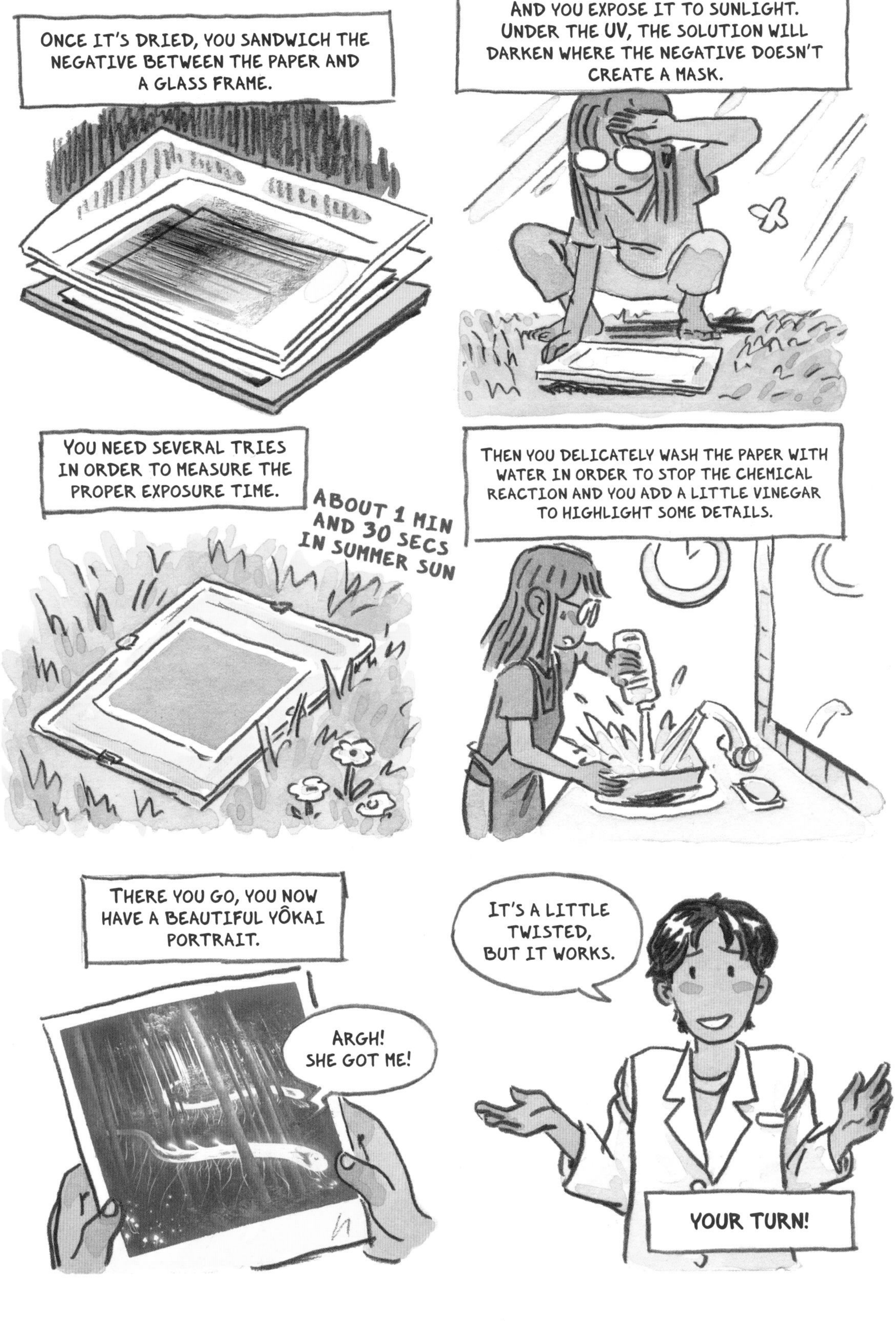
ONCE IT'S DRIED, YOU SANDWICH THE NEGATIVE BETWEEN THE PAPER AND A GLASS FRAME.
AND YOU EXPOSE IT TO SUNLIGHT. UNDER THE UV, THE SOLUTION WILL DARKEN WHERE THE NEGATIVE DOESN'T CREATE A MASK.
YOU NEED SEVERAL TRIES IN ORDER TO MEASURE THE PROPER EXPOSURE TIME.
ABOUT 1 MIN AND 30 SECS IN SUMMER SUN
THEN YOU DELICATELY WASH THE PAPER WITH WATER IN ORDER TO STOP THE CHEMICAL REACTION AND YOU ADD A LITTLE VINEGAR TO HIGHLIGHT SOME DETAILS.
THERE YOU GO, YOU NOW HAVE A BEAUTIFUL YÔKAI PORTRAIT.
ARGH! SHE GOT ME!
IT'S A LITTLE TWISTED, BUT IT WORKS.
YOUR TURN!

Glossary

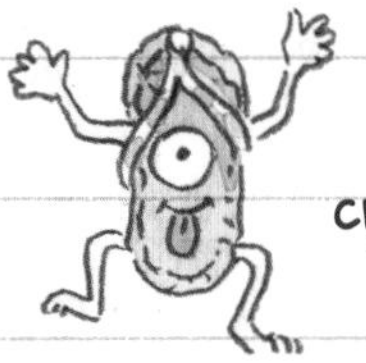

YÔKAI
SUPERNATURAL
CREATURES THAT LIKE
TO PLAY TRICKS ON
PEOPLE.

JIZÔ
BODHISATTVA
STATUETTES OFTEN
SOLICITED TO PROTECT
CHILDREN.

ONIGIRI
RICE BALLS
GENERALLY WRAPPED
IN NORI SEAWEED.

ONIBI
WILL-O'-THE-WISP
THAT PRECEDE
YÔKAI APPARITIONS.

TORII
GATES SYMBOLIC
OF THE SEPARATION
BETWEEN THE REAL
WORLD AND THE WORLD
OF SPIRITS.

TEMPURA UDON
FRIED SHRIMP AND
THICK WHEAT NOODLES
IN A BROTH.

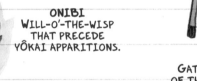

ONSEN
NATURAL HOT SPRINGS.

YEN
JAPANESE CURRENCY.